Dead ball

L190   23.95

DUE DATE			

DEAD BALL

DEAD BALL

A HARVEY BLISSBERG MYSTERY

R. D. Rosen

Walker & Company ✺ New York

First published in the United States of America in 2001 by
Walker Publishing Company, Inc.

Published simultaneously in Canada by Fitzhenry and Whiteside,
Markham, Ontario L3R 4T8

Library of Congress Cataloging-in-Publication Data
Rosen, Richard Dean.
Dead ball : a Harvey Blissberg mystery / R. D. Rosen.
p.   cm.
ISBN 0-8027-3366-2 (alk. paper)
1. Blissberg, Harvey (Fictitious character)—Fiction.
2. Private investigators—Massachusetts—Boston—Fiction.
3. Boston (Mass.)—Fiction.   I. Title.
PS3568.O774 M4   2001
813'.54—dc21   2001026574

Series design by M. J. DiMassi

Printed in the United States of America

2 4 6 8 10 9 7 5 3 1

To Tom Friedman and David Bloom especially, this time around, for so unselfishly and astutely watching over me and this book.

And for their endless friendship and support: Chuck Dawe, Jim Friedman, Joyce and Lev Friedman, Pam Galvin, Simon Gavron, George Gibson, Gail Hochman, Merrill Markoe, Cathleen McGuigan, Steve Molton, Harry Prichett, Laurence Rosen, Robert and Ellen Rosen, and Paul Solman.

To my remarkable parents, for their ageless example; to Diane McWhorter, for helping shape this novel's soul; to Peter Gethers, for supplying crucial pieces of the puzzle; to Allyn Reynolds, for her quotability and expertise; to Lou Narcisso and Vince Sullivan, my other reality consultants; to Ben Mondor for his baseball hospitality.

To all my teammates through the years, without whom I wouldn't know how the game is played.

To the late Ann Hall, who loved the Dodgers for good reason, me despite my faults, and life despite its injustices.

Finally, and most of all, to my daughters, Lucy and Isabel, beautiful inside and out, who keep lighting the way back to where I am.

DEAD BALL

AGAIN, Moss Cooley was the last player in the Providence Jewels' locker room. For over a week now, the press hadn't left him alone after a game. They hung on his every word as if what was about to emerge from his mouth was the name of the second shooter in Dealey Plaza and not one of the clichés that all major-league baseball players seemed hardwired to recite. Still, it was extraordinary even to Cooley himself, these last seven weeks of freakish consistency. He'd never experienced it before, not even in Little League. The ball looked like a huge scoop of vanilla ice cream out there.

The elderly clubhouse man, a fair ballplayer once in the Negro League, shuffled toward him with an armful of dirty towels, saying, "It's just you and Joltin' Joe now, boss. Old Charlie Hustle's hurtin' tonight."

Cooley buffed the toes of his Bruno Magli slip-ons with his towel and tossed it on Jimmy's load. "I'm not going to get worked up about it. DiMaggio can't even see me in his rearview mirror. What do I need now?" As if he didn't know that the greatest record in baseball, maybe in all of sports, was thirteen games away. Provided he hit safely in all of them. A detail.

"Twelve to tie, thirteen to be immortal."

"It ain't gonna happen so I'm not gonna worry about it," Cooley said, reaching into his cubicle for his Armani sport coat. The whole thing made him uneasy—the mounting pressure, the increasing isolation, the sleeplessness. It was enough to make him long for mediocrity.

Jimmy bent over to pick up a jockstrap from the middle of the clubhouse floor. "Nobody accuse you of overconfidence, Cool."

"It's not in my hands, Jimmy."

"You got that right. But there's no harm in letting the man upstairs know how bad you want it. Here, let me get the back of that jacket for you."

Jimmy tossed the dirty laundry in a canvas hamper and came over and brushed off the back of Cooley's coat with his hand.

"Looking as good as you do," the old clubhouse man said, picking a last bit off the shoulder, "I hope you got something good going on tonight."

Cooley laughed his wheezy laugh. "If I did, I sure as hell wouldn't tell *you*. I tell you, and it'd be all over the American League." He pulled a silver money clip out of his pocket and peeled off a twenty.

Jimmy raised a big black arthritic hand in protest. "Stop giving me that hard-earned money of yours."

"Just spreading the wealth, Jimmy." Cooley stuffed the bill in the breast pocket of Jimmy's white shirt. "Just spreading sunshine wherever I go."

"All right then. Much appreciated," Jimmy said. "You're a good man, Moss Cooley, and I don't mind saying so. Some of these boys—" He waved the rest of the thought away in disgust and shambled off to get his mop to begin on the bathroom.

"'Night, Jimmy," Cooley said, watching him go.

No twenty-dollar tip could begin to close the gap between

them, the one who played in splendid obscurity before Jackie Robinson integrated the game and the one the ravenous white press couldn't get enough of now. But Moss Cooley's mama hadn't raised a fool. Black was black, and white was white, and if he ever forgot it, he only had to read his hate mail.

Moss Cooley patted his pocket to make sure his keys were there and headed for the clubhouse door, stopping at the remains of the buffet. A solid hour of postgame interviews had kept him from chowing down with the others. Now he quickly ate a few chicken fingers and meticulously wiped his fingers on a paper napkin.

He heard a noise and looked up. Mike, one of the young attendants from the players' parking lot, a nice kid with a buzz cut, from Pawtucket, was pushing a hand truck through the clubhouse door. It was loaded with a plain cardboard box, about three feet high, a couple of feet square.

"There you are," Mike said, wheeling the hand truck up to Cooley. "Special delivery."

"What is it?"

"No idea. It was sitting outside the gate to the street with your name on it."

There, on top of the box, in heavy black marker, were the words: "Please deliver to M. Cooley."

"It's heavy," Mike said, sliding the hand truck's plate out from under the box. "Want me to open it for you?"

"No. Just leave it. Thanks."

"Twelve more to go."

"That's what they tell me. Here." Cooley held out a folded ten-dollar bill between his index and middle finger.

"Forget it."

"Better take it, Mike, or I'll give you even more." Cooley smiled. He was anxious to get going. It was one of Cherry Ann's nights off, and she was waiting for him at her loft in the Jewelry District.

"Okay, you win," the guard said, taking the money. "See you later. Have a good night."

The crap he got from fans: teddy bears and Toast-R-Ovens and homemade cookies. Nothing this big, though. Cooley tried to push the box with his foot.

He took a chef's knife from the buffet table and slit the tape over the flaps on the top of the box. The inside was filled with foam packing peanuts. He dipped his hand into them until he felt a rough metal object. Some kind of statue, he thought. With both hands he lifted it slowly from the box, all forty or fifty pounds of it, shedding foam peanuts everywhere. An envelope came out with it and fell to the floor.

It was a cast-iron Negro lawn jockey, about two feet tall and speckled with rust, hunched over in a submissive posture, left hand resting on its hip, right outstretched, holding an iron hitching ring. It was wearing a red vest.

Cooley had grown up around them in Alabama, knew them as "Jockos," these last public tokens of racism dotting the lawns of white neighborhoods. Under normal circumstances, they were just an unpleasant reminder of another time.

But this one was addressed to him.

And it had no head.

He stared at the decapitated jockey for several seconds, feeling a dense fury gather itself inside him. It rose slowly, spreading to his chest. When it reached his arm, he picked up the chef's knife and plunged it again and again into the cardboard box.

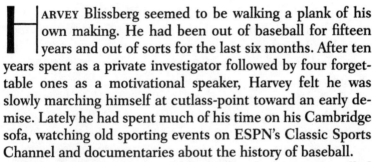

1

HARVEY Blissberg seemed to be walking a plank of his own making. He had been out of baseball for fifteen years and out of sorts for the last six months. After ten years spent as a private investigator followed by four forgettable ones as a motivational speaker, Harvey felt he was slowly marching himself at cutlass-point toward an early demise. Lately he had spent much of his time on his Cambridge sofa, watching old sporting events on ESPN's Classic Sports Channel and documentaries about the history of baseball.

When the phone rang, he paused a documentary called *When It Was a Game* that he was enjoying for the third time that week, brushed the tortilla chip crumbs off his shorts, and croaked a hello into the receiver.

"Professor?" a voice said. "That you?"

Professor. No one had called him that for years. It was like hearing a childhood nickname called out at the end of a very long hallway.

"Felix?" Harvey said, meaning Felix Shalhoub, his manager during his last year in the majors with the expansion

Providence Jewels, and now—Harvey still followed the game just enough to know this—the franchise's general manager.

"Yeah, yeah, it's me. How are ya?"

"Outstanding."

"Good to hear your voice. I heard you were doing some motivational speaking."

"Not anymore."

Harvey had been possibly the least motivated motivational speaker ever to address three hundred pharmaceutical salesmen in Orlando or three dozen managers of export documentation for dangerous cargo in Bayonne, New Jersey. How had this happened, that a man who prided himself on his avoidance of cliché should end up peddling platitudes about courage, teamwork, and the will to win? Because a man named Cromarty, who operated a second-rate speakers' bureau in Boston, had heard Harvey address a group of high school coaches and told him that midsize companies who couldn't afford Norman Schwarzkopf or Fran Tarkenton would still shell out good money for a tall, personable, former major-league outfielder with good teeth to pump up their troops.

Cromarty's proposition came at a time when Harvey had lost interest in exploring the bleaker secrets of his fellow human beings. It turned out there was a limit to the amount of evil a man could investigate, even at a certain professional remove, without eventually feeling contaminated by some virus of moral degradation. Before Harvey knew it, he was on a plane to the first of many sales meetings with themes like "Simply the Best," "The Future Is Now," and "Tomorrow's Our Middle Name" to explain to a ballroom of captive employees the fundamentals of a positive outlook that Harvey himself had never quite mastered. When he was through spewing slogans, there was invariably a stampede of grown men to the podium. They peppered him with questions about his baseball exploits, which they remembered far better than he, or tried to solicit his predictions for various pennant races and free-agent signings. It was depressing to Harvey that so many otherwise functional adults would want to shake the hand of a .268 lifetime hitter. And finally, he was out of that game too.

"You still with Mickey Slavin?" Felix asked.

"Still together, still not married. You know, she's now a sideline reporter for ESPN. She's on the road a lot." Fifteen years ago, when they met, *he* had been the star and she had been an oddity—a female sportscaster, albeit in Providence's tiny market. Now she was on national television, and he was—well, he was on the sofa, merely watching it.

"Now that you mention it, I feel I've seen her around the league this year."

"So how's the team doing?" Harvey asked.

"Whaddya mean, how's the team doing? You don't follow the game anymore?"

"Oh, off and on."

Where to begin Harvey's list of grievances with the national pastime? Overentitled players, selfish owners, and soaring ticket prices that left many ordinary Americans outside the ballpark. Worse, the game itself was buried beneath an avalanche of inane sports talk radio, round-the-clock cable coverage, and merchandising of team apparel and vintage sportswear. The game seemed to Harvey little more than a sideshow, the raw material for the finished product, which were the highlights that ran around the clock on several channels, a frenzy of home runs and annoyingly complex graphics. Instead of being a refuge from the clutter of daily life, baseball was now just part of that clutter.

"We actually got a shot," Felix was saying. "And thanks to Cooley we're selling out. His streak's the biggest thing to hit Providence since the hurricane of 'thirty-eight."

"I see where he's flirting with history."

"More like French-kissing it. Last night he pulled even with Pete Rose and Wee Willie Keeler."

"Twelve more, and he'll do the unthinkable," Harvey said.

"The Daig," Felix said in a reverential whisper. "Joe DiMaggio."

Whose very visage had appeared moments ago on Harvey's TV screen. The documentary he'd been watching consisted of 8- and 16-millimeter home movies of baseball players, games, and ballparks shot by players, their families, and fans between 1934 and 1957. It was like opening up a box of old baseball photographs to find they had all come quietly to life in faded color: DiMaggio himself, Gehrig, Ruth, Robinson, Greenberg, Dickey, even old-timers like Honus Wagner, Ty Cobb, and Cy Young, all liberated from their black-and-white prisons, yet still innocent of television and everything it would do to the game, to the very expressions on men's faces. The home movies gave these players a particular poignancy, a simple clowning humanity.

The documentary captured some of the game's now forgotten rituals: comical pepper games, train travel, afternoon crowds in hats, ties, and fur stoles. In the 1940s, ballplayers were still leaving their gloves—poor little scraps of leather—on the field rather than carrying them to the dugout, as if to say the field was hallowed, as if leaving a sacred piece of themselves there until they returned. Harvey had retired in the 1980s, much closer to the present than the days the documentary depicted, but it was only with the grainy, earnest realities of baseball's past that he felt any connection at all.

"You wouldn't recognize Rankle Park, not since Marshall redid it and renamed it The Jewel Box. We're packing 'em in. It's a real carnival atmosphere."

This was pure Felix. The hoary bromides of baseball were his specialty; "carnival atmosphere," "a real donnybrook," and "a day late and a dollar short" just rolled off his tongue. Not that Harvey was anyone to cast the first stone; he'd made a living off the clichés of competition for the last few years. He'd even stolen a few of Felix's.

"You want to know something funny, Felix? I used to use a few of your favorite sayings in my motivational speaking."

"Be my guest."

"Remember that sign you had in the clubhouse? 'Winners Are People Who Never Learned How To Lose.'"

"I believe that with all my heart."

"I know you do, Felix. And that's why I passed it on to thousands of office supply salesmen across this great country of ours."

"You doing okay, Professor?"

"I'm fine." But the fact that he was wearing an embroidered polyester-blend Mexican shirt with four pockets suggested otherwise, that dark forces were at work. Of course, he could try to justify the guayabera on the basis that, in early middle age, he needed more pockets than ever: for reading glasses, cell phone, bottle of Advil, tiny address book for numbers he could no longer remember, the TV remote control, a tin of Altoids. But without question his sartorial style, which Mickey referred to as "a lot of denim, a little suede, and a great deal of olive green," had taken a nasty, leisure-wear turn. Time had swallowed him up, as he had seen it do to other middle-aged men.

"Look," Felix was saying, "all the more reason for you to come down and see me tomorrow night. I want to talk to you about doing some work for us."

"Do what?"

"We want to hire you as the team's motivational coach."

"You can't be serious."

"A team that's on the verge of winning might as well be losing if it can't get over that last hump of inferiority."

"You just make this shit up, don't you?"

"I need you down here, Professor, to gas these boys up."

"I've been out of baseball a long time, Felix."

"Which gives you that important fresh-blood factor."

"My blood is very tired at the moment."

"That's because you're not out here at the ballpark, where you belong."

"Right here on my sofa is where I belong."

"I'm talking about showing these overpaid boys how to put the finishing touches on their self-esteem. I'm talking about instilling in these boys the peace of mind needed for victory. I've cleared it with Marshall."

"I have nothing to say."

"You're underestimating the value of your experience."

"Don't be so sure."

"I want you to come down here to The Jewel Box. I'm offering you a free skybox seat to a game you'd never be able to get into otherwise. We'll sit and drink Narragansett and talk about my proposition, and you'll see how you feel about this great national pastime."

"I know how I feel about it."

"I'll leave your name and a pass to the owner's box at the Will Call window. Campy would love to see you."

"Campy Strulowitz? I thought he was dead."

"He *is* dead, but he keeps showing up at the ballpark, so we figure we might as well just let him coach third base."

Harvey laughed, perhaps for the first time in weeks. Felix Shalhoub and Campy Strulowitz still working for the Providence Jewels? After all these years? It was like hearing your family had survived a tornado.

"So it's a deal?" Felix said.

When Harvey got off the phone, he took a long swig from the quart bottle of Gatorade he kept on the end table and stared at the image on his television screen, frozen in pause mode: it was President Eisenhower throwing out the first ball at a Senators' opener in Griffith Stadium. Eisenhower, the Senators, Griffith Stadium—all gone now.

For the first time in a while, Harvey remembered what it was like to stand three hundred feet from home plate and pick up the flight of a ball the instant it came off the bat, how it felt to be connected by a thread of pure desire to that sphere as it rose and cleared the background of the upper deck, arching against the summer night sky as he sprinted deep into right center, Harvey already knowing, with a certainty that was wholly lacking in his present life, that he would consume the ball in full stride a few feet from the warning track and feel the warmth of the fans' applause on the back of his uniform jersey as he loped, full of humble triumph, back to the dugout.

Harvey bit off the corner of a tortilla chip and chewed it thoughtfully. He had the sinking feeling he was about to push himself off the end of the plank, into his shark-infested future.

T was almost midnight by the time Moss Cooley turned into the dapper development in western Cranston where he'd bought a seven-thousand-square-foot home over the winter after signing his new deal with the Providence Jewels. He was the only black man in Roger Williams Estates, a distinction that added a tincture of guilt to his love of the house and its amenities. The truth was, his neighbors left him alone, a courtesy for which he was grateful now that he had to spend two or three hours a day talking to reporters and evaluating endorsement offers. He had helped beat the Baltimore Orioles this evening by sending a hanging curve into the Providence bullpen, making him the sole owner of the second-longest hitting streak in major-league baseball history. Forty-five straight games.

He looked at his hands on the steering wheel and tried to remember what they had been like when he was a scrawny kid hitting rocks into the clover field behind his house with a broom handle. Now his hands, and the thick wrists to which they were attached, had entered history. *Sports Illustrated* had compared them to Hank Aaron's. He smiled at the absurdity of it all. He couldn't wait to call his mama. She'd still be up waiting to hear from him. When he was ten and newly cut from his Little League team, she had paid a personal visit to Coach Lloyd and browbeat him into taking her little Maurice back. "My boy has greatness in him," she told Lloyd, as she reported to her son years later. "He has greatness in him, and I won't have that greatness sitting around the house all summer, moping and getting into what-all kind of trouble."

As he pulled into the driveway, past the parched lawn beyond the redemption of sprinklers, he wondered if he was in any kind of trouble now. The hate mail didn't faze him, even the worst of it. You reached a certain prominence, and that was part of your job—providing a target for the ranting of unhappy people. As his mama liked to say, "Don't you make other people's unhappiness your business." Just like there were some folks who had to get in the TV shot, mugging and waving like anyone gave a shit, there were a certain number of people in America who just had to write you a letter telling you what a black cocksucker you were.

But the lawn jockey last night had thrown a scare into him. It was different, he thought as he pushed the button for the garage door and waited for it to complete its slow ascent. It had taken more than a 34-cent stamp and a trip to the mailbox to get it to him.

He started to pull his Range Rover into the rightmost bay, next to the mint-condition 1979 Caddy he had bought for the simple reason that he could afford to and that it was the car he had wanted most when he was a child, watching Dr. Drexel cruise around the town of Starrett in his.

Because he was lost in thought, and because he was admiring the Caddy, he was halfway into the garage before he saw it. He applied the brakes. Had he not, it would have hit the windshield.

It had been tied to a piece of twine and hung from the garage ceiling. It dangled in midair, eyes bulging, swaying slightly now in the entering breeze.

2

I T was the instant you crossed the border from life's chaos to baseball's magnificent green order.

It was the moment that baseball writers fell back on when fresher metaphors escaped them—and yet, there it was, it couldn't be denied that the game's divinity was somehow contained in it. You came up the sloped stadium ramp toward your seat, seeing only sky and perhaps a light tower or a fragment of scoreboard, and as you got closer, the field itself seemed to rise up to meet you. At the crest of the ramp, you stopped, startled by the vivid grass, the scope of the park, the immortal discipline of the diamond. And if it's a night game and the summer sky is turning that bottomless, evening blue, you would be forgiven for thinking that God's a fan.

When Harvey came up the ramp of the jam-packed Jewel Box, né Rankle Park, he was stung by a sadness that this beautiful game had gone on without him. Baseball was an archetype, an institution through whose turnstiles he had come to play his small historical role before being ejected back into the world. And now he was back as just another fan. Or rather, a motivational coach, whatever the hell that was.

As he looked for an usher to give him directions to the owner's box, he took in the new, improved home of the American League East's Providence Jewels. The charming irregularities that highly paid design and architectural firms had created from scratch with the new generation of retro ballparks in Baltimore, Cleveland, Detroit, Pittsburgh, San Francisco, and Houston, Pro-Gem Palace had achieved as the result of a long organic process. When the expansion Jewels had first moved in sixteen years ago, Rankle Park was a former minor-league park, a steel, brick, and concrete affair down by India Point on the Providence River. It looked like the deformed offspring of a World War II battleship and a nineteenth-century mental hospital. In the years since, owner Marshall Levy had made improvements, culminating in a $30 million facelift. Levy had added new seats, a big scoreboard with all the trimmings, and a grassy knoll beyond the left-center-field fence where fans could put out blankets and picnic. No amount of refurbishing, however, could conceal the fact that the stadium was a hodgepodge. But it conformed to the current vogue for asymmetry, and The Jewel Box was included in any discussion of baseball's architectural treasures.

Harvey was watching the Jewels warm up on the field below when an usher wearing a hunter green jacket with silver epaulettes asked to see his ticket. When Harvey showed him his pass to the owner's box, the man said, "Well, well—give my regards to the boss," and pointed a bony forefinger back up the ramp toward a private elevator.

When he arrived at owner Marshall Levy's skybox high above the field, both Levy and general manager Felix Shalhoub rose from their upholstered chairs to greet him. Levy, with his big features, even tan, and good head of hair, didn't look like a man in his seventies. His Pro-Gem Inc., the last surviving big costume jewelry manufacturer in Rhode Island, had expanded into picture frames and automotive dashboard trim, and his success had helped him patiently nurse the Jewels to good fiscal health after the rough, noncompetitive years. Personally and professionally, he knew how to survive in style.

"Gosh, you look good," Marshall said, pumping Harvey's hand.

"And look at you," Harvey said.

"Professor, you can't be more than a couple pounds over your playing weight," Felix said with equal charity, embracing him in a bear hug. Felix had lost weight, and although well into his sixties by now, looked healthier in his Italian sport coat and salt-and-pepper crew cut than when he'd managed Harvey. While Felix had been an indifferent, at times pathetic manager, executive life seemed to agree with him. The bumbling was gone, replaced by something approximating dignity. He laughed heartily, advertising capped teeth. "Why, I'll bet I could put you in center field right now. And I've half a mind to do just that. Andy Cubberly can't buy a hit. It's like Moss has stolen all his luck the last few weeks."

Cubberly. The name meant nothing to Harvey. Just another name clogging the box scores he only glanced at. "If it's all right with you," he said, "I'd just as soon sit up here and enjoy the view."

Owner Marshall Levy chortled. "Well, you can see what we've done with the old sandlot, Professor."

"Amazing. A true baseball palace."

"We exceed every requirement of the Americans with Disabilities Act. You can take your wheelchair everywhere in this place. How about the new unies?"

"Outstanding."

"We've got alternative ones for both home and road. We put in twenty-four fully equipped hospitality suites. We're completely up to speed, and we're pulling people in from all over Rhode Island, eastern Connecticut, southern Massachusetts. We've become a real regional draw, Harvey, and with the sixth lowest payroll in the league. Not bad for one of these old mill cities. Heck, we got Brown and RISD kids walking over from College Hill to get away from their books." Marshall could sound more like a brochure than any man Harvey knew.

Harvey helped himself to a boiled shrimp from the little buffet. "Can't hurt that Cooley's closing in on DiMaggio."

"Can't hurt?" Felix said. "It's the goddamn Second Coming. I've got a good feeling about this streak."

A greet cheer arose from the stands, and Harvey turned and looked through the skybox Plexiglas to see the Jewels taking the field in their brilliant white uniforms trimmed in the team's color scheme—hunter green and orange. He watched the center fielder jog out to his old hunting grounds—Harvey could barely make out the "Cubberly" on the back of the jersey—and begin trading long easy throws with Moss Cooley in left. Harvey's stomach tingled with the memory of that pregame excitement; funny how the physical memory had been stored, perfectly preserved, inside him. From the facing of the left-field upper deck hung a sign that read, "HEY, MOSS! 46 WOULD DO THE TRIX!" The press enclosures next to each dugout were teeming, like refugee lifeboats, with photographers. From the skybox, Harvey could see a slice of glittering Narragansett Bay over the center-field bleachers. A fat Fuji blimp plowed the evening sky. It seemed like the whole world had descended on Providence, Rhode Island.

"Wouldn't it be super if he actually did it?" Marshall asked.

"Obviously you don't believe in jinxes," Harvey said.

"You mean that business of not talking about it? I don't believe in jinxes, Harvey. I believe in preparation. Chance favors a prepared mind, and a prepared bat."

"Just don't get your hopes up," Harvey said.

"Why not?" Marshall asked.

"This guy Ed Purcell, Nobel laureate in physics," Harvey said, selecting a cherrystone on the half shell, "he studied all

streaks and slumps in major-league baseball history and concluded that DiMaggio's fifty-six-game hitting streak was the
only sequence that is so many standard deviations above the
expected that, according to him, it should never have happened in the first place. He called it an 'assault on probability.' How many players have even hit in as many as
thirty-seven straight games in the recorded history of baseball? I'll tell you. Eight. Nine with Cooley now."

Marshall eyed him suspiciously. "You just know that?"

"There's not a savvy baseball student alive who doesn't
think the streak is the single greatest athletic accomplish-
ment ever," Harvey went on. "Twenty years ago Tversky—at
Stanford—proved that hot streaks—whether you're a player
or a team—are an illusion. The probability, that is, of getting
a hit in your next game is not in the least increased by your
success getting hits in previous games, no matter how many
straight previous games. Statistically speaking, there is no
such thing as momentum. Every streak is essentially a random fluctuation of the statistical norm. Every game, every at-
bat, you're starting over with the same allies—your skill and
your luck. Okay, now, DiMaggio had the benefit of a break or
two during his streak. I think there were a couple games in
which his only hit was a cheapie. Plus he got a few sweet calls
from the official scorer. Correct me if I'm wrong, but I believe
that the three hits he got in game four of the streak were all
suspect. And a dubious call in his favor saved his ass once in
Chicago. Nonetheless, DiMaggio's streak was made possible
by some sort of divine intervention or cosmic oversight. Plain
skill, enhanced by luck, can't begin to explain it.

"Look," Harvey said, gesturing with a johnnycake, "just
think about it. A hitting streak flies in the face of baseball's
basic irrationality. Unlike home runs. Home runs are rational.
If you hit the ball far enough and fair enough, it's a home
run—and even that is subject to the variables of different
ballparks. But getting base hits is not the inevitable outcome
of either force or distance. You know, you can hit it a ton to

deep center for a four-hundred-foot out, or nick it for an ex-
cuse-me single that rolls thirty feet up the line."

"But you've got to have consistency of contact," Marshall
suggested.

"Absolutely," Harvey agreed. "You start there. But a lot of
players have that. Low strikeout average, high-percentage hitters, always getting wood on the ball. How come more of
them haven't hit in even thirty straight games? There's just
too much damn luck involved. Too many variables. The location of the pitch, the positioning of the defense, outfield dis-
tances, the degree of bat-on-ball contact, the length of the
grass, the wind, the barometric pressure. Injuries. Over the
long haul—over a season—sure, Tony Gwynn's going to bat
three hundred, but get a hit in thirty, let alone fifty-six straight
games? You need more than talent on your side. More than
the umpire and the official scorer. You need *God*."

"Always the Professor," Felix said. "Always thinking."

Harvey felt a rush of shame. The truth was that, once
roused by Felix's call the previous afternoon, he had phoned
his brother Norm, renowned baseball nerd and now chairman
of Northwestern's English Department, to discuss Cooley's
hitting streak. As usual, Norm was off and running. Purcell,
Tversky, deviations from the statistical norm—all the erudi-
tion was his older brother's. Too late now to give credit where
it was due. "I'll bet you a thousand bucks right now Cooley
doesn't even get to fifty," Harvey's only sibling had concluded.
"DiMaggio's streak was a once-in-an-eon event, just like your
relationship with Mickey. What is it now—fifteen years, and
you're still not married? Talk about streaks."

"Can I have something to drink?" Harvey said. If streaks
and slumps were illusions, what explained the fact that he
was having the psychological equivalent of a fifty-six-game
batting slump? He felt many standard deviations below the
expected for days spent in a really bad mood.

"What'll it be?" Felix asked, just as the PA announcer
asked everyone to rise for the national anthem.

"Beer's fine." Harvey saw Felix turn and mumble something to a black steward in a white shirt and tie lurking in the doorway of the skybox.

When the anthem had been sung, the drinks came, and the three men settled into the nubbly chairs facing the field. Marshall Levy was drinking Scotch on the rocks, and Felix was sucking Canada Dry ginger ale from the bottle.

"Where's your beer?" Harvey asked him.

"I've been in recovery for almost twelve years, Professor."

"I didn't know. Congratulations." Harvey flashed on Felix pounding down the Genesee Cream Ales in his little clubhouse office loss after loss.

"First I ended my relationship with my wife, then my relationship with booze."

"Good for you," Harvey said, referring to both the booze and the former Frances Shalhoub.

The PA announcer announced Baltimore's lead-off hitter, a lithe little lefty, and Marshall said, "Speaking of Joe DiMaggio, you know his brother Dom was called 'Little Professor'? I guess 'cause of the glasses."

"Must be a hundred ballplayers had the nickname, Marshall. All you have to do is look like you can read and write."

Felix belched. "If I'm not mistaken, you actually used to read whole books."

"Still do, Felix. Bad habits die hard. As you know."

At the crack of the bat, Harvey looked up to see a liner off the lead-off hitter's bat slice down the left-field line, where Moss Cooley, moving well for a big man, made a nice backhanded running catch. The Jumbotron reacted to Cooley's catch with a prerecorded voice that yelled "Priceless!" and a blinking, expanding and contracting message that read, "Y'ALL BE COOL!"

"Yes!" shouted Marshall, pumping his fist. "I *love* the fact we've got Cool for four more years. The Beast of the East! The Big Green Machine!"

"That's a very hyperactive scoreboard you got there, Marshall."

"Worth every penny!"

How strange, Harvey thought, that in this dark corner of New England there had arisen the possibility of baseball greatness and posterity in the sculpted form of Maurice "Moss" Cooley, of Starrett, Alabama, a newly re-signed, twenty-seven-year-old left fielder whose highest batting average in three years with the Jewels had been .314 and who until now had never hit safely in more than twelve consecutive games. His forty-five-game streak—this extremely rare union of skill and prolonged good fortune—had separated him from the ranks of baseball's mere mortals. Moss Cooley had given baseball fans everywhere a new reason for living. This was baseball at its best, gathering up all the loose ends of human aspiration, the bits of excitement that life had sloughed off, all the misplaced enthusiasm in millions of American lives, and shaping it into one huge, hard, shiny hope.

The next Oriole grounded out to second.

"Moss is getting quieter the longer this goes on," Felix said.

"He's probably just trying to protect himself from the media," Harvey suggested while watching the Providence starting pitcher, someone named Clark Pevere, landscape the rubber with the toe of his right shoe.

"Well, hell yes, there's that," Felix said. "It's like being followed around by a pack of annoying little dogs. That's what Moss calls 'em: the Chihuahuas. They've been nipping at his ankles since the streak hit twenty-five."

Harvey nodded. "The media makes everything harder. Makes it harder to operate in your own sphere."

"DiMaggio had the media," Felix said.

Harvey snorted. "A bunch of middle-age guys in fedoras who've tacitly agreed not to mention your private life? C'mon, they were kept men, paid by the ball clubs. There's no comparison."

"He did have some crazy fan sneak into the dugout during the streak and steal his favorite bat."

"But they got it back."

As they all watched the number-three batter in Baltimore's lineup drop a banjo hit in short center for a single, Harvey's cell phone began to warble the opening bars of "Take Me Out to the Ball Game." He'd changed the ringing option that afternoon from the funereal "Fuga."

He pulled the phone out of his pants pocket and said, "Hello."

"It's me." It was Mickey. "Just checking in to see how you're doing." Since his recent confinement to the sofa, she made a point of calling once a day to make sure he hadn't harmed himself.

"I'm fine. Where are you?"

"I'm at your old stomping grounds. ESPN is doing the Jewels-Orioles game in Providence, which you'd know if you still followed the game."

"I do follow the game," Harvey said. "As it was played many years ago." He stood to get a better look at the field. "Where are you exactly?"

"I told you. The Jewel Box."

"I meant, where in the ballpark." It was symbolic of their relationship these days that they should be in the same place and not even know it.

"Okay," Mickey said, "I'm wedged in the first-base-line press enclosure, hoping to get two seconds with Moss Cooley after his at-bat."

He saw her now, a splash of auburn hair among the gray paparazzi jockeying for position in the little pen next to the dugout. "I see you."

"You see me? Where are you, Bliss?"

"Look over your left shoulder and about seventy feet up."

"You're here? Where?"

"Look up at Marshall Levy's skybox. There's a sad middle-aged man waggling the fingers of his right hand at you. That would be me."

"This is too much. Wait—there you are!" Harvey could see the tiny oval of her face break into a smile. "*What* are you doing there?"

"Felix thinks he wants to hire me."

"To do what?"

"Motivational coach."

"Don't be ridiculous."

"My sentiments exactly."

"Why'n't you come down and see me?"

"Come up and visit us in the skybox."

"Tell her she's my guest," Marshall said loudly, then dropped his voice to mutter, "Best-looking woman on TV. Better-looking than Hannah Storm. Or that woman on *The X-Files*."

"Maybe later, if I can get away," Mickey said. "Maybe after the game."

"You know where the elevator to the skyboxes is?"

"I think I can find it."

Harvey, Marshall Levy, and Felix Shalhoub watched as the Providence pitcher retired the Orioles without further damage, and the PA system sprayed the park with loud rock music as the Jewels trotted in for their first at-bat.

Providence Jewel second baseman Arturio Ferreiras roped a single to left to lead off the top of the first, then stole second.

"Way to go, Artie!" Marshall yelled, banging the arm of his chair. "God, I love this game!"

Center fielder Andy Cubberly came to the plate and waved at two high fastballs from Baltimore pitcher Jack Bustow.

"This guy can't handle the high stuff," Harvey observed.

Felix snorted. "Every housewife in Woonsocket knows he can't handle the high stuff. Marshall," he said, turning to his boss, "remind me to talk to Terry about dropping him down in the lineup until his mojo starts working again."

"Leave the skipper alone," Marshall said. "He knows what he's doing. You know from personal experience, I don't believe in a lot of front office interference."

"What're you talking about? You're forgetting it was you who once let my ex-wife sit in the dugout."

"I let you make your mistakes when you were at the helm," Marshall said, not interested in Felix's view of ancient history, however accurate.

Cubberly struck out on a change-up, and a tide of clapping and hooting signaled Moss Cooley's slow progress toward the batter's box.

3

I n DiMaggio's day, nobody looked really good in a baseball
uniform. This could not be said of Moss Cooley. Flannel had
given way to form-fitting synthetics, chewing tobacco had
given way to sunflower seeds and strength-and-fitness training,
and Cooley was a testament to the virtues of this evolutionary
process. His jersey with the big green "14" looked as if it had
been spray-painted on his sculpted upper body. Felix was saying that for someone with a power hitter's build—six-two, two
hundred and five pounds, according to the program—Moss
could hit extremely well to all fields.

"And he owes a lot of that to Campy," Felix said, referring
to the Jewels' elderly batting instructor, whose ministrations
sixteen years ago had helped Harvey hit .300 for the only
time in his career. "He convinced Moss that he was essentially a contact hitter with power, not a power hitter. Campy
convinced him to shorten his stroke, learn to hit inside out,
give up ten or twelve home runs a year, hit for the average, be
the table setter for Barney and Monkman. Pure genius on
Campy's part."

Cooley paused just outside the batter's box and rotated his head several times in each direction to loosen up his neck muscles. Baltimore's Bustow stood patiently on the mound, perhaps contemplating his disadvantage as a lefty facing the game's current best right-handed hitter. Ferreiras wandered a little off second, waiting for the fans to get a grip on themselves and Cooley to step in.

"One thing about Moss," Felix was explaining, "is that he'll surprise you sometimes and go after the first pitch. On the other hand, last week he had this great at-bat against the Indians. He fouled off a few iffy pitches, waited out the walk, and got a rally going. All this despite the fact he'd gone hitless in the game and would probably get only one more at-bat, which is what he got, and doubled off the scoreboard."

"Let's go, Cool!" Marshall shouted.

From the stretch Bustow delivered his first pitch, a waist-high slider on the outside corner that Cooley promptly drove to the opposite field in a low parabola. It dropped thirty feet inside the foul line and fifty feet in front of the right fielder. Ferreiras chugged around third to score. The crowd erupted. Cooley stood calmly on first base, peeling off his batting gloves with the decorum of a gentleman caller, and said something to the Orioles' first baseman, who laughed. The Jumbotron went into unspeakable gyrations involving a likeness of Moss Cooley's face and the phrase "46 STRAIGHT!"

When the cheering finally subsided, Levy leaned toward Harvey. "No chance involved there, eh, Professor?"

"Touché," Harvey admitted.

What impressed him was Cooley's effortlessness, as though he were merely demonstrating an opposite-field hitting technique rather than executing one of the most difficult hand-eye feats in all of sports: hitting an eighty-five-miles-per-hour major-league slider thrown from a distance (when you calculated the actual point of release) of fifty-four feet. Harvey was thinking about how Cooley must feel, getting his hit out of the way early, like a man who steals a successful kiss early on a first date and can relax for a while.

"Professor," Marshall said, "what did Felix tell you over the phone about our wanting to hire you?"

"He said the two of you thought you needed a motivational coach. But I've got to tell you—"

"He was lying, Harvey." Marshall rotated his glass of Scotch in a tight circle, the melting cubes chattering against the glass.

"Not that we don't think your presence will be influential," Felix said as Guercio, the designated hitter, stepped in. "Teach these boys that winning's up here." Felix jabbed a finger at his own head. "That baseball's a game of fund*amentals*. Get it? Mentals."

"I get it," Harvey said, snapping a carrot stick between his teeth. "Suppose one of you tells me what's going on."

"Officially, we want you to be our motivational coach. Unofficially—"

"Can I get you gentlemen another drink?" The black steward was suddenly at their sides. "Some spicy chicken wings?"

"No, thank you, Robert," Marshall said, and the steward deftly retreated.

"Unofficially?" Harvey prompted the Jewels' owner.

"Unofficially—and we're completely at the mercy of your discretion on this matter, okay?"

"Understood," Harvey assured him.

"We want you to protect Moss Cooley."

"From the Chihuahuas?"

"Oh, no," Marshall said, swirling his Scotch. "Something worse than Chihuahuas."

"Cool got something the other day," Felix said. "An ugly thing that worries us."

"What?"

"We'll show it to you after the game," Marshall said. "Let's just say the gist of it is that someone doesn't want him breaking DiMaggio's record."

Harvey knew enough not to push it. This was the owner's skybox, after all, not the dugout. But it made him edgy as hell. It was only the first inning, after all. "Why'd you make up all this bullshit about a motivational coach?" he asked Felix.

"Everybody said you weren't taking on any cases. That you'd lost the taste for it. So I had to get you down here some other way. Even you have to admit what a hard sell you are."

In the eighth inning, with the Jewels comfortably out in front 6–2, Cooley got his second hit, a topped grounder he beat out by a step, and the fans cheered as lustily as though it had cleared the remote 417 FT sign in center. "*There's* your chance for you," Harvey tweaked Marshall Levy.

"Cool'll get his hits," the owner said smugly. "One way or another."

By now, it was really beginning to annoy Harvey, the way Marshall kept using the nickname "Cool." It reminded him of the way parents ingratiate themselves with their children by using their lingo, the way his own late father, for a year or two in Harvey's adolescence, had kept referring to things in Harvey's presence as "boss."

"Does Cooley know about me?" Harvey asked.

"Not yet," Marshall replied as Jewels catcher Ray Costa flied out to end the bottom of the eighth. "But soon."

Just after Jewels closer J. C. Jelsky sealed the Jewels' 6–3 win, meaty storm clouds began rolling in from the west. It was as if nature had politely waited for the national pastime to conclude its business. Within minutes The Jewel Box was under a thick dome of gray licked by lightning. The temperature dropped ten degrees. To the accompaniment of thunder and under the first big raindrops, the grounds crew removed the bases and drew the big tarpaulin over the infield. The tarp itself billowed like a great green cloud before settling down. The crowd drained out of the park and was replaced by the maintenance crew snapping back seats and sweeping the fans' litter into the aisles.

Harvey, Marshall, and Felix retired to Marshall Levy's glassed-in office right behind the skybox to talk baseball. Marshall sat in a Naugahyde executive chair behind his desk sipping Scotch, while Felix and Harvey sat in molded plastic chairs opposite him, both now nursing ginger ales. The office looked as if it had been furnished after a fifteen-minute stop at Office Max. On Marshall's otherwise sparsely populated desk sat a big brown cardboard shipping box.

After several minutes, their conversation was interrupted by a portly, shortish middle-aged man poking his head in the door. He had lost all his hair on top, leaving a friar's fringe of brown hair, but had retained, like many stout men, a boyish face bulging with good cheer. He wore a sport shirt open at the neck under a summery linen sport jacket with a light check.

"How 'bout dat, gentlemen? History in the making!" the man said in a rumbling singsong baritone, and Harvey knew at once from the overmodulated voice that he was a broadcaster.

"Snoot Coffman," Marshall said, sweeping his open palm from Snoot to Harvey. "Harvey Blissberg. Snoot here does the games on radio for WRIX. And Harvey used to play this game."

"I remember the Professor," Coffman said. "But you traded in your bat for a gun, as I recall."

"For a while, anyway."

"You here for Cooley?"

Harvey glanced at Marshall.

"Snoot knows," Marshall said.

"We thought he might have some insight," Felix added. "He knows what goes on with the ballplayers as much as we do."

"That's what I get from having to interview them ad nauseum."

"And he can keep his mouth shut," Marshall said, "although you'd never know it."

"You can bet Granny's bustle on that," the broadcaster said with a resonance entirely unnecessary for casual conversation. This, Harvey thought, was a man in the throes of a love affair with the sound of his own voice.

"So I guess I'm the only one here who's still in the dark," Harvey said.

"Not for long," Felix replied.

Coffman rubbed his hands together briskly. "Well, I'll leave you gentlemen alone."

"You have any thoughts, Snoot?" Marshall asked.

"Nope, but give me a chance to think about it. I love a good mystery. Really, I just stopped in to commend you on another fine victory and share my excitement about Moss. You know, DiMaggio was great the moment he came up, but Moss has really blossomed overnight. I'm honored to be broadcasting this amazing streak. As you were," he added, sliding back out the door.

When he was gone, Harvey said, "Snoot?"

Marshall laughed. "Hey, I don't name 'em; I just pay 'em. No one can say he hasn't brought a lot more pizzazz to the broadcasts. Not that there was anything wrong with Scott Sipple, our play-by-play man before last year. But Scott was a little . . . subtle. Snoot's one those big fans of the game. He's got half of Providence saying, 'Now how 'bout dat?'"

Sipple. He was now one of ESPN's stable of anchors Harvey would occasionally catch at three in the morning on a sleepless night. Harvey wondered if Mickey knew him.

Soon after the lights of The Jewel Box started to go out in an orderly procession around the park, there was another knock on the door, and Moss Cooley himself came in, larger than life. He wore an expensive navy blue shirt with a nice drape to it, brown slacks, two-tone fabric-and-leather shoes. His espresso-colored face was topped by a nest of six-inch dreadlocks that fell about his head in a moplike fashion. He wore one thin gold chain around his neck and two gold rings on his left hand. He was carrying, incongruously, a brown paper lunch sack. Harvey wondered if it contained a sandwich. That would make good copy—baseball's biggest hero brown-bagging it.

Harvey watched as Cooley's eyes fell on the cardboard box on Marshall's desk. There was a slight ripple in his composure, signaled only by a blink, and then his eyes were up again, surveying his hosts, who had risen.

"Congratulations, Cool," Marshall said. "I hope it never ends." He came around the desk to bang fists with Cooley, like one of the brothers.

"Everything comes to an end, Mr. Levy," Cooley replied.

"Way to go," Felix said, opting for a traditional handshake. "Moss, this is Harvey Blissberg, who played center field for us many years ago."

"Oh, yeah," Moss said. "I had your card once. You played for Boston before you ended up in this dump."

"Five years."

"'Course, I was just a little thang back then." He put his hand, palm down, at knee level.

"And now look what happened to you," Harvey said.

"He got bigger," Marshall said.

"And luckier," Moss added with a smile that revealed a gold bicuspid. "Thank God for that hit in the first inning. I'd be ashamed to keep the streak going on that sorry-ass squib in the eighth."

"Chance favors the prepared mind," Marshall suddenly said. "And the prepared bat."

"Wiser words have never been spoken," Moss said, humoring the man who signed his enormous paychecks.

"Actually, wiser words *have* been spoken," Harvey said. "Just not by Marshall Levy."

"How true," Moss said, laughing.

"Have a seat, Cool," Marshall said. He motioned him to an empty chair and retreated to his own. They all sat. "You're probably wondering why we brought Harvey down here from Boston."

"I was?"

"Well, in any case, you may be seeing a lot of him. Harvey's a licensed private investigator."

"Wait a second," Harvey said. "I haven't agreed—"

"Of course not," Marshall said, making a meaningless adjustment of his eyeglasses.

"I'm a little confused," Moss said.

"You're not alone," said Harvey.

"Wait a second." Moss looked from Marshall to Harvey and back. "You want him to look after me?"

"With your permission," Felix said. "Look, I think we all agreed yesterday that, for the time being, the less attention we call to this thing the better. You know what the press would do with something like this."

Moss nodded. "For the Chihuahuas it's like fuckin' crack."

"And we agree, if I'm not mistaken," Marshall added, "that we don't want to involve the Providence police."

"They'll talk to the Chihuahuas."

"Plus, once this gets out, you've got to worry about the copycats getting into the action," Marshall added. "We need to handle this quietly, if we can, and let you go about your business."

Harvey listened, looking at the box.

"We're going to do a routine security upgrade here at the park," Felix said. "But we're mum about the threat, right?"

"That's right," Moss said. "Let's keep it low."

There was a knock at the door. Marshall and Felix quickly exchanged looks and shrugs. "Who's there?" Marshall called out.

"Mickey Slavin. I'm looking for Harvey Blissberg."

Harvey was out of his chair in an instant, opening the door only a foot or so. "Hi," he whispered.

"Can I come in?" She asked. Her complexion was orange from her TV makeup.

"Not right now."

"Who's in there?"

"Nobody."

Mickey craned her head for a better look. "That looks like the back of Moss Cooley's head."

"It's not."

"Bliss, what's going on?"

"Nothing. We'll talk later."

"Okay. Meet you at Haven Brothers?"

"Give me an hour."

"Okay. Bliss, that's the back of Moss Cooley's head."

"Whatever."

"And, if I'm not mistaken, that's Felix Shalhoub's leg."

"No comment."

"And you're in Marshall Levy's skybox office."

"That I can't deny."

"Something's going on."

"We're having a motivation meeting. I'll see you in an hour."

When Harvey sat back down, Moss was shaking his head, muttering, "Chihuahua."

"More like a fox," said Marshall Levy. "Is she going to be a problem, Professor?"

"Meaning?"

"Nobody can know about this, not even Mickey."

"She won't be a problem."

"You two an item?" Moss said.

"More like a deeply flawed long-term proposition."

"Then I apologize for my comment."

"Forget it," Harvey said. "I don't like the press, either. Now where were we?"

"The cops," Marshall said.

Moss shook his head. "No way."

"Exactly," Felix said.

"Not until we know what we're dealing with," Marshall said. "Which is where Harvey comes in."

"Anyway, Harvey was a private investigator after he left baseball," Felix explained to Cooley. "Till he entered the lucrative world of motivational speaking. But we'd like him to keep an eye on you."

"I don't need a bodyguard," Moss said.

"Just think of him as handling the situation," Marshall said calmly. "Officially, we'd be bringing him on as a motivational coach. You'd have to go along with that. Look, Cool, there's just too much at stake. You've got a chance to make history."

Harvey coughed lightly. "What's in the box?"

"Yes, the box," Marshall said, standing, placing his hands ceremoniously on top of it, as if it were the Torah or something. The box had no markings on it. "Two nights ago, someone dropped it off outside the gate to the player's parking lot. It was addressed to Cool."

"We figured it was just another gift from a fan," Felix said.

"You wouldn't believe the shit I get," Moss said. "Someone sent me a Toast-R-Oven. Note said, 'DiMaggio's streak is toast.'"

"This is no Toast-R-Oven," Marshall said, opening the top flaps of the box. "Give me a hand, Cool." With Marshall's help, Cooley reached in the box and, grunting, lifted out the headless lawn jockey.

"Lovely," Harvey said.

"Wait till you see the note," Marshall said, handing him a piece of white paper folded in thirds.

Harvey opened it. The note was made up of letters cut from magazines and glued to the page:

diMAggiO   EvADeS   aPprEHenSiON.
do NoThinG In   GreATEsT gAMe.
        EsCApE RetRIbuTiOn.

"'DiMaggio evades apprehension,'" Harvey read aloud. "'Do nothing in greatest game. Escape retribution.'" He looked up at the others. "Christ, that's got to be the wordiest death threat ever."

"It's kind of like a fortune cookie fortune," Marshall said. "Without the cookie."

Harvey was confused. The threat's verbosity had the effect of undercutting its menace. What psychopath bothers to use words like *evade* and *apprehension*? On the other hand, the size of the jockey and the labor involved in transporting it suggested someone going to great and serious lengths to scare Cooley.

Moss passed a huge hand across his forehead. "I'm one big-ass target. A big black buck with a forty-six-game hittin' streak, a white girlfriend, and a Jewish bodyguard."

"You've got a white girlfriend?" Harvey asked.

"Same as you, my man."

"Let's not get ahead of ourselves," Marshall said. "It's probably nothing to worry about. A prank. Remember what Hank Aaron went through in 'seventy-three and 'seventy-four. One good thing, Cool, is that they don't know where you live."

"Not so fast," Cooley said.

Marshall twitched. "Excuse me?"

Cooley picked up the brown paper bag at his feet, placed it on Marshall's desk next to the headless lawn jockey, reached in, and removed a grinning lawn jockey's head. Its rust-dappled red cap matched the torso's vest.

"Jesus," Marshall said.

While the others watched, Cooley leaned over the desk and placed it gently on top of the jockey's body, where the irregular planes of the severed neck and body were perfectly joined.

4

ARVEY was as skilled as the next person at avoiding his feelings. Actually, for the past six months or more he had been considerably more skilled than the next person. Now he stared at the reunited lawn jockey and felt nothing for a moment. It was as if none of this could possibly have anything to do with him. Then everything came slowly back into focus—Marshall's office, the concerned faces in it, the headless figure on the desk. His slumbering instincts kicked in with the force of a controlled substance crossing his blood-brain barrier.

"Where do you live, Moss?" he asked abruptly.

"Cranston. In one of those developments."

"A gated community?"

Cooley shook his head.

"Does your house have a security system?" Felix and Marshall were now looking at Harvey as if he had just awakened from a coma and begun reciting Shakespeare.

Cooley said that the first floor was wired.

"Motion detectors?"

"No. Just the doors and windows."

"Sound detectors? Pressure mats? Pressure switches on the stairs, anything like that?"

"No, no, and no."

Harvey leveled a look at Marshall. "We've got to get him the hell out of that house."

"Hold on, Harvey," Marshall said, holding up his hands to stop Harvey's verbal onslaught. "Can you be so sure this threat's serious? I mean, it's just a lawn jockey." Minimizing the very reason they had summoned him from his funk in Cambridge.

"Marshall, this is not like getting a piece of garden-variety hate mail. We're talking major-league harassment." Out of the corner of his eye, Harvey could see that Cooley was registering this opinion of the danger to him with a tightening of his neck muscles.

"You want to move him out of his own house already?" Marshall said, stroking his upper lip to a point with his thumb and index finger.

"Marshall, I'm happy to go back to what I was doing this afternoon."

"What was that?" Cooley asked.

"Sitting on my sofa watching an HBO documentary about baseball's golden days."

"Tell us what you have in mind," Marshall said.

Harvey turned to Moss. "I know a broker in town that deals in executive transfers. I'll see what she's got lying around. What do you drive?"

"Range Rover."

"Not anymore." Harvey pivoted his head to Marshall. "You must know someone in the car business in Providence."

"Max Malise is an old friend. Malise Motors."

"What kind of cars?"

"Subarus, Hondas."

"Good. Call Max tomorrow morning and tell him you want to rent two nondescript cars from him in your name.

Tell him you'll turn them in in a few days for two more. And that you might keep doing that for a while. If he asks you why, don't tell him. Have the first two cars delivered to the players' parking lot tomorrow morning. Make sure they have tinted windows."

Harvey thought of his five-shot Smith & Wesson .38 Detective Special sitting in a lockbox on the highest shelf of his closet in Cambridge. Good thing he'd gotten requalified two months ago at the firing range in the basement of the Cambridge Police headquarters—he'd scored 267 of a possible 300. His concealed firearms permit was valid only in Massachusetts, though. Rhode Island didn't honor Massachusetts permits, so it might take weeks to get a Rhode Island pistol permit if he didn't have someone run major interference for him with the AG's office. He wondered if Detective Linderman, who headed up the Rudy Furth investigation fifteen years ago, was still with the force. Harvey's mind was on fire.

"Moss," he said, "I don't know what your autograph policy's been—"

"Cool is very good about autographs," Marshall said with paternal pride.

"Not anymore. Until this blows over. I'm sorry. Also, I don't know where you hang out after hours—"

"I got a couple bars where I know the owner—"

"Well, you're going to have to change your routine for now. If there's really somebody out there who wants to whack you in the knees, or worse, we're going to make it hard for him to find you. Are you with me?"

Cooley looked at Harvey as if he were an oncologist with bad news.

Felix said, "What about the ballpark? Talk about being exposed. We've got a ten-game home stand."

"The park's where he's going to be safest. Especially since, unlike, say, Wrigley Field, there're no buildings outside that would give anyone a shot at Moss."

"I don't want to become too hysterical, Professor," Marshall said, listing a bit as he spoke so the lawn jockey didn't come between them, "but what about a guy on the roof of *this* place with a high-powered rifle and a telescopic sight? . . . Sorry, Moss, but we've got to cover the possibilities."

"First, Marshall, you're going to eliminate all access to the roof, if you haven't already. That aside, there're just too many opportunities to be seen, especially with a rifle, which can't be concealed from forty-five thousand potential witnesses. And then there's the problem of getting away. You think it's easy to get out of a stadium in the middle of a game after shooting someone? Gentlemen, if someone's going to take a crack at Moss, it's going to be where he can go one-on-one, with the element of surprise completely on his side and the getaway assured. Where Moss is vulnerable. Going in and out of his home, in and out of the bars or restaurants where he's known to hang out. That's why we've got to change everything about your routine, Moss. Your habits."

"Damn," Cooley said.

"Hey," Harvey said, trying to leaven the mood with a little laugh, "if Campy can change your stroke and turn you into the game's most consistent hitter, I can change your lifestyle for a week or two and keep you alive. Marshall, can you put Moss up tonight in your home?"

"Sure."

"Wait a second," Moss said. "I've got plans with my lady."

"Tell her you're temporarily indisposed. Marshall has a very nice house, and I'm sure you'll be comfortable there tonight until I can get back from Cambridge tomorrow with a change of clothes and my gun."

Cooley looked up. "Gun?"

"I'm good with a purse, Moss, but I'll feel safer with my .38."

"Damn."

"I'll see if I can come up with a new house for you by tomorrow. In the meantime, I don't want you anywhere near your own."

"I need to go home and change my threads," Cooley said.

"No," Harvey said, then quickly: "Look, we all hope this is nothing. These things often are." He let the reassurance hang there in the air for a moment before it quickly dispersed on its own, like a puff of cigarette smoke.

"Maybe we ought to clue the rest of the team into what's going on," Felix suggested. "So they can be looking for any unusual activity, suspicious characters?"

"Let's wait on that," Harvey said. "Let's stick to the motivational-coach cover for now. By the way, I wouldn't mind having that for a little while." He pointed again at the headless jockey standing politely on the table between Marshall and him. Harvey didn't think he had seen one of them in anyone's yard for twenty or thirty years.

"Be my guest," Marshall said, taking off his designer eyeglasses and wiping each lens tenderly on a handkerchief. "All right with you, Cool?"

"It's cool with Cool," the ballplayer said, and Harvey felt a stab of disappointment to hear Moss indulge in the celebrity vogue for referring to oneself in the third person.

"Should we get it fingerprinted?" Felix asked.

"I assume it's already been handled enough to make the search for usable prints futile."

They struggled to get the lawn jockey—and its head—back in the box, and Marshall beckoned Robert the skybox steward and gave him instructions to get the package down to Harvey's car in the players' parking lot.

Five minutes later Harvey stood with Moss Cooley in the clubhouse while he gathered up some toiletries and extra clothes from his cubicle. They were alone except for a twentyish clubhouse assistant, collecting dirty postgame dinner plates from the food area and sponging off the two long dining tables. A much older black gentleman was vacuuming the clubhouse's indoor/outdoor carpeting.

"I don't need this shit," Cooley muttered as he began to lay his belongings carefully into a small green nylon duffel bag with the Jewels' logo silk-screened on the side. "I don't need you all in my business."

"Don't blame you," Harvey replied, careful not to say too much or make a bad impression. He and Moss, who had had no relationship at all until an hour ago, had been thrown rudely together now, like contestants on *Blind Date*. "Listen, I'd appreciate it if you used a different bag. I'd rather you didn't carry anything that might identify you."

Scowling, Cooley took the two hangered items—a pair of slacks and a silk shirt with a brown-and-tan geometric pattern—and held them out to Harvey. "Here, you take them then." He disappeared around the corner into the food area, returned with a plastic grocery bag, and dropped his toiletries and some other items into it.

"I want you to do something for me tonight, Moss, while you're enjoying Marshall's hospitality. I want you to make a list of every place you go regularly in and around Providence at least once a week. Gas stations, movie theaters, restaurants, you name it. Any place you go on a regular basis. Plus any place where you're known to make an appearance. Any place the papers have reported you going to."

"What're you tryin' to do, man, invade my life?"

"No, I'm trying to save it."

"Let's get out of here. Mr. Levy said to meet him in the parking lot in fifteen."

"I want you to make a second list."

Cooley rolled his eyes.

"This one's got your habits on it. You jog? Good. Put it down, including the route. You play miniature golf? Good. When and where? You gamble? Fine. I want to know who your bookie is."

"I don't gamble," Cooley said flatly.

"Moss, anything you're used to doing, you're going to stop doing until your streak is over. Let's be optimistic and say you break DiMaggio's record. You're twelve games away. That's two weeks. We can do that. We're going to change your life fast so that you don't have to think about it. You can get back to the game and let me do the worrying for you. Okay?" Twelve games away from the record? It was a vast distance—unthinkable that his luck would hold out—and Harvey was calmed by the thought.

"Okay."

"One other thing."

"What?"

"Your girlfriend."

"Cherry Ann. What about her?"

"Does she live with you?"

"No. She comes over a couple of times a week. I go there some. But we get together at odd hours. We both got night jobs."

"Let me ask you a question, Moss, and don't take it personally."

"Go for it."

"Are you just getting laid, or is this a love project?"

"A lot of the first and some of the second. She's not some bimbo of mine. She's a student at Johnson and Wales. She's studying to be a chef. Open her own restaurant."

"Do you trust her, Moss?"

"Meaning?"

"Can she keep a secret? Would she ever betray you?"

Cooley furrowed his brow. "What kind of question is that?"

"It's a good one, Moss. A young woman is dating a famous ballplayer making several million a year. People might offer her money for information about you or your whereabouts. I'm talking about tabloid journalists, or even worse."

"I don't believe she'd ever do that."

"It's hard for the best people to keep their mouths shut about knowing a celebrity. Especially about sleeping with one. I'm just being realistic. Do a lot of people know you see each other?"

"I haven't seen it in the papers, if that's what you mean. We've only been dating since May, and we're very careful."

"Does she know about the death threats?"

"No. I've just told her I get letters."

"What about the jockey?"

"Haven't told her that yet."

"Where'd you meet her, Moss?"

He hesitated slightly before answering. "At Teasers."

"Teasers?"

"It's a strip joint in the Jewelry District."

"She likes to go to strip clubs?"

"She doesn't like to go there. She works there."

"Great," Harvey said.

"It's not what it seems. She's not the person you see up there."

Harvey didn't want to touch the philosophical and onto-logical edges of that one. "I'd like to talk to her."

"She'd never be involved in this shit."

"Not knowingly. Look, Moss, I don't know about cooking school, but a strip joint's not the kind of place I'd want to have my name bandied about, and frankly, it wouldn't surprise me if she's been boasting about you."

"She's just stripping for money. It's not her life."

"Moss, it's not like it ever occurred to me she was doing it for the dignity and self-fulfillment. Look, tomorrow's a night game, right?" Cooley nodded. "Maybe you, Cherry Ann, and I can get together in the late afternoon before you're due at the park?"

"I'll try."

"Meanwhile, don't mention the lawn jockey to her. Don't say anything about me, either."

Cooley nodded reluctantly. "I don't like this."

"Whereas, of course, I'm really looking forward to spending the next couple of weeks wondering when some-one's going to jump out of the bushes and attack the two of us."

"You know," Cooley said, "you're all right, Bagel Boy." He clapped him on the shoulder.

Harvey looked in Cooley's eyes, inspecting them for any sign of hostility, and decided there wasn't any. "I may be a Bagel Boy, but at least I don't get my hair done at Snakes R Us."

"C'mon, this hair cost me two bills."

This was good. At least they wouldn't be wasting time skating around on thin, politically correct ice. "Oh, I think you can afford it," Harvey said.

"Damn right I can."

"I've gotta tell you something, Moss."

"What?"

"At least Bagel Boy beats Professor."

"Must be ten thousand Professors in baseball."

"I know. Nothing more original ever stuck. Bagel Boy," he mused. "Just don't wear it out."

They walked out of the clubhouse and into the long hallway that led to the players' parking lot, their footsteps clapping against the concrete floor and bouncing off the walls.

Mike, the security guard, pushed opened the metal door for them, saying, "Good night, Cool, and congratulations." The thunderstorm had left the blacktop littered with puddles. There were only a handful of cars left in the lot, none worth less than thirty grand. Cooley fished in his pocket for his keyless remote and pressed one of the buttons. Thirty feet away a Range Rover, beaded with rain, chirped and blinked its headlights at them.

"We're not taking your car," Harvey reminded him.

He jammed his keys in his pocket. "When you're black," he suddenly seethed, "you don't ever get a day off. Every fucking day, your job is being black."

Harvey put a hand on Cooley's shoulder. "You know, Moss, I think this could be the start of a beautiful relationship."

"Over here, Cool," Marshall Levy called through the window of his Jaguar, which was idling by the gate.

Harvey closed his eyes. After four years of dawdling in the

shallows of motivational speaking, he was back on the high dive, stepping off now, no turning back, the dark current coming up fast to meet him. He had wondered how he would ever re-enter the river of time, and now he knew.

"Moss," he said, "is there anything you know about these threats that you didn't want to say upstairs?"

"You mean, do I know somebody who wants me dead, but I'm not fucking telling you?"

"Something like that."

"Shit, no. Cool's everybody's friend."

Harvey handed Moss his hanging clothes. "Not anymore."

5

EVERY afternoon at four, for as long as most people in Providence can remember, a lunch wagon hitched to a truck cab has pulled into a couple of parking spaces on Fulton Street next to the Second Empire–style City Hall and remained there until dawn. Set on an angle atop the wagon, a small neon sign blinks "HAVEN BROS. DINER." The diner is like some alien aluminum creature from another world, a fossil of the 1940s that seems to have crawled out of urban America's unconscious, a film noir artifact spliced nightly into the city's present. Throughout the night, in the shadow of the floodlit old Industrial National Bank Building on Kennedy Plaza, a trickle of the city's powerful and powerless, Ivy League–educated and semiliterate, sleepless and snack-deprived, climb the portable steps of the diner for a bowl of red beans or a steamed hot dog.

Haven Brothers is no culinary mecca. Its specialty is inedible—a serving of romantic desolation—and in that regard it was probably no accident that Mickey Slavin had suggested that they meet there. Their relationship had seen better days, which is true of most relationships that last more than a few months, but Harvey felt keenly that they had lost something that needed to be found again, or else they needed to find something they had never had in the first place.

When Harvey pulled his Honda up to the curb at the Biltmore, a hundred feet from City Hall, he could see Mickey's Jetta parked in front, and Mickey herself sitting on the second step of the building's splayed granite staircase, sipping from a cardboard cup of coffee. She wore her television clothes—an expensive navy blue blazer over a silk scoop-neck blouse. Her bare legs, which Harvey was always delighted to see, had a light, even midsummer tan. She was wearing high-heeled sandals of such subtle construction that Harvey could barely figure out how they stayed on. She seemed to be looking into her coffee cup, her shaggy auburn bob obscuring most of her face.

Unseen, Harvey watched her for a moment from behind the wheel. Love has a hard time surviving its own complexity, and he relished this stolen glimpse of her, with its illusion of innocence. For a moment she was once again the willowy twenty-five-year-old daughter of New York civil rights lawyer Arnold Slavin who had converted a Princeton education, a solid knowledge of American sports, and a traffic-stopping face into a job as Providence's first female television sportscaster. In the whole world he knew no one better, nor was he by anyone better known. The downside of that, of course, was that each had a metal detector's unerring knowledge of the other's concealed vulnerabilities. And lately, they were getting too good at setting off each other's alarms.

People met, fell in love with only the slightest notion why, and then spent years obligated to each other. They made as much sense as they could of the investment. Still, it was a strange streak indeed, their never marrying. Was it their perfectly balanced ambivalence about each other, or about marriage itself? Was there a tacit agreement between them, now perhaps too late to amend, that marriage was somehow not good enough for them, that their bond was too fragile, or too important, for the degradations of matrimony? After all this time they shared most of the great indignities of marriage, anyway—from the exasperating familiarity with each other's quirks to long bouts of sexual apathy to aging parents. All they lacked, really, was children. No small thing, they knew—the topic still came up—but Mickey's biological back was against the wall.

"Haven Brothers is about the only thing that hasn't changed in this town," she said when he sat down next to her. "The city's got sushi bars now and parking lots where it costs five dollars for the first half-hour. They took the Providence River and turned it into a canal with gondolas and started calling the town Renaissance City. They've got hit TV shows that take place here. They've got bars with secondhand sofas in them, for chrissakes, just like Manhattan."

When Harvey played ball here, it was still being referred to in college guidebooks as "the armpit of the East." It was his suspicion that people were sentenced to live in Providence for unspecified Kafkaesque crimes, or else were paying down some horrible karmic debt. But now it was a city where people actually chose to live, and with good reason. From its ashes had risen a jewel of a city. Harvey hardly recognized it. It was like a child of a previous marriage who'd grown up in his absence. He loved it, but at a painful, befuddled distance.

"Now they've even got a ball club you could care about," she said. "No offense, Bliss."

"None taken."

Mickey pointed over to the left, toward the old Amtrak station. "See that over there. They even put in an outdoor skating rink, just like New York, but cheesier."

"What do you expect from a state whose mascot is Mr. Potato Head?" The papers had reported this strange development in the last few months. "What other state's got a mascot that's a children's toy?"

"It was invented here," Mickey said. "Hasbro invented it."

"I know Hasbro invented it. So what? Is the mascot of Massachusetts Tickle Me Elmo?"

"Tickle Me Elmo wasn't invented in Massachusetts."

"I *know* it wasn't invented in Massachusetts. It was just an example." Lately, there were these ridiculous, literal-minded misunderstandings, as if their relationship hadn't been founded on finely tuned irony. "I was only trying to point out that Providence is still Providence." How could two people who knew each other so well suddenly understand each other so little? They had gone to couples counseling a few years ago, but the effect had worn off. They again appeared to prefer a murky discontent, as if what sustained them were grievances they were too lazy to even name.

A Camaro skidded to a stop in front of Haven Brothers. Two toughs got out and started play-fighting, air-punching as they called each other "mothafuckas," before disappearing into the lunch wagon.

"You're baby-sitting Cooley, aren't you?" she said, taking a studied sip of coffee.

"No, I'm not."

"Just like you baby-sat Dave Kasick all those years ago." Kasick, his old Red Sox roommate, had gone AWOL on the eve of guest-hosting a late-night network comedy show. Harvey had dug him up and gotten him through the ordeal, only to find himself then investigating the death of the show's executive producer.

"They want to hire me as a motivational coach."

"Pardon me while I gag, Bliss. Right now you couldn't motivate a rosin bag."

"Be that as it may," Harvey said.

"How can you not tell me? I'm your best friend."

"You're also a correspondent for ESPN."

"So it *is* something juicy."

"See what I mean. You can't wait to get your hands on it. Except that it's nothing."

"Bull."

"Look, Mick, even if it *was* something you're not supposed to know, I wouldn't want to tell you and put you in the
bind of holding a scoop you can't use. I love you too much for
that."

"Double bull. You know, you like keeping secrets too
much. Why's that?"

"I can't divulge that information."

"Look, the black man's creeping up on whitey's big
record. The racist underbelly has found a new focus."

"Now you're talking like the daughter of a left-wing civil
rights lawyer that you are."

"C'mon, Cooley's even got a teammate against him."

"Who's that?" The two toughs now emerged from the
diner with wieners and zoomed off in the Camaro, disappearing into downtown Providence's dark web of eighteenth-cen-
tury streets.

"Andy Cubberly, who hits in front of him."

Harvey tried to appear uninterested.

"Cubberly almost single-handedly ended his streak on
Sunday in Detroit."

"Be serious."

"Seventh inning. Jewels down by one. Cubberly leads off
with a drive to right center. A gapper. Except that Desch does
a nice job of cutting it off before it goes through. Cubberly
runs right through Croker's stop sign at first and slides under
the tag at second for a double."

"So, with first base open, the Detroit pitcher has to intentionally walk Moss Cooley," Harvey reasoned. "Depriving him
of an at-bat."

Mickey nodded, raising her perfectly plucked, ready-for-
prime-time eyebrows. "That's right."

"Let me guess. Cooley's hitless so far in the game."

"On the schneid. Oh for three."

"So you're saying Cubberly tries to take the bat out of his
own teammate's hands? And succeeds."

"In a situation when it makes no sense at all for him to try for an extra base. Cavanaugh chewed him out pretty bad after the game. Cubberly claimed he just wasn't thinking, didn't see the sign."

"Well, maybe that's the case."

"He did it another time, Bliss."

"Really?"

"You know Scott Sipple, who used to do the Jewels' games on radio?"

"I see him on ESPN."

"Well, Scott pointed out the other instance to me when I was talking to him about Sunday's game. We went back and looked it up, and sure enough, last Thursday against Cleveland, sixth inning, Cubberly hits a one-out infield single and promptly steals second base."

"So Cooley gets intentionally walked again in a game where he's gone hitless?"

"Correct," Mickey said. "Under normal circumstances, Cubberly's done a good thing. Tie game. Cubberly's stealing percentage has been above seventy percent. Get a rally going. Just one thing, Bliss: it's a very unfriendly thing to do to a man who's working on a long hitting streak."

"Unless Cubberly's just not a thinking man," Harvey suggested.

"No one's ever confused him with Tielhard de Chardin." She still liked to show off her comparative religions major from time to time.

"Well, that's all very interesting."

"Is it?"

"I'll keep an eye on Cubberly from my new perch as motivational instructor."

"Something's happening," Mickey said. "And you're not telling me about it."

"Can we continue this conversation at home? Or rather, not continue it at home? I was hoping I might get lucky tonight."

"With anyone I know?"

"Only barely." Harvey stood, giving Mickey his hand and pulling her to her feet.

"It'll cost you," she said. "There's no free funch."

"Right." He laughed. "Sure." He walked her to her Jetta. "I'll race you to Cambridge."

They walked to their separate cars for the one-hour drive back home. For the first time in months he felt stuffed with purpose, and pleasantly in the present.

6

THE next morning, while Mickey slept late upstairs, Harvey went to his little study off the living room of the Italianate stucco house in Cambridge they called home. It had been months since he'd sat in his nail-head leather swivel chair to do any work. A manila folder next to his blotter contained copies of his boilerplate motivational speech, and he shoved it into a compartment of the oak rolltop desk. He eyed his black box of Schminke watercolors and his canvas brush caddy in one of the desk's larger cubbyholes. Spring and summer were usually reserved for bouts of painting, but his initiative had been failing him there too.

With a sigh he picked up the phone and dialed the number of Debbie Rubino at a real estate firm in Warwick, Rhode Island, that handled the housing arrangements for executive transfers in and out of the state. She had found him the apartment on Benefit Street he rented the year he spent in Providence, and they had dated for a couple of months B.M.—Before Mickey.

"Harvey Blissberg," she said. "My God, it's been a long time. How are you?"

"I'm just fine, Debbie. You?"

"I'm still here."

"That's just what I was hoping."

"So what's going on? What're you doing? And where're you doing it?"

"I'm up here in Cambridge, you know, being an ex-athlete. Doing some motivational speaking."

"You married?"

"Well, I've been with the same person forever, but—"

"That sportscaster?"

"Mickey Slavin."

"Good for you."

"Fifteen years now. No kids, though."

"Wish I could say the same for myself. I've got three. At least they're old enough for me to be back at work part-time. What's up?"

"I need a short-term house down there. I'm going to be doing some work in Providence for a month or so, and I can't stand the damn commute every day."

"A month? That's tough. What're you looking for?"

"Something secluded. Country squirish. Big lot. Preferably surrounded by woods, but a big yard in front. Mowed. Two-car garage with remote door opener."

"Jeez," she said with a laugh, "what color walls do you want in the living room? People who want a rental for a month can't be too choosy. Why don't you just stay in a hotel?"

"It's not that kind of job, Debbie," Harvey said as he heard Mickey coming down the stairs. He kicked the study door shut with his foot.

"Okay, for you I'm looking," she said. "I've got a house here in Warwick where I could stuff you. But it's a development with half-acre lots."

"Needs to be secluded." He heard Mickey open the front door.

"Boy, this is getting more mysterious by the minute. Here we go. There's one in Exeter, off Route One-oh-two. It's a yuppie development. Huge lots. Let's see. Four bedrooms. Thirty-six hundred square feet. Three-car garage, alarm system, woodsy, but a big yard. It's a nice shingled colonial. The former tenant just got transferred to San Francisco, and most of their furniture's still in there until he and his wife get settled."

"Perfect. How much?"

"I'll let it go for three grand a month, but you'll have to pay a month's security."

"Fine."

"This is unorthodox, Harvey."

"I know. I'd like you to handle all the utilities and the phone bill. I'll reimburse you in cash. Just makes things easier for me."

"Okay, okay. When do you want to look at it?"

"Today."

"That's fast."

"Can you show it to me if I'm at your office by eleven?"

"Harvey, I've got to tell you, this doesn't sound like a motivational speaking job."

He called Marshall Levy to let him know about the house and ask about the cars.

"Two Subarus'll be at the park by this afternoon."

"Excellent. How's Moss doing?"

"The perfect houseguest. Made his own bed, too. Hospital corners."

"Put him on for a minute."

Cooley came to the phone.

"Did you sleep well?" Harvey asked.

"Okay."

"Did you call Cherry Ann?"

"She can't make it today. But she said I could come by her place late tomorrow morning."

"That'll have to do. Now, listen, can you hang at Marshall's till two or three this afternoon? I think I've found a house for us. I want to check it out, and then I'll pick you up, and we can go to your place and get your things."

"I feel like I'm in the Federal Witness Protection Program."

"You're not, Moss. You're in the Blissberg Protect-Your-Black-Ass Program."

Harvey flipped through his Rolodex until he found Professor Roy Hinch of the University of Rhode Island's Crime Lab in Kingston, where he trained a lot of the Rhode Island BCI forensic people.

"Remember me, Hinch?" Harvey asked.

"I remember hearing you were out of the detective game."

"I still like to get my feet wet now and then. Can I bring you something later today?'

"My people are more backed up than a bus station toilet."

"I just want you to eyeball something and give me a low-tech opinion. Nothing fancy."

"When?"

"Let's see," Harvey said, trying to plan his day. If he saw the house by eleven-thirty and liked it, he'd need to make arrangements for heightened security. . . . "One this afternoon okay?"

"I'll slip you in," Hinch said without enthusiasm.

"Hinch, you still into dessert wines?"

"More than ever."

"Good. I'll make sure there's something in it for you."

The next call was trickier. Detective Linderman had retired soon after he investigated the death of Harvey's Providence Jewels' roommate Rudy Furth fifteen years ago. Harvey hadn't talked to him in years, and wasn't even sure he was still alive. Linderman answered his home phone on about the tenth ring.

"What took you so long?" Harvey said when Linderman uttered a rumpled hello. "Couldn't find your walker?"

"Blissberg?"

Harvey had to smile. It was like Old Home Week. Felix, Marshall, Campy, Debbie Rubino, and now Linderman. "It is I."

"Don't laugh. My knees don't work so good anymore."

"Then why aren't you in Scottsdale with the other retired cops?"

"I *got* a place in Florida, whaddya want? But it's frickin' July, Harvey. I like to spend the summer near my granddaughter. I hope you're not calling me for money."

"Something far more valuable. I was wondering whether you could run me a little interference with the Rhode Island AG's office."

"What makes you think I still got friends there?"

"Just give me a yes or no."

"Not until you tell me more."

"I've got a job in your state, and I need a pistol permit for my thirty-eight because your pathetic state won't honor my Massachusetts concealed firearms permit. I need someone to get my application pushed to the top of the pile. I'm not waiting thirty days. I don't have that kind of time."

"Why should I do this for you?"

"How about because I need to prevent a terrible catastrophe from occurring in your beloved state?"

"What's the job?"

"Only if you can keep your mouth shut."

"You want your permit or not?"

"One of the Jewels needs protection."

"The mob?"

"Nobody knows. The ballplayer doesn't think he has any enemies."

"All right, I'll make the call for you. When are you planning on showing up at the AG's office to fill out the application?"

"Later today."

"Don't forget to bring IDs, a recent photo, and your fingertips."

"I never leave home without them."

Harvey was leaning back in his chair, hands folded behind his head, basking in the unfamiliar glow of his own competence, when a knock on his study door was followed immediately by the appearance of Mickey Slavin in a loosely cinched bathrobe.

"You were very loving last night," he said. "I appreciate that."

"Bliss, I hope this doesn't come as a shock to you, but you have a headless lawn jockey in the backseat of your car."

"I wish you wouldn't go through my things."

"Well, I'm sorry, but I went out to my car to get some files, and I noticed a big box sitting in the backseat of your car, and I just thought I'd have a little peek. You can imagine my surprise."

"Don't worry. I've got the head."

She glowered at him. It was amazing how good she'd gotten at glowering in recent years.

"I was going to surprise you with it for our anniversary," he said.

"Anniversary of what?"

"Fifteen years of living together? I'm pretty sure it's the headless-lawn-jockey anniversary."

"Don't be a jerk."

"It's just something I picked up at a yard sale. They're collectors' items now."

"I'm sure. Especially with a severed head. You know what I think?"

"I have a good idea."

"The team's hired you to protect Moss Cooley because he's been receiving death threats, one of which has taken the form of said lawn jockey."

"It's too early in the morning for this," Harvey said. "Did you make coffee yet?"

"You just expect me to sit on my hands?" Mickey said as they ate bowls of Familia in the kitchen.

"Yes," Harvey said.

"For how long?"

"Until it's no longer a problem. Then it'll be your exclusive. That's your reward for putting up with me all these years."

"Just tell me this."

"What?"

"Where did the headless lawn jockey show up?"

"At the ballpark."

"And the head?"

"It showed up later," Harvey said tersely, head bowed over his Swiss cereal to indicate his disinclination to continue. "What's your schedule the next couple of days?"

"I fly to New York this afternoon to do the Yankees–Devil Rays tiff tonight." Unlike Felix, Mickey used sportscaster clichés ironically, and merely to taunt him. "Tomorrow night I'm in Cincinnati for the big Reds-Cubs clash."

"I'm glad we've been able to spend this time together."

"Don't give me that shit. You've been just as unavailable."

"I've been right here on the sofa."

"Emotionally unavailable. I'm only geographically un-available."

"Don't flatter yourself."

"You're suffering from sad man–ism, Bliss. You're so deep inside sad man–ism I can't reach you."

"Every guy's entitled to a few years of total dysfunction-ality."

"Just remember to put me on your mailing list when you notify folks that you're fully functional again."

"I'm coming out of it, Mick. I'm now officially attached to the hip of the best hitter in baseball."

"Come here," she said, motioning him closer with her finger.

Harvey leaned in, hoping for a kiss.

Instead Mickey raised her paper napkin to his face. "Let me wipe your chin," she said. "You've got more Familia on your face than a two-year-old."

7

A MAN carrying a gun is exponentially different from a man without one. A gun has the power to alter any reality into which it enters. But it's also a beautiful fusion of form and function; a poetic, metallic extension of the hand; deadly jewelry. Shooting a gun has a hard elegance about it not entirely related to its deadlier duties, which is why you can always find cops in the bowels of a police station at two in the morning firing off a couple hundred rounds for the sheer brain-changing, soul-satisfying pleasure of it. At a certain level, firing a gun is just another explosive physical challenge, like hitting a golf ball well, a first serve, or a hanging curve.

Guns were not in Harvey's blood. He had come to them late, in his thirties, when his new profession demanded it. His rapport with his gun was clouded by a healthy aversion to violence. While Mickey was in her study downloading files from her ESPN producer on the Yankees and Devil Rays, Harvey got down his nickel-plated Smith & Wesson .38, removed its chamois swaddling, and laid it on the bed next to a box of hollow-points and the little clip-on buckskin cross-draw holster he used to carry it inside the left side of his belt. History could not be undone, gunpowder uninvented, and so he accepted his gun as an inevitable and morally justified advantage in situations that might otherwise end badly as far as society in general and himself in particular were concerned. But every time he pulled the trigger at a firing range, each shot seemed to leave on his soul a trace of dread, a memory of the damage he might have done. The idea that tools of such instant and remote-controlled violence were available to ordinary citizens—above all teenagers who either had not yet tasted mortality or had become impervious to it—still shocked him.

Harvey dressed in a dark blue short-sleeved sport shirt that draped comfortably over his linen pants. The shirt had been expensive, far more expensive than polyester ought to cost. He was feeling a little Rip Van Winkle-ish these days, rubbing his eyes at a changed world and its oxymorons: expensive polyester, beautiful Providence, The Jewel Box, gun-toting Blissberg. He wiped down his pistol with an oily cloth, then clipped the cross-draw holster inside his pants about eight inches to the left of his belt buckle and slid the gun into it. He practiced drawing it a few times, lifting the tail of his shirt up with his right thumb as he grabbed the checkered walnut grip and raised the pistol into firing position, his left hand gripping the bottom of his right for support.

He put everything—gun, bullets, holster, oily cloth, and cleaning kit—into a small leather bag. Then he packed a week's worth of clothes and his toiletries in a nylon duffel and put it in the trunk of his Honda, along with his gun bag, his Toshiba laptop, two bottles of Muscat de Beaumes-de-Venise 1997, and a pair of dark blue coveralls with the name "Stanley" stitched on the left breast in white thread.

When he came back in the house, Mickey was still at the PC. Harvey went back to his office and called Jerry Bellaggio, the former FBI special agent and Boston private detective under whom Harvey had once worked in the 1980s to earn his license. Bellaggio was retired and almost always at home now, thanks to his emphysema. Leaving the house required him to drag along a portable oxygen tank about which he was self-conscious.

"I need some basic research," Harvey said.

"Hey, what happened to motivational speaking?" Bellaggio said.

"I was highly motivated to stop motivating people."

"What's up?"

"I've just been hired to bodyguard Moss Cooley."

"Can't say I'm surprised. Aaron had one, you know, chasing Ruth."

"Some joker left him a headless lawn jockey with a note, then hung the head from his garage ceiling."

"Any evidence there's more than one person involved?"

"Not yet. Why?"

"Two or more, and it falls under possible FBI jurisdiction. Title 18, U.S. Code 241, Conspiracy against Rights."

"Right now we're not trying to shine a big light on it. It could just be some asshole showboating."

"Who knows about it?"

"The team's top management and me, basically."

"They haven't gone to the locals?"

"No. I'm their insurance policy right now against having to open the thing up to a public viewing. That's why I need you."

"Well, go on, give me my marching orders."

"First of all, can you get on the Web while I'm baby-sitting and find out everything you can about Negro lawn jockeys, especially cast-iron ones—who still makes them, who distributes them in Rhode Island, any news stories or legal cases involving lawn jockeys? This one's about two feet tall, goes about fifty pounds. He's hunched over, wearing a red vest and cap, and he's holding a hitching ring in his extended right hand. His head is a caricature—bulging eyes, obsequious grin. You still have access to FBI databases?"

"I've got a friend in the BAU, but the bureau frowns on the abuse of database privileges."

"Doesn't it count for anything that you're a proud member of the Society of Ex-Special Agents?"

"Yeah. That and six dollars will get me an FBI souvenir key ring. I don't like to call in too many favors, Harvey. It puts my buddy at risk."

"Oh, for chrissakes, Jerry, I'm feeding you data the FBI can use in their profiling."

"But it's not their case."

"Some day it might be theirs. I just need to run with it for a while."

"Well, tell me what you want," Bellaggio said, wheezing.

"I need to know about any right-wing or racist activity in southern New England, especially groups or incidents where death threats involving lawn jockeys or other segregationist symbols are the signature. Also anybody in southern New England currently under federal surveillance for suspected hate crimes."

"All right. Let me see if I can get my buddy to tap in for you. What about the note?"

"What about it?"

"Is it handwritten or typed?"

"Neither. Cut-out letters from magazines."

"Did you know that ninety percent of those are written by the so-called victims themselves?"

"You're kidding," Harvey said.

"Nope. It's a curious fact, since the bad guys would be better off using that technique, but for some reason they insist on writing or typing them themselves. Bureau's got a huge repository of death threats and ransom notes to draw on, but cutouts aren't going to help you."

"In any case, I seriously doubt that Moss Cooley sent himself a decapitated lawn jockey with a note telling him to lay off DiMaggio's streak. He doesn't need publicity that bad."

"No, I suppose not. So where do I reach you?"

"I'll be on the fly, Jerry, so use my cell phone number the minute anything lights up."

On the way out of the house, he gave Mickey's ass a fierce squeeze, and she gave him two sheets of computer down-loaded printout, folded in thirds, saying, "Read this before you see Cooley today."

As Harvey drove from Boston to Providence, there was a mo-ment—it was soon after he hit the straight leg of 95 that began around Norwood and shot south to Rhode Island's capital—when he felt like he was passing through a membrane from one world to another. It was hard to explain to others, the un-canny feeling he had about Providence, that it existed in an-other place and time. Maybe it went back to his childhood outside Boston. Providence was only fifty miles away, yet he had never gone there as a boy. It lurked on the edge of his awareness, like an aunt too eccentric to visit. That he had fin-ished his playing career there, in the costume jewelry capital of America, only enriched its personal mythology for him.

No matter how many television shows were set in Provi-dence, no matter how much they gussied it up with canals and urban renewal, it was still a city ensnared in the past. In fact, it was the only major American city whose entire downtown was listed on the National Registry of Historic Places. For forty years, from the late 1920s to the late 1960s, there had been virtually no money for new building downtown. Despite its recent growth spurt, the city continued to exhibit what a *Christian Science Monitor* journalist once called "a curious lack of bustle." Who could explain Providence? The New Eng-land mob, with roots in Prohibition, when Narragansett Bay was a rum-runner's paradise, made a Federal Hill storefront its headquarters, while only a mile away, on College Hill, Brown University and the Rhode Island School of Design churned out the power elite and the avant garde. In this tight town, everything was a stone's throw away from its contradiction. Its

mayor was a man who had once extinguished a lighted cigarette on the forehead of a man he suspected of sleeping with
his estranged wife, but now sold "The Mayor's Own Marinara
Sauce" on the Internet.

On the empty straight stretch of 95, Harvey unfolded the
printout Mickey had given him, propped it up on the steering
wheel, and read it in snatches. It was a short item from *Sports
Illustrated,* published almost six years ago, headlined "Farewell
to Al Molis."

Journeyman catcher Al Molis was
found dead last week in an Ohio motel, apparently of a self-inflicted gun-
shot wound to the head. Thus ended
one of the saddest major league baseball careers in recent memory. Molis,
35, who had been released this spring
by the St. Louis Cardinals, failed to
catch on with another team and at
the time of his death was contemplating a coaching offer from an undis-
closed minor league team, according
to his estranged wife Jeannette.

He had a major league lifetime batting average of .244 with six teams,
but was perhaps best known for his
highly unorthodox political activities
in a sport not known for its players'
political involvements. A professed
right-winger and member of the
rogue white supremacist group Izan
Nation, based in Virginia, Molis recruited fellow major leaguers to his
cause. As a member of the Colorado
Rockies, Molis was arrested, along
with teammates Andy Cubberly and
Rod Duquesne, for disrupting a
Black Pride parade in downtown
Denver by shouting racist slogans
and hurling white paint-filled bal-

loons at the marchers. The charges
were eventually reduced, and all
three were required to perform community service.

On the field, Molis was twice repri-
manded by the league for his habit of
whispering racist comments to black
batters from his position behind
home plate, but his defensive skills
and knack for handling pitchers—yes,
even African-American ones, as long
as they were his teammates—kept
him in the league for twelve years.

Always prone to erratic behavior
and drug use, Molis's troubles seemed
to worsen over the winter. Police in
his hometown of New Welford, Ohio,
arrested him in January for possession
of crystal methedrine and had to subdue him with pepper gas.

Molis once said to a reporter who
asked him what it was like playing for
so many different teams: "I've only
played on one team my entire life—
the white team."

Harvey gunned his Honda southward. As he approached
the gleaming domed Rhode Island State House off 95, just
north of downtown, he was surprised by Snoot Coffman's
face smiling down on him from a billboard. Coffman was
holding up a baseball glove, which seemed to be catching the
line of copy "CATCH EVERY JEWELS' GEM ON WRIX WITH SNOOT
COFFMAN." A cartoon bubble coming out of Snoot's mouth
contained his signature "Now how 'bout dat?"

Harvey stopped at the AG's office to fill out his pistol permit application and get fingerprinted, then got back on 95
South, making Rubino's Warwick real estate office by eleven-
fifteen.

The house in Exeter was just right: a dark, shingled colonial on the far loop of a high-end development, set well back from the street, protected from its equally affluent neighbors by phalanxes of evergreens. Inside, it was tastefully furnished and boasted a fully equipped designer kitchen. Harvey trailed behind the matronly Rubino, now only faintly reminiscent of the buxom blond he had once wooed, as she led him from one room to another. She pointed out each of the house's virtues with that absurd zeal only real estate brokers can summon while keeping a straight face. With the possible exception of the first seven years of sex with Mickey, Harvey had never achieved the levels of enthusiasm Debbie Rubino expressed as she pointed out the flagstone fireplace and the northern light in the master bedroom. Harvey occupied himself with mentally calculating the added security arrangements he would have to make to keep them secure at night until Cooley's hitting streak was over.

Back at Rubino's office, Harvey wrote out checks, received two sets of keys in return, thanked her profusely, and retired to his Honda to call a local home security firm with whom he'd had dealings on a few occasions. Within half an hour he was walking through the colonial again, this time with two of the firm's installers, indicating where he wanted motion and sound detectors, pressure mats, and pressure switches on the stairs to the second floor. He left the men his second set of keys so they could begin work as soon as possible and then took off for the University of Rhode Island's Crime Lab, glancing over his shoulder now and then to make sure the box containing the lawn jockey was still wearing its seat belt.

"Don't see many of these anymore, not even with their heads on," Professor Roy Hinch said once Harvey had lugged the boxed lawn jockey upstairs and hoisted it onto his office desk. Although Harvey had done all the heavy lifting, it was Hinch who dabbed his forehead with a neatly folded handkerchief, took a plastic comb out of his shirt pocket, where it had been hiding behind a trio of cheap Paper Mates and a rectangular magnifying glass, and carefully tucked the hair on his graying temples back behind his ears. As he groomed himself, he never took his eyes off the jockey and the grinning head that lay gruesomely on the desk next to it. Professor Hinch worked his lips, saying nothing for the longest time. He picked up the head and examined its surfaces, then ran his finger over the severed neck of the figure.

"What do you want to know?" he said, touching an index finger to his lips. He looked more like a man who knew a lot about wine, which he did, than a man familiar with the microscopic intricacies of crime.

"How was it decapitated? Blunt object?"

"Oh, I doubt that, Harvey. I doubt it very much. Cast iron's very brittle. A blow would've broken or shattered the head. Even if it was wrapped in a towel. No, this was done with a Sawzall."

"A Sawzall?"

"An electric reciprocating saw made by Milwaukee." Hinch indicated a rapid forward-and-backward motion with his hand flattened into a knife's edge.

"Oh, of course," Harvey said, who didn't know his power tools very well.

"You can tell by the unevenness of the cut," he said, again running his index finger over the severed neck. "Cast iron's hard to cut, and a Sawzall will make reasonably fast work of it, but because the blade moves back and forth at a high speed, it's a little tough to control, which explains the undulating planes of the cut here. Now, you can cut cast iron with a hacksaw, and you'll get a cleaner cut because its teeth are finer and the blade's not shaking like a fat lady without a girdle, but it'll take you forever."

Harvey took the two bottles of Muscat de Beaumes-de-Venise 1997 out of his backpack and brought them down, one in each fist, on the professor's desk.

"That's very kind of you," Hinch said.

"I take it a Sawzall's not something you'll find in your average joe's garage?"

"Well, now, that all depends if you're a plumber, or the kind of joe who has to cut a lot of metal."

Harvey was back in Warwick by three, making his way up the crushed stone drive to Marshall Levy's nouveau French Provincial mansion on Narragansett Bay. The lawn jockey was now locked in his trunk. He was let in the house by Levy's Cambodian maid, who showed him to a flagstone patio where the hottest hitter in baseball sat shirtless, reading a magazine by the pool in Oakley shades.

"You know what a Sawzall is, Moss?"

"You fixin' to cut some pipe?"

"You know anyone who's got one?"

"Not offhand. Oh, I get it. The jockey."

"I met with a forensic friend who's pretty sure that's what they used." Harvey checked his watch and said, "C'mon, we should probably head over to the park."

"Whatever," Cooley said, trying to appear indifferent, although Harvey could sense Cooley's anxiety—and his own—gathering like an angry crowd outside the gates.

"Where's Marshall?"

"Massah Levy, he out da house."

"Very funny," Harvey said.

Cooley put the magazine on the matching redwood table next to his chair and rose. "I'll get my stuff."

In the driveway, he walked to the rear of the car, opened the trunk, put on his cross-draw holster inside his waistband, and stuck his .38 into it, illegally for now. He also pulled a soft straw hat out of his duffel. When he got into the driver's seat, he told Moss to put it on. Cooley didn't protest.

"Noticed any strange behavior in any of your teammates?" Harvey asked as he pulled out of the driveway.

"Yeah, I notice strange behavior in them all the time. Ross

Monkman has to smoke a cigar before every game. J. C. Jelsky has to spend an hour in front of the mirror checking for hair loss. Craig Venora's got to kiss his wristbands before he can step in the batter's box. And Hugh Croker, he's always spitting in the first-base coach's box. By the eighth inning, he's knee deep in his own saliva."

"I think you know what I mean, Moss. How about Cubberly? You get along all right with him?"

"Andy? He's a harmless cracker. Grew up around a million like him. He was probably so poor growing up, he was afraid he might wake up black one day."

"You know he cost you a couple at-bats last week?"

"He stole second in Cleveland, then stretched a single into a deuce in Detroit. Both times I get a free pass. You can bet I talked to the Cub Man about that."

"You don't think it was deliberate?"

"Cub Man's too stupid to think that far ahead."

"Here—read this." Harvey handed Cooley the printout and waited for him to finish.

"Goddamn," Cooley said, "I didn't know that about the Cub Man. I wasn't even in the league back then."

"Does that change your mind about him?"

"Let's say he *is* trying to undercut me. Goddamn it, let Cavanaugh drop him down in the batting order so he isn't batting in front of me. Hell, the Cub Man can do my streak more damage *on* the field, and maybe that's exactly what he's been doing."

"Maybe he's got friends," Harvey said, winding through leafy streets. He pulled his cell phone out and speed-dialed Jerry Bellaggio's number. "Excuse me," he said to Cooley.

"Jerry, it's Blissberg. One more thing for you. A rogue white supremacist group called Izan Nation, based in Virginia as of six or eight years ago. Thanks." He turned to Cooley, who was slumping noticeably in his seat. "As I was saying, Moss, maybe he's got friends."

"You want to know something, Bagel Boy? I'd feel a lot better if I knew you were carrying that hardware you were referring to last night."

"It's right here." Harvey patted his Detective's Special. "How's your mood now?"

Cooley smiled, gold bicuspid catching a bit of the afternoon sun through the windshield. "Improving."

"So's mine," Harvey said.

8

I
T was two hours before game time against the Orioles, and the Jewels players were enjoying the asylum from the real world that is baseball in general and the clubhouse in particular.

"What do you think?" Moss whispered to Harvey at his cubicle.

Harvey took another look at the glossy photograph of Cherry Ann Smoler in his hand, shielding it from the view of Cooley's clubhouse neighbors. She was wearing only a spangled thong and appeared to be fornicating with a brass pole on the stage of a strip club. She eyed the camera lasciviously under blond bangs, lips parted, her mind elsewhere. The name "Ivette" was printed at the bottom of the photo, but the handwritten inscription read: "To M.C. with love, C.A.S."

"You'd go for some of that, wouldn't you?"

Sexual vulgarity was the coin of the clubhouse realm. During his playing days—and, to be honest, after them as well—Harvey had enjoyed his fair share of uncensored exchanges about the vagaries of the female body. Under the circumstances, however, he found Moss's comment inappropriate.

"She's your girlfriend, Moss. Not something on the dessert cart."

"Forget it, Bagel Boy." Moss smirked, snatching the photo from Harvey's hand and sliding it facedown on the top shelf of his cubicle beneath some folded undershirts.

"Don't get me wrong," Harvey said. "She's a fox, but I don't think you should have that photo in your locker."

"But she's my good luck charm," Moss said, turning his attention to his sanitary hose. He worked them on with womanly care, smoothing the wrinkles out of the toe before unrolling the sock up his calf. Most ballplayers were slaves to rituals of preparation; suiting up for games had a religious quality to it. The cubicles were shrines to personal grooming, with their neat rows of deodorants and powders, vitamin jars and cans of protein supplements, hairbrushes and blow-dryers.

Harvey wandered off toward the office of Jewels manager Terry Cavanaugh. It was time to make his presence felt as the team's motivational coach.

The Jewels clubhouse, renovated and enlarged with the rest of the ballpark, no longer resembled the seeping grotto of Harvey's one year with the team. Now it combined the attributes of an inner-city health spa with those of a Store 24. The effect had been accomplished with wall-to-wall carpeting, harsh fluorescent lighting, and two large refrigerated cases containing soft drinks, fruit juices, and mineral water, quart containers of half-and-half, even a plastic tub filled with baby carrots floating in ice water. Although it was only an hour before game time, one long counter was already covered with chafing dishes of rice, beans, spare ribs, and fried chicken. Another counter was devoted to coffee, condiments, and commercial-size boxes of David sunflower seed packets, Bazooka bubble gum, Twizzlers, and Total cereal. Considering that after the game, win or lose, another spread would be

awaiting the players, it was no wonder that baseball players
had the biggest asses in professional sports.

Jewels players in various states of undress, most of them
wearing plastic shower clogs, kept coming by to lift the lids
off the chafing dishes to check on, and sample, their contents. Other players stretched their hamstrings in the middle
of the floor or slid new bats out of the Louisville Slugger
boxes over their cubicles and took a few slow-motion swings.
A few disappeared down a hallway to the team's new fitness
room filled with Cybex equipment and free weights. Still others sat at a table in the dining area, signing balls, or reading
and answering mail. A few sat on a sectional sofa beneath a
TV, tuned to ESPN, bolted high on the wall. The great variety
of body types was a testament to baseball's democratic nature: Height, weight, strength, and speed did not get you to
the majors as fast as some quirky genius—learned as easily in
a cornfield as a city lot, as easily by a slow, squat kid as a
scrawny one—for throwing a nasty little curve, or putting the
fat of the bat on it, or making perfect throws from the shortstop hole, or, like Harvey in his prime, vacuuming up everything hit in your direction.

As game time approached, the chatter subsided. Some
men sat meditatively on their folding chairs, staring into their
cubicles. Despite the competing strains of hip-hop and salsa
pouring out of ghetto blasters in opposite corners of the clubhouse, Harvey was aware of an underlying silence he remembered all too well: the sound of ballplayers taking refuge from
their vulnerable public lives, taking advantage of the last few
moments before battle.

When Harvey poked his head into the manager's office,
Cavanaugh was striking the classic Baseball Manager in Re-
pose pose: stocking feet on his desk, Diet Pepsi in one hand,
the lineup card before him. Harvey remembered Terry as a
utility infielder from the Florida panhandle who played pri-
marily in the National League and later worked his way up

the managerial ladder in the minor leagues. His last job before making it to the majors was managing the Jewels Triple A
farm club, the Evansville Emeralds.

"Excuse me, Terry."

Cavanaugh raised his tired eyes over the frames of his
dime store reading glasses. He still had a youthful mop of
sandy hair, but the weathered face beneath it gave his hair the
air of a toupee.

"Reporting for duty as your motivational instructor." Harvey flung two fingers off his forehead.

Cavanaugh pulled his legs off the desk and pointed Harvey into the chair across the desk. Harvey pushed the door
shut behind him and sat. It was a windowless office, a cin-
derblock bunker of a room whose salient feature was a gray
array of metal file cabinets. On Cavanaugh's desk was a copy
of the current issue of *Sports Illustrated* with Moss on the
cover and the headline "Cool Stays Hot."

"At ease, Coach." Cavanaugh turned his head to fire a siz-
zling stream of tobacco juice into a metal wastebasket near
his feet.

"So," Harvey said, "are there players in particular you'd
like me to motivate?"

"Not that I can think of," Cavanaugh said, tipping some
Pepsi down his throat.

"Or would you prefer that I motivate en masse?"

"I don't think it really matters either way."

"Then how would you like me to proceed?"

"As far as I'm concerned, you don't have to motivate anybody."

"No?"

"The way I look at it, all that matters is that everybody
knows you're the motivational coach. It doesn't matter if you
do anything. Everyone will think you're motivating someone
else. Just the fact that you've been hired to motivate them will
suggest to them they are not sufficiently motivated, and that
in itself will be a motivating factor."

"What should I do in the event I get the sudden urge to motivate?"

"I'd avoid sudden urges to motivate, Harvey. Look, let's cut the bullshit. I know why you're here. Felix told me this morning."

"Oh." It would be nice if Felix kept him abreast of the expanding circle of cognoscenti.

Cavanaugh sent another stream of blackened saliva into the wastebasket. Harvey wondered whose job it was to empty it at the end of the week. The manager picked up the lineup card and scowled at it. "If you were me, what would you do with Cubberly?"

Funny how all roads so far seemed to lead to Cubberly. "Meaning?"

"He's not hitting. His on-base percentage is still decent, since he draws a lot of walks despite his problems with the high pitch, and I hate to juggle a good lineup unnecessarily. But he's hurting Cooley."

"You mean, on the base paths?"

"And at the plate."

"Is something eating him?" Harvey asked.

"Personal problems?"

"Yeah." Harvey nodded, waiting for Cavanaugh to take the bait.

The manager pressed his lips together thoughtfully and looked off. "Well, his wife and kid are back in Cincinnati. Sometimes that gets to a guy, living alone. But my view's always been that the slump gods are irrational." He picked up a pencil and gnawed on the eraser. "I could bat Verona in the two spot," he said, mostly to himself.

"Cubberly got something against Moss?" Harvey asked.

Cavanaugh looked at Harvey. "What?"

"Something against Moss?"

"Cubberly?"

"Yeah."

"Interesting you say that."

"How come?" Harvey said, bracing himself for a revelation.

"Well, Moss has always been a bit aloof, from blacks and whites. And Latinos, for that matter. It's his nature. As I recall, you were a bit like that yourself, Harvey."

"And without the talent."

Cavanaugh smiled. "See, with the year Moss is having, that exacerbates how he rubs some guys the wrong way. Now that he's having a career year, what used to be just keeping his distance now strikes some people as a superiority complex."

"Is Cubberly one of those people?"

"Are we talking now about the lawn jockey?"

"We are."

"Say it *is* someone on the team," Cavanaugh said. "What's the motive?"

"Maybe somebody's got a mean streak that's a hell of a lot stronger than his team spirit."

"Maybe you've got a paranoid streak."

"Terry, since I've been out of baseball I've seen people do far worse for far less rational reasons than making sure some record doesn't fall into a black man's hands."

"I would caution you against stirring things up on the team," Cavanaugh said. "There's a pennant I'm still trying to get my hands on. I've got mouths to feed at home. I didn't claw my way back to the majors to see my team's chances destroyed by suspicion and allegation."

"It's hardly my intention." For all of Cavanaugh's apparent reasonableness, he was getting Harvey's back up—not that he wasn't born with his back already in the upright position.

"I wonder how Monkman would do in the two spot," the manager mused, squinting at the lineup card. "I think that's too much beef high in the order."

"I'll stay out of your way, Terry, but I need to count on you to maintain my cover."

"You've got my word there, Harvey."

Drawn by an irresistible impulse, Harvey left the man-

ager's office and wandered by Cubberly's cubicle, where the
outfielder, fully suited up, was cramming a stick of Wrigley's
Spearmint gum into his mouth. He was a rangy, big-boned
farm boy with a high waist that accentuated the length of his
powerful legs. His face, though, looked as if he had borrowed
it from a different man. It was bland and doughy and freckled, as forgettable as an eleven-year-old boy's.

"Just wanted to introduce myself, Andy. Harvey Blissberg.
I played center here for a year back when you were probably
in junior high."

"Sure," Cubberly said, kneading his wad of Wrigley's between his molars. "How's it going?"

"Pretty good, pretty good." Harvey had no illusions that
Cubberly had recognized his name. Most players today
couldn't identify Maury Wills, Brooks Robinson, or Roberto
Clemente, let alone a Harvey Blissberg. They lived in some
eternal, overpaid present.

"I heard you were here to motivate this bunch of losers,"
Cubberly said, a light drawl emerging. According to the program, he hailed from Clawson, South Carolina.

"That's right," Harvey said and picked up a bat that was
leaning against a clubhouse pillar. "I'm here to fill all your
motivational needs."

"Okay," Cubberly said, out of irony's range.

"It's tricky," Harvey said, speaking to Cubberly's back.
"Motivating implies a criticism—you know, that they haven't
been doing something right. People are so thin-skinned."

Cubberly lifted both hands to his cap and reset it with a
minute gesture, like a waiter at a swanky restaurant placing a
hot entree before an important customer and giving the plate
that little extra turn, as if fastening it to the tablecloth. "I ain't
thin-skinned about nothin'."

Then he raised his arm to take his glove off the top shelf
of his cubicle. The glove was a scuffed and weathered open-
webbed Wilson, spotted with stains and creased and creviced

with crow's feet. Harvey, thinking how human leather was, almost missed the tattoo on Cubberly's upper right arm that his reach had revealed.

"Hey, let me have a look at that," Harvey said, lifting the sleeve of Cubberly's uniform with his finger.

The tattoo was the word *IZAN* intersected by a lightning bolt. "*Nazi* backward, huh?"

"A crazy phase I went through," Cubberly said. "I've seen the light."

"What light is that?"

"Live and let live. That's the light. As the Reverend King said, 'Let freedom ring.'"

"You've come a long way."

"Life's a journey," Cubberly said. "Nice meeting you." He pivoted and walked off toward the clubhouse door.

As Harvey watched Cubberly go, third-base coach Campy Strulowitz, wearing nothing but a jock strap and shower clogs, came up and clapped him on the back. He was as old as baseball itself. His pale, hairless body was pleated with folds of skin, and his long Polish face had become exaggerated with age.

"Hum babe, Harv babe, hum-a-now," he jabbered, throwing his arms around Harvey and holding him close for a moment. It was like being embraced by a very large plucked chicken.

"Jesus, Campy, you look great," Harvey said, holding him by the shoulders at arm's length. Strulowitz's face had spent most of the last seventy years in the sun. It was as though someone had held him by the feet and dipped his head in a vat of mahogany stain.

"I look like shit, and you know it," Campy said, pulling at the loose skin on his left tricep. "Look at this—I'm falling off the bone."

Harvey tapped Campy's skull, bristling with short white hairs. "But that's what counts. There's a lot of baseball up there. I see what you've done with Moss."

"That's because he respects his elders. Most of these boys, they don't get it. That's why Felix brought you back."

"Yeah," Harvey said dubiously.

Campy leaned close to Harvey's ear and whispered, "But I don't know if I'd wear a piece in the clubhouse. Felt it under your coat when I hugged you. Either that, or you're glad to see me and have a strange way of showing it."

"You know?"

"Nothing gets by Campy. But hum babe's the word."

Harvey lowered his voice. "Do you know if anybody on the team's involved in any right-wing activities? The only reason I'm asking is that this thing Cooley got was left near the entrance to the players' parking lot."

Campy shrugged. "I wouldn't know, Harvey. I remember back in the fifties, when I was with the Indians, Larry Doby got all sorts of threats."

"How about white prayer groups on the team? Any of that?"

"Not that I'm aware of."

"Cubberly?"

Campy shook his head. "But I'm just a crumbly old man, Professor."

"But you will keep your eyes open for me, won't you, Campy? Just in case something's not completely kosher here at the old ball yard."

"You the one, babe," Campy said, putting his own arm around Harvey's waist, where his hand fell against the .38. Campy patted the butt of it, saying, "Hum babe, you the one, babe."

Harvey smiled. "You don't know how glad I am to see you, Campy. You, Felix, and Marshall are the only familiar faces around here."

Campy did an absurd little dance, rocking out for an instant in his jockstrap. Then he danced away, his buttocks flapping, saying, "Tell Moss I'll see him in the batting tunnel in five minutes."

✦

Moss Cooley sat in his uniform at one of the tables in the kitchen area, reading and sorting a mound of mail into two piles.

"Mind if I sit?" Harvey asked, pulling out the chair next to Cooley.

"Go ahead."

Harvey pointed at the much bigger of the two piles of letters that Moss had slit open and read. "Marriage proposals?"

"It's not marriage they're proposing. It's enough to make Cherry Ann blush." He laid a hand on the smaller pile. "Now this shit's a different story."

Harvey unfolded the top letter on the smaller pile and read: "You crazy spearchucker you better leave the game of the baseball to us I am sick and tierd of seeing your big lips and your big nostrels everywhere." It was handwritten in an unschooled mixture of small and capital letters. Unsigned and postmarked Floral, Massachusetts.

He opened another: "I've got some good friends who'll see to it you don't take Joltin' Joe's record away from him. A word to the wise is sufficient, but since your just another dumb nigger, let me put it this way: you better find a way to go hitless in the next few days or they'll be feeding you through a tube for the rest of your life." The envelope was postmarked Joliet, Illinois.

"You know what I hate about playing up here?" Moss said as Harvey unfolded the next letter.

"What?"

"No fried okra. Can't find fried okra anywhere."

"You keep the other hate letters you've gotten?"

"They're in my cubicle."

"You mind if I take a look at them?"

Moss stood and disappeared briefly, returning with a stack of twenty or twenty-five letters, neatly secured with a rubber band, and two bats.

Harvey took today's haul and added them to the stack. "My homework," he said.

"And here's mine." Moss handed him a single sheet of paper, folded into a square. "My lists. And now," he added, grabbing three bats leaning against the table, "I'm off to see the wizard."

As Harvey shoved the stack of hate mail in his jacket pocket, he had a disturbing thought. Last night in Marshall's skybox, when Felix suggested talking to Cavanaugh about dropping the slumping Cubberly down in the lineup—a move that would prevent Cubberly from sabotaging Cooley's streak, if that's what he was doing—Marshall was quick to object, saying he didn't believe in interfering with his manager's prerogatives. A hypothesis swept across Harvey's brain like a brush fire: What if Marshall Levy himself was behind a conspiracy to use Cubberly to prematurely end Cooley's hitting streak? What would his motive be? All Harvey could come up with was that Levy might be trying to depress Cooley's market value so Levy could save a few bucks at contract renewal time. But Cooley had just signed a multi-year deal, so that made no sense. Moreover, Marshall Levy was a good liberal. And the whole notion of one teammate threatening another in so elaborate a fashion just didn't wash fifty-five years after Jackie Robinson. No, this was pure paranoia, an occupational hazard. Harvey recognized the weakness: the absence of actual progress had pressured him into manufacturing some of his own. He needed to be patient, wait for his pitch.

He stepped outside the clubhouse into the bleak concrete corridor under the grandstands and used his cell phone to dial Marshall Levy's skybox office.

"I need to see you," Harvey said.

9

ARVEY came up the tunnel into the dugout, the field at
eye level before him a thicket of legs. Foul territory was
swarming with players, coaches, reporters, TV production people. Security men in dark green blazers already ringed
the ball field, their backs to the field, hands clasped behind
their backs. Scanning the stands, Harvey saw that Marshall
Levy hadn't wasted any time beefing up security with uni-
formed Providence Police patrolmen. The air was sticky and
stank of oversalted commercial popcorn. The seats were fill-
ing with early birds, Cub Scout troops, and old men who had
lived most of their Providence lives without major-league
baseball and weren't about to miss a single moment of the
team's first summer of glory. Someone had unfurled a bedsheet over the left-field upper deck facade that had a crudely
painted bull's-eye painted on it and the words "47 WOULD BE
BASEBALL HEAVEN."

Aided by the names on the backs of their unies, Harvey
introduced himself to some of the players lingering in the
dugout. Serious-faced second baseman Arturio Ferreiras.

Twitchy third baseman Craig Venora, pacing and picking at his uniform, as if removing cat hairs. Catcher Ray Costa, built like a six-slice toaster. First baseman Jeff Barney, built like an SUV. Coffee-colored shortstop Amos Owens, pounding his glove as gleefully as a Little Leaguer in anticipation of the game. With each of them, Harvey struggled—vainly, he thought—to produce the sort of ebullience he imagined was expected of a motivational coach. The players regarded him with varying mixtures of suspicion and confusion, as they might a friend of a friend who had been allowed into the dugout for no apparent reason. Harvey found the charade depressing.

He was rescued from his discomfort by Moss, who bounced down the dugout steps after taking fungoes in the outfield. He slapped Harvey on the butt with his glove and dropped it on the dugout's top step. Overhead, young fans were pleading for him. Several of them lowered autograph books on the end of strings for him to sign. They dangled in midair like bait.

Harvey was going to whisper something reassuring to Cooley—say again how safe the ballpark was—but he could see that death threats were the last thing on Moss's mind. He was already deep inside the game.

"Campy had some nice words to say about you," Harvey said.

"Man's like Yoda," Moss said, sliding a couple of his bats out of the rack.

Small bats, Harvey thought, for such a big man. "I'll tell you how good he is. He added a good twenty points to my average. And *that* wasn't an easy thing to do. What size bat is that, Moss? Looks like a thirty-three."

"Thirty-three inches, thirty-three ounces. Campy wanted me to go lighter, and it's worked. This one"—he handed Harvey one of the bats, its upper shaft black with pine tar residue—"this one here's my baby."

Harvey held it for a minute cocked in a batting stance,

taking its measure. For an instant he felt the old electricity of the game flow through the bat into his body. "You got a special name for your bat?"

Moss took the bat back and raised the head of it in front of his own face. "Yeah. I call it Bat." He laughed an easy, wheezy laugh, and pretended to be talking to it. "Bat, get me a goddamn hit today, Bat."

With that he bounded up the dugout steps toward the batting cage. As soon as he emerged onto the field, the fifteen thousand fans already in their seats started a rolling tide of cheers, which Cooley ignored as if it had nothing at all to do with him.

A moment later Harvey climbed the steps as well into the dusky golden air and made his way toward home plate through little clouds of mosquitoes, stepping over television cable and ball bags. He could see manager Terry Cavanaugh standing just in front of second base, hand on jaw, watching his players take batting practice, quietly studying their swings, seeing who was ready to play that night. Not every manager did that, and Harvey, standing near the on-deck circle, was wondering whether he should revise his low opinion of him when he heard a burnished baritone voice over his shoulder.

"God love this game." It was Snoot Coffman, the Jewels' radio play-by-play man. He was carrying a loose sheaf of papers in one hand—stat sheets, rosters, scrawled notes.

"Mr. Coffman."

"Oh, hell, call me Snoot."

"Snoot," Harvey said.

"Millions of radio listeners know me by that name."

"Where'd it come from?"

"I got it when I was ten or eleven. I had a buddy who thought I was a little uppity. Always had a lot of opinions. Guess that's why I had to become a broadcaster."

Cooley overswung on the first batting practice pitch and topped a weak roller to third.

"Where were you a kid?"

"Oh, that was in Tennessee. But I grew up all over. Army brat."

"Some great baseball announcers come from the South," Harvey said. "Mel Allen, Ernie Harwell, Lindsay Nelson. You."

"I guess we just like to talk so much they had to invent a profession for us."

Cooley sent the next pitch soaring into the left-field upper deck, not far from the sheet with the bull's-eye.

"That one was strictly for the fans," Coffman said, watching the ball disappear into the stands. "In games, he leaves his home run swing in the dugout. Cool's the new poster boy for patience. You've got to admire the discipline involved. We live in a society where everything's got to be bigger, faster, more sensational. See, the home run's the celebrity of baseball. And our country is addicted to celebrity. Your McGwires and your Sosas may put fannies in the seats, but your Maurice Cooley'll win you a pennant. I wish Cool's values would rub off on these other clowns."

"You think there's a pennant involved here?"

Cooley lined the very next pitch into the right-field seats, and Coffman said, "He's just trying to get it out of his system before the game. Pennant? Well, let's see, it's July eighteenth, and the Jewels are eight games out. It's entirely possible if the starting rotation stays healthy. They've won thirty-one of forty-seven during Cool's streak." Cooley sliced a long drive that made the right-center-field fence on one bounce. "They're on the cusp. I have high hopes. Incidentally, Harvey, one of my hopes is that you'll come up to the booth some time during the home stand and give me an interview."

"I don't have much to say."

Coffman affected astonishment. "Harvey Blissberg, charter member of the Providence Jewels? A man who solved the worst crime ever committed in baseball? Who's now back in Providence with a mandate to motivate a team that's on the cusp of greatness? And you don't think you have a lot to say?

Well, *I* say that a million radio listeners would love to hear you tell a story or two."

"I'm not talking about Moss's difficulties."

"Of course not. How's it going?"

"High-priced baby-sitting."

"You've got to wonder what kind of lowlife would pull a stunt like that. The jockey. That's ugly."

"You're the man with the overview," Harvey said. "What do you see?"

"What do I see? A sick society. A society that still hasn't recovered from that first boat full of African-Americans that landed on our shores. We're still grappling with that single monstrous fact, Harvey—of one man owning another. I don't care how many black multimillionaires we manufacture out of our need to be entertained." He cast his eyes toward the field and said in a low tone, "Actually, I'm mulling over a crazy notion." He paused.

"What would that be?"

"It's between you and me, right?"

"As always," Harvey said. The last thing he needed was an amateur detective in the mix.

"Every team's got fault lines, you know. Hidden dissensions. The one aspect of this that concerns me is that this lawn jockey shows up at the gate to the players' parking lot. How the hell did someone manage to leave a big box there during or right after a game without being detected? Who could get away with that?"

"Someone in a truck posing as a delivery man," Harvey said.

"Or a player." Coffman bit his lower lip, Bill Clinton–style. "Go on."

"I know Moss rubs some teammates the wrong way. He's seen as arrogant."

"He's not, though. He's a quiet kid who makes a lot of money and suddenly finds himself in the spotlight."

"I hear he's got a white girlfriend."

"I wouldn't know about that."

Coffman inspected Harvey's face. "Well, put it all together, and some teammate's imagination could've been inspired."

"Are you nominating, or just speculating?"

"I don't want to say any more until I've given it some more thought. I want to look into the backgrounds of a few players."

Harvey looked askance at the radio man. "I'd be careful, Snoot. I'd rather you just come to me with your suspicions."

"You wouldn't mind?"

"Of course not. In any case, if it turns out to be a teammate, I'll actually be relieved. Better a disgruntled teammate than some stranger with a serious grudge."

Coffman nodded thoughtfully. "Anyway, rest assured I'm not trying to do your job. My daddy was an army colonel, and I must've gotten his gene for maintaining order." He looked off. "Ladies!"

He beckoned to a short woman and two teenage girls who were walking toward them on the grass. The woman was fighting middle age in a too-tight summer dress that said too much about a body that wasn't what it had been. She was in obvious competition with her daughters, who wore matching halter tops, inside of which their breasts trembled like Jell-O molds.

Coffman introduced his wife, Cindy, to Harvey, who took her plump hand.

"C'mon, Daddy," the taller of the two girls said. "I want to say hi to Moss."

"My family," Coffman said to Harvey. "God love 'em. These are my precious jewels, if you'll pardon the expression, Tara and Tiffany. This is Harvey Blissberg, who used to play baseball."

The daughters had no interest in anybody who "used to" anything. "Nice to meet you," they mumbled without meeting his eyes.

"You must be big Moss Cooley fans," Harvey said to them anyway.

"They've been fans since we had some of the ballplayers over for a clambake a while back," Coffman said.

"He picked me up and threw me in the pool!" the shorter one said in a voice that sounded carbonated.

Coffman hugged this one to him and kissed her hair. "I think Tara's more impressed by that than the streak. You have any children, Harvey?"

"Sadly, no."

"There's nothing sweeter than family. Nothing sweeter."

"Oh, stop pontificating," Cindy said, elbowing her husband affectionately. "Leave the poor man alone."

"Yes, dear," Coffman said, winking at Harvey. "Nothing sweeter. So you'll think about being my guest on the pregame show? Don't fret. I'll do all the talking. In fact, I insist on it."

"As usual," his wife deadpanned, fondling an earring.

"Here comes Moss," Tiffany said as Cooley swaggered slowly out of the batting cage. But he walked right past Harvey and Coffman's avid, giggling daughters, oblivious to all of them. He kept his eyes down, lost in some deep ritual of mental preparation, some private preserve where the hollering of history could not reach him.

"Mr. Blissberg."

Harvey turned. Now it was a big young man in his twenties standing next to him in a pale blue polo shirt and slacks. He had a hard face and ballpark franks on his breath. His shaggy brown hair was expensively cut, but his shoes—Vibram-soled clunkers—gave him away as a cop.

He excused himself from the Coffman family and turned to the young man. "Yes?"

"I wonder if I could speak with you for a moment. My name's Joshua Linderman. Detective Joshua Linderman of the Providence Police Homicide Division." He extended his hand.

Taking it, Harvey felt a smile spread across his own face like a pool of warm syrup. "Oh, my God," he said. "You're his son."

"Nephew, actually."

"Well, I'm a big fan of your uncle."

"And he's a fan of yours."

"So, you're in the business too now."

"Yes, sir."

"Part of the security detail here?"

"No, sir. I'm off duty. I came to see you."

Joshua Linderman was at the age when youth and authority were awkwardly blended in him, especially out of uniform. Harvey was tempted to cure him of all these yes sirs and no sirs, but *he* was at the age when he was actually beginning to enjoy a little blind respect. "What about?"

"I'll make it quick. I know why you're here."

Harvey's heart began to sink. "It doesn't seem to be a secret the team's hired me temporarily as a motivational coach."

"More of a security consultant, I'd say. You're here as a bodyguard for Moss Cooley."

A roar went up as Ross Monkman, the Jewel's starting right fielder, parked one in the upper deck. "Why do you think that? Did your uncle tell you?"

"No, actually a member of the force, a friend of mine, who moonlights here at the park. He overheard you and Mr. Cooley talking alone in the clubhouse."

Of course. The twenty-something guy who was cleaning up late last night while he and Moss were talking by his cubicle.

"Who else knows?"

"Him and me. I thought you might let me in on what's going on."

"Don't take personal offense at this, Josh, but if something's going on and the police haven't been brought in on it, it's for a reason. And it's not my decision. For the time being, it's important for me to be able to operate alone."

"That's not always a good idea."

"Let me make a deal with you. If you and your friend will keep quiet about this for now, I promise you that if the situation changes and I need help, I'll come to you for it. Give me space now, I'll make sure to cut you in on the action later." Harvey held out his hand. "Shake?"

Young Linderman hesitated. "I don't like it."

"Of course you don't like it. If I were you, I wouldn't, either. Look at it this way, Josh. If I get lucky, you get lucky. Ask your uncle about that."

"All right." He took Harvey's hand. "As long as you don't break any laws, Mr. Blissberg."

"I appreciate that."

"Here's my card." The detective gave it to Harvey.

"And don't put anyone on my tail. You can't begin to imagine how badly that would fuck everything up. Okay?"

"I hope you know what you're doing, sir."

"That makes two of us."

As Harvey watched the young detective vault the low wall by the dugout and disappear into the stands, he saw Terry Cavanaugh sitting on the bench talking to Andy Cubberly. Cubberly looked straight ahead, nodding once or twice, as Cavanaugh talked.

High in the owner's skybox, Marshall Levy, general manager Felix Shalhoub, and Harvey watched the grounds crew drag the infield in preparation for the game.

"Tell me about Cubberly," Harvey said.

Marshall and Felix exchanged enigmatic smiles.

"What?" Harvey asked. He felt like a child at the dinner table whose parents shared a secret.

"You thinking about the soup can, Marshall?" Felix said.

"Yep."

Felix laughed, turning to Harvey. "Andy was rehabbing a little problem in his right shoulder last season, and the team doctor told him to take a soup can in his right hand and perform a certain series of exercises every day."

"So a couple of weeks later," Marshall said, "Dick asks

Andy how it's going, and Andy says his shoulder's no better. Well, Dick says, are you doing the exercises? Well, no, not exactly, Andy says. Well, why not? Well, Andy says, because I don't have a soup can."

"He's not the brightest bulb in the chandelier," Felix said.

"How long has he been here?"

"Second year. We got him from Cincy for two young pitchers in our system."

"All in all," Marshall added, "he's held down center field pretty well for us. Last season he sprayed the ball around pretty good. Unfortunately, word's got around the American League that he can't hit the high stuff, and his average has suffered."

"What about his political activities?" Harvey asked.

"What political activities?" Marshall said.

"Are you talking about that thing a few years ago with that nutcase," Felix asked, "the catcher who killed himself?"

"Al Molis."

"That's the one."

"He was arrested with Molis and another guy for disrupting a Black Pride parade in Denver when he was with the Rockies," Harvey explained for Marshall's benefit.

"Andy's a cracker," Felix said.

"Who twice last week tried to sabotage Cooley's streak." Harvey recounted the two incidents for them.

"I missed that," Marshall said. "I wasn't on the road trip."

"So you're trying to put two and two together," Felix said.

"I was just wondering whether you knew anything about his life up here in Rhode Island."

Felix spoke. "I think he's got a condo in Wayland Square. His family stayed in Cincy."

"What about the minorities on the team? Owens? Barney? Ferreiras? Guercio? Who's that black middle reliever you've got?"

"Arnell," Felix said. "Wakeen Arnell."

"Cubberly friends with any of them?" Harvey said.

"I'd say he keeps his distance," Felix said.

Marshall looked out the skybox window. "I think you're pressing, Professor."

"Maybe."

"You know, a baseball team's just a microcosm of society," Marshall said. "People stick to their own kind."

"I don't suppose you could get me a list of the players' phone numbers and addresses?"

"It'll just take a second." Marshall picked up the phone next to his chair and pecked out an extension. "Martha," he said, "would you mind walking a players' telephone and address list up here? Thanks." After hanging up, he dug in his pants pockets and brought out two sets of car keys. "Before I forget," he said, tossing them to Harvey, "the Subarus are in the players' lot. License numbers are on the keys."

When the public address announcer announced the starting lineups just before the game, Andy Cubberly was no longer batting second in front of Moss Cooley. On the Jumbotron in center, the Jewels' lineup looked like this:

Ferreiras 2B
Venora 3B
Cooley LF
Guercio DH
Barney 1B
Monkman RF
Cubberly CF
Owens SS
Costa C

Harvey wondered if Cavanaugh had been talking to Cubberly about the lineup change in the dugout, and that was all.

"Your doing, Felix?" Harvey asked.

"Didn't say a word to Terry, swear to God."

Harvey sipped his beer and looked at the haystack. Technically, his job wasn't finding the needle. It was keeping Cooley alive while Cooley kept his hitting streak alive, which he did in the bottom of the first with a standup triple—his first triple of the streak—down the right-field line.

Forty-seven games. For the first time, Harvey sensed, Joltin' Joe was looking over his shoulder.

10

HARVEY excused himself in the second inning and made his way down from the skybox and out to the players' parking lot.

"Is that Cubberly's car?" he asked the parking lot attendant, pointing at random to a black Mercedes.

"No," the attendant said, "that's his over there. The Jeep Cherokee Laredo."

Harvey went to his own car and took out of the trunk his dark blue coveralls with "Stanley" stitched on the front. He wiggled into them in his car, checked the players' address list again, and drove the short distance to Wayland Square on the city's residential East Side, not ten minutes from the ballpark.

A drive-by showed that Cubberly's residence was better for his purposes than the condo Felix had described. Cubberly was in fact renting a small stucco-and-timber Tudor a block from the business district, an old house that would provide easier access. Harvey circled the block and parked on the street just down from Cubberly's driveway. It was now after eight and getting dark, and the streets were empty except for four kids playing street hockey with an orange Day-Glo ball. A few lights in neighboring houses signaled the transition from dusk to night. With a metal toolbox in hand and a pretext in mind—if stopped, he'd say that Cubberly had left him the key so he could measure for some built-in bookshelves—Harvey walked boldly up the driveway and around the back, where a freestanding garage, an unpruned boxwood hedge, and two maples in full foliage gave Harvey excellent cover as he used his lock-pick set to easily open the latch-bolt on the door into the kitchen. Cubberly hadn't even bothered with a chain lock.

With its avocado appliances and sheet linoleum, the Tudor's antiquated kitchen evoked a vague and dreary series of memories from Harvey's childhood. In the fading light, he would have to work fast or risk turning on suspicious lights. A glance at the uncluttered Formica countertops suggested that Cubberly didn't spend much time in the kitchen. Harvey walked through an arch into the dining room, depressing with its yellowing wallpaper, scratched mahogany table, and narrow casement windows. Again, no signs of Cubberly's current life. With his family back in Cincinnati, Cubberly had more important things on his mind than nesting.

In the living room there was a pile of unopened mail on the coffee table—bills and circulars and credit card offers—addressed to Andrew Cubberly. Next to it sat a half-drunk cola, the brown beverage having drifted to the bottom of the glass beneath a layer of water formed by long-melted ice cubes. There was a Mission-style easy chair with cracked leather cushions facing a television. An almost empty bag of pretzel rods on the coffee table completed a sad tableau that lacked only Cubberly himself, killing an evening in front of the tube. There was a pile of sports, business, and entertainment periodicals on the floor near the television, and with a burst of hope Harvey quickly leafed through them, looking for clipped-out headlines. It was too much to ask that Cubberly was dumb enough to try intimidating Cooley into ending his streak prematurely *and* dumb enough to leave the evidence lying around the living room.

The entire first floor was disturbing in its otherness, a musty museum of brown furniture and cheaply framed prints. What could explain a highly paid baseball player choosing to live in such secondhand squalor? Perhaps he had grown up in poverty so overwhelming that he could still not escape it and re-created it as best he could out of the raw material of these rentals. Harvey's emotions swung wildly between paranoia and unwanted compassion. He felt some simple relief as he climbed the olive-green-carpeted stairs to the second floor, with its promise of more light.

On the landing, where the stairs turned, he passed an antique sword leaning against the wall. He stopped to pick it up. With his right hand on the leather grip and his left on the worn leather scabbard banded and tipped with brass, he pulled the sword out, its long and gently curving blade emerging like a deadly snake. The metal had tarnished to a dull gray but held its edge. Stamped at the base of the blade was "Hyde & Goodrich" and underneath it "New Orleans" and underneath that "1862." He hefted it in his hand, marveling at how a Confederate soldier or, more likely, given the ornate guard, an officer—smaller than men of today—could wield such a heavy weapon effectively. Harvey doubted that the sword had come with the house, leaving him to wonder whether Cubberly collected Civil War memorabilia or the sword had passed down to him through the generations from a rebel ancestor. He carefully replaced it against the wall, thinking that, whatever its provenance, Cubberly probably kept it there in case of intruders just like Harvey himself.

On the second floor he was met by a spindly floor lamp with a fringed mustard shade and a telephone table on which he was hardly surprised to find a rotary-dial telephone. The rest of the floor consisted of three bedrooms, each one smaller

than the next, and a bathroom with a shag bath mat and a
shower curtain cloudy with scum and mildew.

Almost all the evidence of Cubberly's occupancy was con-
centrated in the largest of the bedrooms, overlooking the
street. It was the only room that had been altered by his presence, although his additions were few: a Torso Track exercise
machine; a set of dumbbells; a CD player and a CD storage
tower filled with a mix of rock and country-and-western music; and a king-size bed with a black lacquered metal head-
board. Atop the painted pine bureau was a pharmaceutical
skyline of Tylenol PM and Motrin bottles, aerosol shaving
cream and deodorant cans, and skin cream dispensers.

Whatever Harvey thought he might find as he went
through Cubberly's drawers—white supremacist literature;
scissors, tape, and unused letters clipped from magazines;
iron dust and a Sawzall—he found only clothes and an X-
rated videocassette called *The Better Bosom Bureau*, whose
box cover guaranteed that all the women featured within
were in possession of their original breasts. He sifted through
the detritus: paper clips, receipts, blank stationery, pens, and
a roll of first-class stamps. A fistful of Providence Jewels
schedules. A rubber mouth guard. A snapshot of an unsmiling
brunette and a boy who looked like Cubberly. There was
nothing lying around, not a scrap of evidence, to indicate he
was still involved in racist groups or activities. An address
book, closely examined, might tell a different story, but Harvey couldn't find one. Cubberly probably had it with him.
Perhaps he had told him the truth, that he wasn't into that
shit anymore.

The bookshelves held one surprise: a smattering of seri-
ous Civil War history books and novels—McPherson's *Battle
Cry of Freedom*, Channing's *A Crisis of Fear: Secession in
South Carolina*, the eyewitness accounts of Gettysburg by
Lieutenant Frank Haskell and Colonel William C. Oates, and
Keneally's *Confederates*, among others.

A bookmark protruding from McPherson's book caught his attention. Harvey took the volume down and opened it.

It was a chapter, heavily underlined, called "South Carolina Must Be Destroyed," and it detailed the final Union offensive of the war, in the spring of 1865, after Sherman had completed his "march to the sea," from Atlanta to Savannah. In February Sherman turned north and began moving his sixty thousand men through one of the last Confederate regions spared Yankee invasion: the interior of South Carolina. Harvey, who, like most aficionados of the Civil War, had read McPherson's history when it came out in the late 1980s, stood near the bedroom window and read the copious underlinings in the dying light.

"As his army had approached Savannah in December 1864," McPherson wrote, "Georgians said to Sherman: 'Why don't you go over to South Carolina and serve them the same way? They started it' . . . Destroyed it was, through a corridor from south to north narrower than in Georgia but more intensely pillaged and burned. . . . The war of plunder and arson in South Carolina was not pretty, and hardly glorious, but Sherman considered it effective. . . . 'My aim then was to whip the rebels, to humble their pride, to follow them to their inmost recesses, and make them fear and dread us.'. . . Sherman was confident that the war was nearly over and that his destruction of enemy resources had done much to win it."

The underlinings continued into the next, and final, chapter of the book, which concerned in large measure the dilemma faced by the Confederacy in the last half of the war: whether to conscript and arm slaves to shore up the South's faltering prospects. The debate raged in southern newspapers and legislatures. McPherson quoted editors of the day: "'We are forced by the necessity of our condition,' they declared, 'to take a step which is revolting to every sentiment of pride, and to every principle that governed our institutions before the war.' The enemy was 'stealing our slaves and converting them into soldiers. . . . It is better for us to use the negroes for our

defense than that the Yankees should use them against us.'"
Conscripting slaves also raised troubling questions about having to promise blacks emancipation in exchange for their
fighting. "It was true, admitted the *Jackson Mississippian*, that
'such a step would revolutionize our whole industrial system'
and perhaps lead to universal emancipation, 'a dire calamity to
both the negro and the white race.' But if we lose the war we
lose slavery anyway, for 'Yankee success is death to the institution . . . so that it is a question of necessity—a question of a
choice of evils. . . . We must . . . save ourselves from the rapa-
cious North, WHATEVER THE COST.'" A deeper contradiction
was pointed out by the *Charleston Mercury*: "'If slaves will
make good soldiers our whole theory of slavery is wrong.'"

Harvey lowered the book, thinking of Moss's comment on
Cubberly in the car: "I grew up around a million like him. He
was probably so poor he was afraid he might wake up black
one day." Outside it was dark now. The chorus of crickets
poured in through the screen window. Harvey was almost surprised to find himself in Providence, and in the present.

To alter the human heart was the world's hardest work.
Campy Strulowitz could add twenty points to Harvey's batting
average more easily than a man could learn to see things dif-
ferently, even for a few minutes. Now Harvey wondered if
Andy Cubberly, long after Appomattox, wasn't somehow still
fighting the Civil War by other means.

Harvey was back in Marshall's skybox by the seventh inning,
in time to see Moss's third hit of the game, a single through
the shortstop hole. The Jewels put Baltimore away with three
in that inning for an 8–2 victory. An hour later, after Moss
had finally extricated himself from the clubhouse tangle of reporters, microphones, and cameras, Harvey whisked him to
the players' parking lot and into one of the rented Subarus.

FROM the shadows of the narrow alley that ran like a dingy fissure between two warehouses across from the players' parking lot, he watched Cooley and the detective emerge from the stadium and walk to an unassuming silver Subaru. Maybe he had overshot with the jockey. He would have liked to have kept it just between Cooley and himself, a step at a time, until he got the message—all he'd wanted to do with the jockey was make the needed impression, cut through the clutter of hate mail without bringing the law into it, it was so goddamn hard to hit the right tone. Like writing condolence letters, he thought, chuckling at the analogy.

Anyway, one private detective didn't exactly qualify as the law, a Jew no less.

He pulled on his second Seagram's miniature, keeping just enough alcohol in his bloodstream to take the edge off his alarm. He had come too far to lose it now. Goddamn Ed, going off and dying without a word, his death the first link in the improbable chain of circumstance that now threatened to hang around his own neck. He wanted the chain around Cooley's.

The important thing was to compartmentalize, that was the key, he'd done it all along and now he just had to keep doing it. At work he had to seem absolutely unchanged, no one could suspect, no one could know. Jesus, what would life be like if you couldn't compartmentalize? All the bad endlessly flowing into the good and spoiling it? Just like the mixing of the races. Good fences make good neighbors. He sucked on the Seagram's. Good and bad had to be kept apart, within and without, if it was all in one box you couldn't make any sense of it. Jesus forgave you for your sins, let you wash them away, not put them in a goddamn box where someone could find them. And after everything he did for Ed's wife.

The guard was letting the Subaru out of the lot now, the Jew driving and Cooley in the passenger seat with a hat mashed down on his head. He had to laugh, since he too was wearing a hat, a thrift shop fedora, he felt like Glenn Ford or George Raft or somebody in an old thriller. The Subaru turned out of the lot and drove off. He had to laugh at the fact they were in a Subaru instead of Cooley's Range Rover. He had to laugh at all their wasted effort and motion. This was his power now, to be able to see all the unnecessary elaborations of the fear he had planted.

Like he was going to follow Cooley. Like he wasn't watching him all the time anyway.

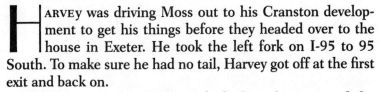

11

ARVEY was driving Moss out to his Cranston development to get his things before they headed over to the house in Exeter. He took the left fork on I-95 to 95 South. To make sure he had no tail, Harvey got off at the first exit and back on.

"Is that necessary?" Moss asked when they rejoined the traffic.

"Listen, I may not have a forty-seven-game hitting streak, but I know how to shake a tail."

Moss pulled his hat down lower on his head. "You're the man," he muttered.

"I want to put this in just the right way, Moss: There are two people in this car who'd rather not be doing this. You and me. But since we have to spend some quality time together, let's just make the best of it."

"You got some suggestions?"

"How do you feel about gin rummy?"

"Don't press your luck."

"We could stay up late and tell each other ghost stories."

Moss snorted. "It beats becoming one yourself."

"Take it easy. I haven't lost a ballplayer yet."

"That's a big load off my mind."

They drove on in silence for a while, Harvey working over Cubberly in his mind. If he wasn't the sharpest knife in the drawer, it was unlikely he would have authored the wordiest death threat in history. Then again, the outfielder had a handful of semi-scholarly books suggesting he still had a hair across his ass about the War between the States. Harvey decided not to bother Moss with his thoughts about the contradictions of Cubberly's personality. In any case, the odds still weighed heavily against Moss breaking DiMaggio's record. The odds were still in favor of the jockey being nothing but a harmless eruption.

Moss, as if reading Harvey's mind, suddenly asked him what he thought the chances were of getting to fifty-six straight games.

"Hell if I know, Moss."

"It gets less likely, doesn't it, the longer it goes on?"

"I'm no statistician, but it's been proven mathematically that there's no such thing as momentum. The fact you've hit in forty-seven straight doesn't work for or against you. Every game you're starting over."

"I could do it, then."

"Of course, in baseball you're at the mercy of so many variables." Harvey was driving through Cranston. "You'll let me know when to turn, right?"

"I won't let you down."

"It's not like you're shooting day after day at a stationary basketball hoop that's always ten feet off the ground. Every pitcher you face is different. The hoop moves to a different place on every pitch."

"What are you saying?"

"I have no idea. I think I'm saying drink plenty of milk, get lots of rest, and lay off the liquor."

"And no pokey on the night before a game."

"Not with me, anyway," Harvey said.

He drove around the development once, looking for suspicious cars, before turning into Cooley's white Mediterranean-style mini-mansion with its little comma of a circular driveway. The lot wasn't big, with woods creeping up within ten feet of the garage, so whoever had left him the lawn jockey's head had probably parked elsewhere and come on foot.

The decor was that of a man with far more money than ideas how to spend it. Each room had two or three large objects in it and nothing else: a giant flat-screen television and a BarcaLounger . . . a stationary bicycle, old-fashioned jukebox . . . a sectional sofa, glass coffee table, and CD rack. There wasn't a rug or carpet in the place. The house looked like an appliance store in the last stages of a liquidation sale. Cooley kept mumbling as Harvey followed him up to his bedroom, "Man hits in forty-seven straight and has to leave his own home . . . has to leave his own fuckin' home."

Harvey pulled the bedroom blinds shut and watched as Cooley took clothes from his immense walk-in closet and carefully laid them in a giant rolling suitcase he put on the king-size bed. He remembered a *Sports Illustrated* article in the 1970s about Pittsburgh Steeler running back Frenchy Fuqua that showed him in his walk-in, suits in every shade, like a decorator's color wheel. Cooley's palette ran more conservatively to blues and earth tones. In the corner of the bedroom was a wicker hamper overflowing with dirty clothes. On the bed lay a copy of *Pro* magazine, a quarterly circulated only to professional athletes, who received it free. Its tiny target audience of about 25,000, most of them millionaires, would find in the current issue tips on investment planning and how to buy extremely expensive watches, as well as an article titled "The Cure for the Common Choke: A Sure-Fire Remedy for Over-Thinking."

Next to the bed was a laptop computer and a tall stack of paperback books. Harvey had tilted his head to read the titles, mostly thrillers, when he was distracted by an object that

Cooley had taken off his bureau and placed facedown on top of some silk shirts. Harvey picked it up, turned it over, had to look twice before he understood what it was.

The old black-and-white photo in a simple frame made from willow twigs showed a young black man, his hands bound in front of him, swinging by the neck from a rope tied to a thick tree branch. The man wore only remnants of his clothes, and on closer inspection Harvey could see that his body was riddled with wounds. The front of one thigh had been filleted open, revealing muscle. Judging from the scrap of clapboard house in the background, it looked like the lynching had taken place in a residential neighborhood. A crowd had gathered, and the photograph's foreground was swimming with white faces—men, women, and even children. Some of them were gazing up at the lynching victim, some of them looked off, and a few white faces were looking right at the camera. Two men, one in a well-creased hat, smiled guiltily right at the lens.

Above them, his head wrenched back on its elongated neck, twisted skyward, as if looking for God, the black youth dangled, so recently a member of the living.

"It's a postcard," Moss said, coming out of the bathroom with his Dopp kit and seeing Harvey. "That's what white folks liked to do. They'd lynch a black man, take a few snapshots for souvenirs or send 'em to their friends and relatives. Sometimes you had a huge crowd in suits and hats, looked like an old-time baseball crowd, except they weren't watching any game. You gotta love those guys in the foreground, don't you? They're just having the time of their lives."

Moss swept a few vitamin and supplement bottles off his bureau top into his arms and dropped them in the suitcase. "I'll tell you an interesting story about that one. The story goes that that dead man there told the mob just before they murdered him to please make sure his wife and young son were sent a copy of the photograph he knew they were about to take of him, so they'd know what happened to him. Seeing as some of the lynchers actually knew the man—he'd done some yard work for a couple of them—they obliged him and made sure his family received the picture you hold in your hands there. I always think about him sliced up and ready to have his neck snapped, and he looks at that redneck photographer and probably says, 'Mister, jes' please make sho' you send one of them pitchers to my wife and my boy. Any one of these men here knows where they is.' I just know he said, 'Please.'" Cooley blinked.

Harvey looked at the image in his hand, a terrible message hurled across time.

Moss grabbed it out of Harvey's hands. "That one there happened in nineteen-thirty-three. You know who the Scottsboro Boys were, don't you?"

"They were a bunch of black teenagers falsely accused of raping two white women on a train. One of the landmark events in American racist history."

"Nineteen-thirty-one," Moss said. "They were convicted again and again in kangaroo trials before all-white juries and spent many, many years in prison, mostly under death sentences, often near the execution chamber where they could hear other men die. At one of the trials the attorney general of the state of Alabama referred to the defendant in court as 'that thing.' In his presence. The Communist Party's defense of them put the Communist Party on the map in this country, although the hero, the boys' defense attorney for many of the trials, was a Jewish lawyer from New York hired by the Commies who wasn't a Commie himself by a long shot. Samuel Leibowitz. Anyway, charges against four of them were finally dropped in 'thirty-seven, more than six years after they were arrested. Another four were finally paroled in the mid-forties. The last one escaped in 'forty-eight."

"Moss, I'm impressed." Harvey had read Marshall Levy's copy of the *Sports Illustrated* piece on Cooley during the game, and nothing in it—the youngest of six children of a steel-

worker and school librarian, the scholarships, the reputation
for hard work and aloofness—nothing had suggested this.

"Don't patronize me. I grew up in the state that put those
innocent black boys behind bars and slowly sucked the life
out of them. It's in my blood, Bagel Boy."

"I've been around ballplayers my whole life, and I've never
heard one of them show any real interest in American history.
They barely show interest in *baseball* history. There was nothing in *Sports Illustrated* about your historical interests."

"You think I'm going to talk to the Chihuahuas about this
shit?" Cooley said, packing three pairs of expensive slip-ons.
"Now, this picture here?" He held it up to Harvey again. "In
thirty-three, two years after their arrest, a judge—an Alabama
judge—set aside the second conviction of one of the Scottsboro Boys, Haywood Patterson, and ordered a third trial. This
riled up a lot of the good white folks, a black 'rapist' "—he set
the word off in verbal quotation marks—"escaping the chair
for the second time, and in their frustration they started
lynching other blacks left and right all over the South during
the summer and fall of 'thirty-three. This one took place not
too far from Scottsboro itself."

The bedroom window blinds were swept by the headlights
of a car and Harvey moved quickly to the window and peered
out between slats at an SUV that turned into a driveway
across the street.

"This picture goes where I go," Cooley said. "Just in case
I slip up and forget who I am. I don't need a fuckin' lawn
jockey to remind me of that."

Harvey left Cooley to finish up his packing and went downstairs to check the first floor and yard for any unusual noise
or activity. All was quiet on the Cranston front. He settled
into the BarcaLounger, turned on the reading lamp, and began going through Cooley's hate mail.

"You cock suckin coon you make me sick"; "stupid fuckin'
nigger kinky-haired Cooney"; "How many spears can a
spearchucker chuck? Who the fuck cares? Just watch your
nigger ass if your ever in Memphis"; "First you jigaboos take
over basketball and football, now we got niggers even in
hockey and a half-breed nigger stinking up in golf why dont
you get out of baseball before you get hurt and I mean hurt";
"your lower than whale shit you piece of turd. What is it like
to look at yourself every day and see that you are the color of
shit?"; "What do you expect from someone who never had
parents a crow just shit on a rock and the sun hatched you";
"You are one uppity junglebunny I saw you innerveiwed on
ESPN and you obviously think you are smarter then the rest
of us when you are another big lipped coon, may you rot in
hell with that other coon, Martin Luther Coon"; "You are
good reason to bring slavry back'; "You are a mother fucker
because I am sure you fucked your own mother."

Moss Cooley's hitting streak had reopened a poorly
healed wound, and it was oozing the same old primordial
racist sludge, unchanged since the beginning of time, seeping
out of cities and towns across the country. It was as though
the words didn't really belong to the individuals who wrote
them, but to a flaw in human nature itself. How else could
you explain the fact that most of these disgraceful letters
were proudly signed and came in envelopes with return addresses—Covina, California; Junction, Texas; Indianola,
Iowa; Gastonia, North Carolina; Hudson, Ohio; New Kins-
ington, Pennsylvania; Springfield, Illinois; Broomfield, Colorado; Newport, Rhode Island?

Cooley came down the stairs with his bag, an emigrant in
his own house.

"You good to go?" Harvey asked, stacking the hate mail
and putting the rubber band around it.

"Do it to it."

Suddenly there was a sound just outside the house, a rep-
etitious beat moving closer. Before he could even think about

it Harvey had his .38 out of his belt. "What's that?" he whispered to Cooley.

"Shit, man, what's *what*? What're you talkin' about?"

"That." The regular beat was getting closer, approaching the door.

Cooley listened for a moment, then stood. "Shit—that's Kevin dribbling his basketball back home from the lighted courts. He lives two doors down."

The doorbell rang, a two-note chime.

"I'll get it," Harvey said. He was at the front door now, back pressed against the wall next to it. "Who's there?"

"It's Kevin. From down the street. Is Mr. Cooley home?"

"Are you alone, Kevin?"

"Yeah, but I can come back another time."

"No, it's all right, Kev," Cooley said, advancing out of the shadows. "Give me a second to turn off the alarm system."

"Hey, Cool!" Kevin said excitedly from behind the closed door. "You were awesome tonight. I watched it on the tube."

"One second, Kevin." Cooley's fingers flashed over the alarm system's keypad.

Harvey holstered his gun and opened the door, letting in the muggy night. Kevin was a gangly teen, cradling a worn basketball, with a teenage boy's standard-issue acne-mottled face. He wore a FUBU jersey and baggy cutoffs. He stood on the stoop, sweating heavily.

"Hi. I'm Kevin Lovick."

"I'm Harvey, one of Moss's friends."

"Hey, Kev, whassup?" Cooley said, knocking fists with him across the threshold.

"Three-for-four! You're crankin'." Harvey knew the kid would be talking about having been Moss Cooley's neighbor for the rest of his life.

"Thanks, man."

Harvey said, "You haven't seen any strangers or strange cars in the neighborhood, have you?" The teenager shook his head. "Listen, Kevin, would you do Moss a big favor?"

"Absolutely!"

"Moss is going to be away from the house for a few days, so I was wondering if you could keep an eye on the house for him. You know, especially at night. Let us know if you see anybody casing the house. Take down a license plate number, that sort of thing."

Kevin looked at Moss quizzically. "But you guys are just beginning a home stand."

"There could be a field pass in it for you," Cooley said. "Hang out with me at batting practice."

"Awesome." Kevin was glowing. "Sure."

"How's the jumper coming? You keeping that right elbow in?"

"Absolutely."

"Good. Well, listen, Harvey and I have a little business to attend to, so I'll dig you later, okay?"

Harvey found a scrap of paper in his pocket and wrote down his cell phone number on it. "This is what you call if you have any news."

"Awesome," Kevin said. "Thanks!" He bounced the ball once excitedly on the front stoop before dribbling off into the darkness.

In the Subaru, on the way to Exeter, a light steamy drizzle began to fall. Harvey set the wipers at a slow interval.

"I don't know if this streak's worth it," Cooley mumbled.

"Well, Moss, having set no records of my own in my brief career, I'm really not in a position to give you any advice on that. All I can say is, on the one hand, I understand it's no fun feeling like your life's in danger. On the other, you just don't want to give up too quickly on a chance to be known as the man who did the impossible."

"What's this?" Cooley said, picking up a videocassette off the dashboard.

"Oh, that's a documentary I thought we could watch in our new home. Seeing as how we're going to have all that time on our hands."

"*When It Was a Game*," Moss read off the label.

"Might appeal to a man with your sense of history. Speaking of which, Moss—before, remember when you were telling me that the lynchers knew where their victim lived because he'd done some yard work for them?"

"Yeah?"

"How'd you know *that*?"

Moss Cooley let the wipers complete their arc before answering. "Because he was my granddaddy."

12

IT was two in the morning. Upstairs slept a man whose grandfather had been murdered and strung up, and who was now one of the most recognizable and revered figures in the country. Only in America, Harvey thought bitterly, sipping some pilfered cognac on the downy sofa the last occupant had left behind.

The rain had kept up, troubling Harvey with the cover it provided for other sounds. Despite the newly installed motion detectors and pressure mats, the loaded .38 lay on his stomach. It had been a while since he had ventured into the land of physical peril, and it was hard to relax. He felt like talking to Mickey, but a call at this hour would probably wake her out of some much-needed sleep. He dug a pack of Export A cigarettes out of his knapsack—the pack was a week old and still half full—and lit one. He sat and smoked, thinking of nothing. That was a cigarette's charm—it offered a brief dopamine-charged release from rumination.

When he stubbed it out, he began thinking again—about how his first career, baseball, had chosen him. He had chosen his second, private investigation, without at first understanding why. Later, knowing that some of life's biggest decisions echoed the obscure mandates of childhood, he wondered if he hadn't laid the groundwork as a boy, when he turned out to have a gift for finding errant baseballs hit into the woods that lay beyond the outfield of his school playground. As he and his friends grew older, and stronger at bat, no game was complete without several balls disappearing into the dense foliage that acted as a short center-field fence. His skill was in greater and greater demand. He had a sixth sense for what had been lost. His gift, though, was complemented by a sense of responsibility to find the ball, whether or not he had been the one to hit it. He took a profound pleasure in it. It wasn't simply that baseball was always more important to him than the others and so he was willing to assume responsibility for keeping the game going; it seemed, in some deeper sense, to be his job to do what was necessary.

"Oh, let Blissberg find it," one of the Orlowsky twins would say, happy to have a breather, perfectly content to move on to the day's next activity. They'd sit on the scruffy grass and watch their skinny friend, whose father would often treat them to submarine sandwiches at his Italian restaurant after their games, as he jogged single-mindedly toward the trees. With his preternatural talent for gauging the trajectory, direction, and speed of a baseball, Harvey would fix his eyes on a point in the forest where he figured the ball had settled. And it would be there. Or nearby, underneath some trillium leaves, behind a fallen branch.

One time he came out of the woods after an unusually difficult five-minute search, only to find that everyone had gone home, leaving him alone with a smudged Rawlings ball and his own strange intensity.

He heard Moss walking above him now, padding to the bathroom in the strange house, unaware that they had something in common. They had both lost family to hate. Harvey's own great-grandmother on his father's side, and her daughter, who was his grandmother's sister, and *her* diabetic husband and two children had been taken to Auschwitz by the Nazis. But there was no photo of their death to keep the horror fresh. In post–World War II America, among Jews who had come long before the war, the Holocaust was not a daily touchstone of racial agony; by the time Harvey began to understand what had happened, the unthinkable events had disappeared behind a scrim of history. Once in a while—even at Fenway, during that brief eternity between pitches—the upstage lights came on, revealing the carnage, and he was shocked, but the shock would end abruptly, like awaking from a bad dream of falling to one's death. Harvey felt stranded at one end of an impossible contradiction.

Two generations after his relatives had vanished, Harvey was just another white man in America. You had to be standing awfully close to see the Jew in Harvey. But Moss Cooley carried his holocaust on him. In him. He continued to wear the badge of difference and humiliation, because it was his skin.

Cherry Ann Smoler lived in a converted loft in the Jewelry District, an area of nineteenth-century brick factories that once provided, through the magic of electroplating, the bulk of America's costume jewelry. The few remaining survivors, like Marshall Levy's Pro-Gem, had long since fled to suburban industrial parks along 95. Now the district housed architectural firms, Internet start-ups, consulting and design groups, software programmers, and an assortment of other young professionals, including Cherry Ann Smoler, who held down what had to be one of the more colorful night jobs.

Just before noon, she opened the door of her loft to Moss and Harvey, wearing baggy sweat clothes in which she had apparently been sleeping only recently. Her copious blond hair was held loosely in place with a plastic butterfly clip. There was a touch of misgiving in her smile at the sight of a second man in her doorway.

"Hi, honey," she said drowsily to Moss, laying a palm on one of his cheeks and rising on her tiptoes to kiss him lightly on the other. She was a Slavic beauty, with wide-set brown eyes, broad cheekbones, and a generous mouth. Behind her, he saw a well-appointed kitchen in a corner of the loft, glistening with stainless steel and copper, and then a cat, a muscular lilac-point Siamese, licking itself ardently on a throw rug. Harvey glanced at Cherry Ann's manicured bare feet. He turned his head away at the thought of them in the towering platform shoes favored by strippers. Harvey didn't fit the standard profile for horny men in many respects, one of them being his distaste for platform shoes, the calf-enhancing sine qua non of exotic dancing. He thought they made women look like R. Crumb drawings. But even without the benefit of platforms, makeup, or a chrome pole, Cherry Ann Smoler was the stuff of men's rawest fantasies and knew it, and her success at denying or ignoring that fact—for there was nothing affected or flirtatious in her behavior now—only endeared her more to Harvey.

"Hi, baby," Moss said, passing his hand up and down her back.

"Did you make a hit last night?"

"Three of them."

"Excellent. I can come watch you play tonight. I'm not working."

"You can sit with this guy," Moss said, jerking his head at Harvey. "He has the run of the place."

Now, at last, she turned to Harvey, looked him up and down, and with hand outstretched said, "I'm Cherry Ann Smoler."

"Harvey Blissberg." He shook it, her warm fingers like a small animal in his palm.

Cherry Ann turned to Moss even before withdrawing her hand. "Is he a cop?"

"Uh . . ." Moss began.

"No. I used to be a baseball player," Harvey said, impressed by her intuition, even as it annoyed him that he, or his responsibilities, would be so transparent. "I even spent a year with the Jewels."

She then did something Harvey found extraordinary. With her right hand she reached out and gently touched Harvey's shirt where it hung over the belt. Her hand came to rest instinctively on the butt of his concealed .38. "But what is it you do now?"

"You don't miss much, do you?" Harvey said.

"Not where men are concerned." She looked at Moss. "You didn't do anything wrong, did you?"

"No," Harvey said before Cooley could answer, "he's doing something right. He's now got the second-longest hitting streak in major-league history. And that's made him a target."

She collected some fugitive strands of hair in the hook of her index fingers and pulled them off her face. "Which your job is to reduce the size of?"

"Yes," Harvey said, resenting that he should have known this woman initially from a photograph in a clubhouse.

Harvey and Moss sat at her long butcher-block kitchen counter, drinking coffee, and brought her up to date on the headless lawn jockey, the letters, the safe house. Cherry Ann listened with a growing expression of alarm.

"Is this streak worth his life?" she asked Harvey.

"If we knew how serious the threat was, it would be easy to answer that question. But we don't. Like so many, it may turn out to be empty, and a hitting streak like Moss's is nothing to sneeze at."

"Men," she said, topping off Moss's coffee cup. Harvey held his hand over his. "Women don't value streaks the same way."

"Except the ones in your hair," Moss said.

"Yuk yuk," Cherry Ann said.

"A man likes to leave something behind," Harvey said and

realized at once that this attempt at pithiness was not going to get by Cherry Ann Smoler.

"And women don't?"

"What I meant was that men are more hung up on concrete accomplishments, like getting their names in record books."

"And on the obituary pages," she said. "I don't want him doing anything stupid."

"Speaking of doing something stupid, let me ask you something," Harvey said. "Have you told anybody about your relationship with Moss? You understand I'm not implying anything here, but you're dating a famous ballplayer, and most people in your position wouldn't keep quiet about it."

"A couple of the girls at Teasers know about it. The two girls I'm closest to. Bobbi and Carol."

"Have you discussed your relationship with anybody else besides the two of them?"

She thought. "My parents."

Cooley lifted his head "Your parents?"

"Don't get excited, honey. My dad's a big baseball fan. Sorry if I broke the rules."

"What rules?" Harvey said.

"We have an agreement," Moss said.

"We have an agreement to keep this as private as possible," she said.

"I'm under a microscope enough, as it is," Moss added.

"Me too," she said, "and I'm not talking about guys staring at my monkey five nights a week. It's more the way they look at you."

"How do they look at you?" Harvey asked, wondering what he looked like to strippers, holding his watery drink and pretending he had wandered in by mistake.

"Like I already belong to them, like they've already had me or something. That's the disgusting part, to see it happen on their faces. Men have two brains, and when I see that second one take over, it's scary. But, hey, it's how I'm putting myself through restaurant school. I don't know if Moss told you, but I'm studying to be a chef."

"Good for you."

"Anyway, Moss and I really don't believe in blabbing about us. Right, honey?"

"Right."

Like hell, Harvey thought, thinking of the eight-by-ten glossy of Cherry Ann Smoler humping a pole that Moss kept in his cubicle. And God knows how much advertising of their affair Cherry Ann was not admitting to. Still, whatever they each did, Harvey saw that they meant it, this pact. Perhaps a shared knowledge of what too much visibility is like was the very thing that gave this relationship some glue. Harvey thought of the endless supply of celebrity relationships that kept the tabloid newspapers in business. It was easier to fall in love with someone in your own field, someone already on the movie set, someone in your own income bracket. But all public figures had something else in common: the experience of feeling owned by others. Celebrity was a kind of highly paid slavery. People objectified the famous; they were the serfs of other people's fantasy lives. DiMaggio and Marilyn Monroe— if it hadn't been for their respective fames—Joe had seen a publicity photo of her, and a business manager had arranged their first date—they would never in a million years have found each other.

"Has anyone at the club asked you about him? Made any comments to you?"

She shook her head.

"And you two haven't been sighted as a couple in the local papers?"

"Not that we know of," Cherry Ann said.

"Think."

Cherry Ann flashed a glance at Moss. "Your friend doesn't give up."

"You know these pushy Jews," Moss said.

"You know what I like about Moss?" Harvey said to her. "For a black man, he's not lazy. The motherfucker actually holds down a job. What about you?"

"I have a heart of gold," Cherry Ann said.

"I thought you might," Harvey said.

"To answer your question again," she said, "no, I don't think we've shown up in the paper. This isn't New York, anyway."

"Cherry Ann, three nights ago somebody broke into Moss's garage and left the lawn jockey's head hanging by a rope." She gasped—the tiniest audible intake of air—and reached out to take Moss's hand. "So," he continued, "there are people who know where he lives."

"He can stay here," she said.

"People know where you live."

"But people don't know about us."

"That's what you say. Until this blows over, I've put Moss in a safe place where nobody can find him. I'm not even going to tell you where that is, because I want you to have deniability. He can always call you, and I'll give you my cell phone number so you can reach Moss or me if you need to." He ripped a page out of his little leather notebook and wrote down the number, nothing else. He handed it to her. "Don't write my name, or Moss's, next to this number, okay?"

"But the ballpark," she said.

Harvey gave her his ballpark rap. "The odds of someone getting to Moss on the street, at night, are a lot better. That's why Moss and I are going to be like Siamese twins for a little while. That's why I'm carrying a piece. Beautiful cat, by the way." The lilac-point male was on the counter, sniffing the contents of the creamer.

"When can I, you know, *see* him?"

"If you two can live without each other for a few more days, I'd feel more comfortable. After that, if the streak's still going, we'll figure something out."

Moss excused himself to use the bathroom, and Harvey used the opportunity to ask Cherry Ann if she was friendly with any other players on the team.

"Absolutely not," she said, insulted.

"Listen, I have to ask these questions."

"I'd hate to have your job."

"And I yours," Harvey said.

She looked at the kitchen wall clock and stood. "Excuse me. I have to throw some clothes on and get over to Johnson and Wales. My associate degree in culinary arts awaits."

Moss came back, saying, "Why don't you let Harvey take you to the game tonight? I think you might bring me good luck."

"Just what you need," she replied. "But okay." She looked at Harvey. "What time?"

"I could leave a ticket for you at the Will Call window. Why don't you show up at seven-thirty? Unless you want to come earlier to see batting practice."

She shook her head. "I've got Baking and Pastry Arts until seven."

"You got a cell phone?" Harvey asked, and she nodded. "Call me when you arrive at the park, and I'll come down and meet you at the gate."

"All right," she said. She gave Harvey her cell phone number and disappeared behind two decorative screens that demarcated the bedroom in the open loft.

Ten minutes later, Moss and Harvey said good-bye to her on Richmond Street in the shadow of the Route 95 overpass.

"I'm just curious," Harvey said to her, "how you knew I had a gun."

She thought for a moment. "You act like a cop. For one thing, honey, your eyes were everywhere from the moment you and Moss arrived. You were taking in everything. Recording and filing away. I have a lot of experience watching men watching me. I know what it is to check out and be checked out. I'll see you tonight, Harvey Blissberg."

"Be careful, baby," Moss said, not kissing her, even though there was no one on the sidewalk to see them in this city with its curious lack of bustle. The two men watched her in silent appreciation as she walked away toward Weybosset Street in her blue jeans and running shoes, with her backpack slung over one shoulder and her hair in a golden ponytail.

"Moss?" Harvey said.

"What is it now, Bagel Boy?"

"Don't fuck with her."

13

MY pregame guest tonight, folks, is someone you older Jewels fans will warmly remember, I'm sure, since he was a member of the Jewels' original team. For five seasons before that he patrolled the main pasture up in the home of the bean and the cod. Since his retirement from the game almost fifteen years ago, he's worked as a private investigator and now as a motivational speaker." Coffman winked at Harvey as he said this. "I'm talking, of course, about Harvey Blissberg, who's been good enough to come up here and chew a little fat with Snoot as we await the opener of the Jewels' three-game set against the first-place Cleveland Indians and a game that we hope—no, we assume—will see the amazing Moss Cooley hit in his forty-eighth straight game. So, Harvey, what brings you back to Providence?"

Harvey fiddled with his headset, which was bothering him. "I guess there's a feeling that my experience as a motivational speaker might come in handy."

"Folks, as you may have read in this morning's *Providence Journal*, Harvey Blissberg's been hired as the Jewels' new motivational coach, although I have to say, Harvey, the way this team's been playing, you may have your work cut out for you."

Harvey laughed. "Yeah, this could be the shortest tenure of any motivational coach on record, since the team is really having a great season."

"You said it, my friend." Coffman turned to him, chin on hand, with an expression of ridiculously solemn interest. "Maybe you can tell our listeners what exactly it is that a motivational coach does."

"Well, basically, Snoot, in the clubhouse before the game I put on a short pleated skirt and grab the pom-poms, and then I do a rousing cheer for the guys that ends with a cartwheel and the splits."

A laugh exploded out of Coffman's mouth, showering Harvey with a fine spittle mist. "Ouch!" he said. "That's gotta hurt!"

"It's more of a modified splits, but of course, I still have to be helped up. Seriously, though, I'm still feeling my way into the job. Trying to see where the problem areas are, what I can do to help certain players prepare better mentally for the game. You know the old saying—failure to prepare is to prepare for failure."

"Well, there's one guy on the team who doesn't need any extra motivation right now."

"Moss Cooley."

"My boy Moss has hit in forty-seven straight games, and tonight he'll be trying for forty-eight, which would put him just eight shy of Joe DiMaggio's remarkable record."

"There's a cute sign out there, Snoot, hanging over the upper deck in right field. I don't know if you spotted it."

"Folks, it's a bedsheet with what looks like a mail slot drawn on it and the message, 'Insert No. 48 Here.' Harvey, you're something of a student of the game and not a bad hitter in your playing days, so you must know how hard it is to hit in twenty straight games, let alone forty. Hard as a week-old biscuit."

"People should keep in mind that DiMaggio's record is

widely considered to be so many deviations above the norm that it's the one record that shouldn't even exist. I know Moss is closing in, but there're a lot of people out there who don't think he has a chance to break DiMaggio's record." Harvey wanted to add, "And there are some who don't think he *should* have the chance, either."

"C'mon, now, Harvey, don't do anything to jinx him."

"I'm just being realistic, Snoot, but you're absolutely right. If anyone is going to do it, it's Moss."

"Let's take a minute for our sponsors, fans. We'll be right back."

They shed their headsets. Harvey stretched.

"Damn funny, your line about the pom-poms," Coffman said.

"Thank you."

"I've been doing a little digging, Harvey. What if I told you that at least one player on this team has been involved in racist activities? I don't know about now, but he's got a bit of a history."

"It wouldn't surprise me," Harvey replied, reaching for his can of Pepsi. "You want to tell me any more?"

Coffman exhaled loudly. "I want to make a few more phone calls."

"Who are you talking to, Snoot?"

"Just some friends around the league. Look, I'm only trying to help. I know you got your hands full taking care of Moss. Anyway, it probably won't amount to much." Observing Harvey's expression, he added, "You don't want me doing this, do you?"

Harvey drained his Pepsi. "Look, I appreciate it, but I don't want us to be tripping over each other."

"Got it. But what if I just make a few last phone calls and let you know what I found out?"

"That's fine." Anything to keep him amused.

Coffman glanced at his engineer and donned the headset. "We're back, fans, and with me is Harvey Blissberg, a man who's done it all. Played center field for the Red Sox and Jewels, been a private detective, a motivational speaker . . ."

Harvey did not want to subject Marshall Levy and Felix Shalhoub to the distracting presence of a ravishing young woman in Marshall's skybox, so they took two house seats along the third-base line and watched Moss Cooley's first at-bat.

"What's the deal with the stupid grinning Indian face on Cleveland's hats?" she said. "It's so demeaning."

Although no slave to political correctness, he nonetheless agreed. "It's like the Washington Redskins logo in football—they've got the profile of a brown-faced Indian chief. It's like putting a rabbi on your hat and calling your team the Moneylenders."

Moss struck out on a wicked split-fingered fastball from Cleveland's ace, Rick Rusansky, and Harvey feared it would be a long evening for the hometown boys. Cooley trudged back to the team's first-base dugout, staring disappointedly at his bat.

"Okay, Moss, you'll get 'em next time!" Cherry Ann yelled, standing up in her tight jeans.

That afternoon, his old mentor Jerry Bellaggio had called back with his preliminary findings, which did little to illuminate Moss's predicament. Due to the lack of interracial violent crimes in recent years, the Rhode Island Attorney General's Office and the Providence Police had disbanded their hate crimes units. Most of the serious violent crime took place *within* new immigrant groups. There were no white supremacist groups based in the state, nor any highly visible or active chapters of groups that were based elsewhere. As for the rogue supremacist group Izan Nation, to which Al Molis and Andy Cubberly had belonged, it was, according to Jerry, a splinter group that became a toothpick and then nothing at all. It did not even show up on the FBI's radar screen. His FBI crony at the Behavioral Analysis Unit had run a check on the agency's computers for anyone with a history of using lawn jockeys to threaten another person and come up empty.

As for Negro lawn jockeys themselves, Jerry had discovered that the earliest "Jockos" (legend had it that George Washington commissioned the first lawn jockey as a memorial to a young black volunteer named Jocko Graves, who had frozen to death holding the reins of Continental Army horses while waiting for Washington to cross the Delaware) were decorative stone tributes to the horse-savvy West African slaves who turned out to be such excellent groomsmen. Soon, despite their indentured status, they proved to be expert jockeys in the burgeoning sport of horse racing. The call to the post at the first Kentucky Derby in 1875 featured thirteen black jockeys in a field of fifteen. Seven of the first thirteen Derbies were won by black jockeys who owned their own horses. But the prominence of blacks in the equestrian world, and the threat emancipation posed to the social order, eventually gave rise to demeaning, caricatured lawn jockeys—stooped, bug-eyed, and grinning—like the one Moss had received. Lawn jockeys, according to Jerry's research, had also played a political role in nineteenth-century America. Along the Underground Railroad, a lawn jockey sporting a brightly colored ribbon, or one with its lantern lit, signaled a safe house for escaping slaves. By the early twentieth century, black jockeys had virtually disappeared from American race tracks, but black lawn jockeys lived on, increasingly divorced from the progressive social reality to which they originally paid homage.

Jerry had found no evidence that cast-iron jockeys were still made, but molded aluminum and cement ones were being manufactured in the United States and Mexico. Jerry had found an Equine Art and Gift Emporium in Florida that custom hand-painted cement-and-aluminum jockeys—four coats usually required—and sold them to thoroughbred horse farms, but neither bought nor sold cast-iron jockeys. The online auction service eBay offered collectible cast-iron jockeys ranging from eleven inches to forty-five inches high, weighing from two pounds to three hundred. (Harvey's own phone calls that afternoon had failed to find a match between a description of any lawn jockey offered or sold on eBay and the one left for Moss.) Oddly enough, despite this friendly trafficking in lawn jockeys, Jerry had been unable to find any information on them in the major Americana, collectibles, and flea market price guides.

Jerry had found only one reported legal case involving lawn jockeys on the Internet. The American Civil Liberties Union litigation docket for 1998–99 included a pending case involving an African-American firefighter in Maryland who had complained about the presence of a black lawn jockey in the station's recreation room in 1991. The station chief had moved it to the volunteer firefighter's area, from which it returned to its original location, this time with a mop in its hand. The statue was again moved and later returned with a noose around its neck. The black firefighter requested and received a transfer and later sued the volunteer fire company, the station chief, and a volunteer firefighter he believed responsible for the act.

Harvey's own calls to the ACLU lawyers representing the firefighter revealed that the lawn jockey in question was made of cement, not cast iron.

In any case, there was a decent chance none of this would matter after tonight's game. Rusansky, already a twelve-game winner with a week and a half left in July, was mowing down the Jewels. Cooley didn't bat again until the fourth, when, on a two-and-two count, he popped up to the third baseman and the crowd grumbled.

"Rusansky's got great stuff tonight. Excellent location, too."

"Location?" Cherry Ann asked.

"Where the pitch is. Pitching's got that in common with real estate. The three most important things are location, location, and location. Most of Rusansky's pitches are right on the black."

"The black?"

"See," he said, warming to the forgotten pleasures of explaining a subject he knew well to a gorgeous young woman, "the strike zone's an imaginary box whose position is determined by the width of the plate and the batting stance of the batter. According to the rules, the height of it is supposed to be from the player's chest—the letters of his uniform—to his knees. Actually, though, it's an abstraction defined by the home-plate umpire. Almost everything else in the game is governed by clear rules and physical boundaries, but the strike zone is this weird exception, the game's most critical set of parameters, and it really exists only in the mind of a middle-aged man wearing a chest protector."

Guercio got out in front of, and underneath, an off-speed pitch and also popped up. Harvey waited until the ball settled into the second baseman's glove before continuing.

"Now, for some reason, the umpires had been shrinking the strike zone over the last several years so that, effectively, it became from the batter's *waist* to his knees. Some sort of tacit conspiracy, I guess, unless they find that the umps had been meeting secretly in the off season. They took away the high strike. Pitchers complained. Batting averages and home run production went up because batters had less strike zone to worry about, and the pitchers were throwing to a smaller target. So, this year, the leagues have ordered the umps to restore the original zone. You follow me?"

"Yes," she said. "But you were going to tell me what 'the black' is."

"Right. Sorry." Sitting next to her had made him garrulous. He was ashamed to admit it even to himself, but he was not immune to her effortless charms. His attention to the game had been interrupted on more than one occasion by a sexual fantasy involving Cherry Ann Smoler and Marshall Levy's skybox. And this had happened despite the fact that (1) she was dating Moss Cooley, (2) he had enjoyed quite respectable sexual relations with Mickey Slavin only two nights before, and (3) Cherry Ann was a professional stripper who, Harvey was old enough to know, was in the business of mechanically seducing strange men into thinking they had a personal relationship with her and her body. No one knew better than a stripper how cheaply a man's full attention could be bought, how shallow a trough his soul could be, how susceptible the gender was to bad music and beer combined with a chance to visually inspect a pretty woman's crotch. Harvey desperately wanted Cherry Ann not to think he was one of those men.

"The black," he said, "is the imaginary outline of the strike zone—the spot where a pitch is hardest to hit and will still be called a strike."

"Ah," she said.

"The black is where Rick Rusansky is *living* so far today. The man is threading the needle at sixty feet. You will notice, by consulting the fabulously expensive Jumbotron scoreboard, that the Jewels have yet to get a hit."

"But Cleveland only has one."

"It's called a pitchers' duel."

"You know, I've only seen him play once before. Before the streak started."

"Can I ask you a question?" Harvey asked.

"As long as it's not, 'How can you let strange guys stare at your monkey night after night?' Or 'Were you abused as a child?'"

"Damn," Harvey said and pretended to sulk.

Cherry Ann was taken in for a minute, then laughed when she realized he was joking.

"I was going to ask you how you and Moss got together."

"That. One night he came to Teasers, watched me dance, and sent me a note backstage. It's the only time I've gotten a note I answered."

"It must've been quite a note."

"Actually, it was very sweet. It said"—she kept her voice low so their neighbors in the box seats couldn't hear—"that he was the black ballplayer in the first row wearing Oakley shades and that he knew what it was like to do your job in front of a lot of people you didn't know. He said he hoped I'd let him buy me dinner because he'd love to see what I looked like with my clothes on. I thought that was so funny I went out with him."

Barney singled up the middle for the Jewels with one out, bringing up Andy Cubberly. "So you *do* have a heart of gold."

"He's the one with the heart of gold," she said. "Though he saw plenty of bad stuff as a kid too. Maybe that's another thing we have in common."

He wondered if she knew about his grandfather, but he was more interested in her childhood at the moment. "And what did *you* see?"

"The usual. I saw people being bad to each other and bad to me. I saw what men were really like at an age when I shouldn't have seen it."

"And stripping's a way to get back at them?"

"Save your psychobabble for someone else."

"I was just trying to save you some shrink bills."

She gave him a sharp look and retreated into a silence that lasted until the bottom of the seventh inning, with Cleveland holding on to a 1–0 lead. Rusansky was pitching a two-hitter—singles by Guercio and Barney. Cooley was leading off the inning, and perhaps Cherry Ann's anxiety about his streak made her want to talk again.

"I didn't mean to snap at you before," she said. She took a sip from the giant cup of Sprite she'd bought in the fifth inning and now kept secured between her knees. "Don't worry, I can tell you're a decent guy."

"C'mon. I hate that."

"There's nothing wrong with being a decent man."

"No, that part I can live with. It's being *called* one that I hate."

"You'd rather be a tough son of a bitch?"

"I can be one of those if called upon." Cooley fouled off Rusanksy's first pitch.

"Well, good for you," she said.

"It's required in this business. Just as it is in yours."

She turned away and yelled. "Let's go, Moss, let's go!"

Rusansky kicked and delivered—a rising fastball over the outside half of the plate. Cooley liked what he saw and uncoiled ferociously, but he got half an inch under the ball's sweet spot and lofted a routine fly that Cleveland's center fielder drifted over in medium left center to put away. Tens of thousands of Jewels partisans groaned in unison, a decrescendo that filled the stadium with its brief sorrow.

"Damn," said Cherry Ann Smoler.

An electronic snippet of "Take Me Out to the Ball Game" began to emanate from Harvey's pants.

It was Mickey. "Tough luck," she said.

"You're watching?"

"ESPN is cutting to Providence every time Moss is up. This is easily Rusansky's best outing of the year."

"I don't know what happened to Moss's fabled patience on that one. I'm worried the pressure's getting to him. Where are you?"

"Cincinnati. The big Reds-Cubs clash. What's new with Cooley?"

"We've got a safe house we're in. Man's being pursued by ten thousand journalists, and we're playing gin rummy in the wilds of Rhode Island."

"Every scoreboard in baseball is tracking his at-bats. The whole world's watching."

"I know. I've got a nasty stack of letters to prove it. And a lawn jockey's head."

"Let's just hope he gets up again," Mickey said.

Harvey clucked. "If Providence can't get someone on base, he won't."

When he got off, Cherry Ann asked who it was.

"My girlfriend."

"Does she know what a decent guy you are?"

"No," he said.

"Oh. So, will Moss get up again?"

Although the scoreboard showed that Rusansky was still throwing in the nineties and Harvey could tell he still had his stuff too, and that meant that Moss might be through for the day, he reassured her. "He will."

And he did, in dramatic fashion. With two outs in the bottom of the ninth and Moss Cooley waiting patiently in the on-deck circle, Jewels third baseman Craig Venora got enough of a Rusansky slider to slice a soft line drive over second, just out of the second baseman's reach. Only the team's third hit.

The crowd was quiet as Cooley stepped in against Rusansky and took a curve for strike one. With a 2–0 lead, the Cleveland outfield played deep. Rusansky missed with a slider. Cooley fouled off a fastball, fouled off a slider, and watched another fastball sail just high.

Unable to sit still any longer, the crowd now rose majestically in unison to watch the two-and-two pitch. Cherry Ann stood, biting a thumb, as Rusansky looked in for the sign. Venora danced off first base, trying to unsettle Rusansky, who made a sullen pro forma throw over to keep him honest. Cooley stayed glued to the batter's box, eyes locked on the pitcher, hands kneading the bat handle.

Harvey stood too, feeling a curious sensation. His jaded feelings about baseball surrendered to a moment of pure appreciation. He was no longer inside the game looking out, but outside looking in, and he saw what any fan could see: baseball's best pitcher and hitter facing each other across sixty feet of grass and soil. It was as though Harvey suddenly understood for the first time in years what fans meant when they talked about how much they loved the game. The game was a stately procession of conflicts, each one a test of will, cunning, and expertise. The team that won the majority of a game's little battles—between pitcher and batter, pitcher and baserunner, fielder and ball, between the manager and all the possibilities at his command—was the team that won the war. Compared with baseball, football was an unintelligible street fight, hockey a beautiful blur from which sense only occasionally emerged, basketball a furious ballet too complex to grasp. But baseball's crucial moments were played out in a kind of naked stillness. Baseball broke the confusion down, strung out the logic for all to see.

It seemed the whole season had been merely preamble to this moment, a series of sketches working up to this masterpiece on which Rusansky and Cooley were now putting the finishing touches. Of the many millions of boys in their generation who had picked up a bat and ball and dreamed of glory, it was these two—one from Starrett, Alabama, one from Oil City, Pennsylvania, who had earned the privilege today of making baseball history.

Harvey felt Cherry Ann's hand in his as Rusansky set himself, turned to glower for an instant at Venora leading off first base, his glance enough to freeze the base runner. Then the pitcher kicked and delivered a slider headed for the outside corner of the plate. The crowd, which had been holding its breath, let out a strange collective sound as Moss got the fat of the bat on the ball and sent it on a line toward right center. Cherry Ann's hand squeezed Harvey's.

Everyone in The Jewel Box could imagine the ball as it found the gap and skipped to the right-center field wall with Indian outfielders in pursuit, Venora racing around the bases as Cooley, now the tying run, pulled into scoring position at second.

But Cleveland's second baseman stood directly in its path. He intercepted the ball's rising trajectory with a timed leap, and the ball disappeared into his glove, demolishing the fantasy as suddenly as it began, so abruptly necessitating a mass revision of hope that the crowd continued its expectant noise for another second or two before it registered the truth.

It was as if the entire crowd had been shot dead. Fans

everywhere stood in a kind of shock, as did Moss Cooley himself, who had pulled up just a few feet down the first-base line. The Indians swarmed Rusansky near the mound. In the Providence dugout, the players quietly gathered their possessions.

The surreal silence was dispelled only when some fans in the box seats recovered enough to begin applauding Cooley. It quickly spread, and within seconds the entire park was paying homage to Moss Cooley's remarkable forty-seven-game hitting streak, the second longest in baseball history.

Cooley, sensing the need to commemorate the crisis, overcame his reserve and gave the fans in the first-base line boxes a shallow bow. He then turned to the fans on the third-base side and did the same. He raised his right hand to the fans in left, center, and right, and then slowly walked to the dugout as the cheering doubled.

It was pure baseball, Harvey thought, everyone doing their job. Rusansky's perfect pitch, Cooley's perfect contact, the second baseman's perfect positioning and perfect leap. Chance too had played its perverse part, nullifying Moss's very best effort. On another day, perhaps, the score would now be 2–1 and Moss would be dusting himself off as he stood triumphantly on second base. But this was not another day; it was this day, and so the crowd began its sad shuffling toward the exits.

Cherry Ann Smoler reached under her seat for her Jansport backpack amid the litter of popcorn kernels, Pepsi puddles, and discarded programs.

When she straightened, she looked at Harvey and said, "Can I have my boyfriend back now?"

Harvey took Cherry Ann inside the clubhouse to stand with him at the back of a crowd of print, radio, and television reporters jostling each other for a better view of Moss, clad only in a towel as he sat on the chair in front of his cubicle and fielded the predictable queries. "How does it feel . . . ? Are you disappointed that . . . ? What were you thinking . . . ? Was Rusansky the toughest pitcher you've . . . ? Are you glad the pressure's off . . . ? Do you think anybody will ever break DiMaggio's . . . ?" He was gracious, nodding thoughtfully at each cliché before answering, as if he had never considered such a question before. He kept his poise in the thicket of microphones and cameras, under the barrage of flashbulbs, even when reporters shouted at him to turn in his direction.

"Cool! Moss! Over here! Look this way a minute! Cool! Let me have a smile!"

"Be right with you," he'd say. "One moment, please."

"This is a switch," Cherry Ann whispered to Harvey as two Jewels, recently showered, casually removed their towels at nearby cubicles for a final blotting of their privates before putting on their briefs. "I'm in the audience looking at guys' dicks."

"Cool! Cool!" a reporter shouted. "Your streak may be over, but the team's still hot. What do you think of the Jewels' chances this year?" His words ran seamlessly and urgently together, uninterruptible.

The voice was familiar, and when Harvey craned his head to see who it was, he felt a shiver in his spine as he spied the *Providence Journal*'s Bob Lassiter on his tiptoes, flexing an outstretched arm, still plying his trade after all these years. Moss Cooley hadn't been thought of yet when Lassiter began covering baseball. Every year, Harvey mused morbidly, physically gifted babies were born who would grow up some day to supply quotes and sound bites for aging men to fill column inches with. It had been a dozen years since he had spoken with or seen Lassiter, now ashen and jowly. Harvey averted his face and told Cherry Ann they should wait for Moss by the entrance to the player's parking lot.

"I think I'd rather dance naked in front of a bunch of dorks than do that," she said as they walked down the concrete corridor under the stands. "Answer all those stupid questions."

"You're in luck. 'Cause dancing naked in front of dorks is your current form of employment."

"You know, for a decent guy you can come pretty close to being an asshole."

"I've been told that I can walk that fine line."

"So, what do you do now?"

"I'm still on the clock."

"You mean, this thing isn't over yet?"

"Our enemies may not have heard the news yet. The team's general manager wants me to stay with Moss at least through tomorrow."

"So Moss and I can't go out and celebrate?"

"Not yet. Anyone's who's sick enough to want to hurt him for approaching DiMaggio's streak may be sick enough to want to hurt him for hitting in as many as forty-seven games."

WON'T Cooley be surprised, he thought as he dabbed the glue stick on the back of the small square of newsprint. For some reason, maybe because the past was on his mind, he remembered LePage's mucilage from his childhood, the tapered bottle with the slanted, red rubber nipple that dispensed the glue from a small slit. You pressed the nipple against the paper, producing a slick film of honey-colored adhesive. If you didn't use it for a while, a dried crust formed over the slit that you had to peel off with your fingernail. Oh, well. He took the tweezers and turned the scrap over, placing it in its proper position and pressing it down with the heel of his hand. The latex gloves made everything feel a little strange. Remote, like the event itself.

The activity steadied him. As a child, he'd loved making models, all those B-29s and Spitfires and Sherman tanks and destroyers. His bedroom was crammed with miniature materiel. They lined his shelves and hung from the ceiling of his bedroom on black threads, spinning slowly in the summer breeze coming in through the windows. He was good with his hands, knew how to apply glue with a toothpick, just the right amount so that the plastic parts didn't ooze excess when he joined them. He took pride in painting the tiny pilots and gun barrels and wingtips, dipping the slender brush into the small bottles of Testors enamel paint and carefully stroking on the paint, always in one direction. He had once dreamed of being a doctor, a surgeon, a man whose job it was to do small, important things well, tying off the sutures to finish up. He'd always been good with knots. Tying a knot was a pleasingly final motion. He thought of watching the ropers with their furious flurry of movements over the prostrate calf, tying off the rope and raising their hands for the judges. Done! It never frustrated him to tie the black threads that cradled his models and suspended them from the ceiling. Done! He could lose himself in it. It was a compartment, a pretty little compartment full of small, important gestures.

Baseball was a compartment. A series of compartments, really, beginning with the park itself, set off from life. Inside the park was the field, set off from every place else by white lines and fences, and within that compartment was the compartment of the infield, more subtly marked by three bases and the plate, and above the plate the compartment of the strike zone, which contained the good pitches and none of the bad. And there were the batters' boxes on either side of the plate to contain the batter, and the stands to contain the fans, and the dugouts to contain the teams, and the scoreboard to contain the information, and most of all the rules of the game to contain the anarchy outside the game.

Now he pressed the last scrap of paper down with the heel of his hand, and he observed his handiwork and saw that it was good. He felt he had hit the right tone, nothing spelled out, but the message lying there just below the surface like a dead body beneath the ice of a frozen pond where a terrible accident had occurred. If Cooley was smart, he would get it and make the right decision. If he wasn't, then the situation would require more than a glue stick and tweezers. He had to seal the slit, the chink in the present through which the sticky past was in danger of oozing, ruining everything.

And he had the same full, no longer lonely feeling he had as a child in his room when he finished a model. He laid the paper next to the doll on the worktable in his basement and began cleaning up, putting the scissors and glue and paper away in the bottom of a cardboard box filled with old Mason jars that he'd found in the little canning pantry in the basement. Canning was another thing that belonged to the past, like LePage's mucilage. He gathered up the magazines and put them in a plastic bag along with the latex gloves he peeled off. He let himself out the basement door, carrying the bag, and took it to the Rubbermaid trash barrel and dumped the bag inside, all the magazines, the magazines that were missing only the letters that made up Cooley's next instruction. His next lesson in keeping the past in its compartment.

When he entered the basement again, he guzzled a Seagram's miniature. Then he plucked a fresh pair of gloves, tissuelike, from the box and put them in his pocket. Now he was free to think about the girl for a few minutes and who she was. In a bigger city—L.A., Chicago, maybe even Boston, New York above all—these things would be known. The rumormongers and the gossip columnists would see to it. But Providence, fucking Rhode Island? Might as well be Missoula, Montana. No one knew anything. And Cooley kept to himself anyway, didn't play with the boys, no one knew anything about his private life, just like that fucking Jew Moe Berg.

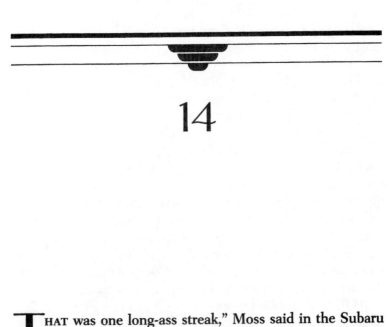

14

THAT was one long-ass streak," Moss said in the Subaru the next morning as Harvey drove him back to his own house to pick up a few things before taking him to the ballpark for the afternoon game against Cleveland and the resumption of his normal life. They'd spent one last uneventful night in the Exeter safe house, watching ESPN and drinking beer. "Yes, sir, I think God made one fifty-six-game streak, and naturally He or She gave it to the white man. But I'll take my forty-seven and be goddamn proud of it."

"Well, there's got to be some relief in knowing you're not an inexplicable number of deviations above the statistical norm."

"I want to tell you something, Harvey." Moss sighed as if he'd been holding his breath for weeks. "I wasn't having an easy time with this, and I'm not just talking about the lawn jockey. I had the feeling I was losing myself. Losing pieces of myself every day that were going out to make up this public figure I've become. Maybe some dudes are good at handling it. It just made me feel like I was living with another Moss Cooley."

"Well, I've got to tell you, big guy, you've been referring to yourself in the third person. You know that, don't you? Been referring to yourself as Moss Cooley."

"Now, you know I'm going to cut that shit out right now. And you better believe that when Moss Cooley tells you he's going to do something, he's going to do it." He looked at Harvey, and his wheezy laugh started up like a car engine on a January morning.

"Very good, Moss. Very funny."

"You know what I've been feeling like? I've been feeling like a cartoon waiting for a caption."

"And now you've got one," Harvey said. "'Owner of the second most goddamn unbelievable hitting streak in major-league history. And you did it without the hitters around you that DiMaggio had.'"

"But I had the smaller strike zone on my side."

"Yeah, sure, but DiMaggio didn't have to contend with better athletes and those huge gloves. I'll bet you lost a hit or two during the streak 'cause of the bigger leather."

"But I sucked against Rusansky."

"If you're going to be that way about it, Moss, you'll just have to start another streak later today. DiMaggio did it, you know—hit in sixteen more straight games." Harvey thought of DiMaggio and *his* caption, the Yankee Clipper, and how high and thick the myth had been constructed, so that it was really only after his death that biographers could bring DiMaggio's hidden, limited self to public light: his obtuseness about, and abuse of, women; his endless, shameless use of others; his insatiable appetite for money; his intellectual and emotional poverty; his profitable association with the mob. Really, greatness didn't care who possessed it, although DiMaggio's case suggested that the people who make the best icons are often those without much substance in the first place, the better to be filled with our needs and fantasies. Was this what had been troubling Moss Cooley, a man with more substance than the public gave him credit for, not less? For while fame could give an empty man a kind of self, for a man already full of self, fame could only deplete it. Harvey could not imagine Moss tolerating DiMaggio's fate—spending half a century and more living inside a moated castle of lies.

"I want those pieces back now," Moss said.

"Even if you'd broken DiMaggio's record," Harvey replied, "you'd have found a way to get them back. Anyway," he added with a rush of good feeling, realizing how much he liked Moss, "I'll always cherish these few days we could spend together."

"The Jew and the black man living as one."

"An interracial, interfaith, intergenerational relationship."

"With the highest combined major-league lifetime batting average of any couple ever."

"With the *only* combined major-league lifetime batting average of any couple ever," Harvey said.

"You got that right."

"Where you going?" Cooley said as Harvey pulled off 95 on an exit ramp. "This isn't my goddamn exit. The next one."

"I've got a Toyota pickup two cars behind me that's been there for a couple of miles," Harvey said, watching the vehicle in his rearview mirror. "I want to make sure I'm not being tailed."

"Tailed? Don't spook me. The streak's over. Don't be so goddamn thorough."

Harvey got off 95, and the pickup stayed on the interstate. "Listen, Moss, whoever sent you the jockey will probably just wither up and die now, but I think you ought to stay away from your routine for a while. Stay away from situations and places where you're known. Stay away from Teasers." Harvey eased the car back onto 95.

"I don't have to go to Teasers anymore to see Cherry Ann in the altogether."

"I know. I'm just saying. You know, Moss, I never came up with a pet name for you."

"I already got one. Cool. And you never use it."

"Everyone calls you that. People who've never met you call you that. The goddamn signs in the stands call you that. I'm talking about a name that's just between us. Like Snake Head."

"Snake Head?" Cooley laughed. "What kind of dumb-ass name is that? What you going to call me when I get a new do? C'mon, you can do better than that."

"The Starrett Stallion."

"That shows no intelligence whatsoever."

"Yo' Mama Head," Harvey said, suddenly laughing uncontrollably.

"You don't calm down, I'm gonna drive."

Harvey got off 95 again at exit 14 and headed toward Cooley's house in Cranston, winding past ranch houses, saltboxes, tag sales, and fruit stands. "Moss," he said, "I'm sorry I never got the chance to show you the documentary about the old days of baseball. You would've liked it. Joltin' Joe's in it— film of him as a kid at Wrigley Field playing in the 'thirty-eight Series. I'll bet you didn't know that the fielders used to leave their gloves on the field."

"I think I heard that, but why the hell did they do it? Did the other team use 'em?"

"Nope. Everybody just left their gloves there. I don't know why they did it. Convenience. Tradition. The league didn't outlaw it until after the 'fifty-three season."

"I wouldn't want to be tripping over somebody's raggedy-ass glove."

"I don't think anybody ever did. Least not in an important game. Otherwise it would've been outlawed sooner, don't you think? They say someone once put a dead rat in Phil Rizzuto's glove. He had a phobia about rats."

"I got one of those too."

"I've never met anybody who actually had a thing *for* rats," Harvey said, pulling into Cooley's circular driveway. "What's that?" he asked Moss, his stomach tightening.

"What?"

"Hanging from your porch light."

"Goddamn motherfuckin' motherfuckers."

They got out of the car and walked up to the front stoop. It was a black Ken doll without any clothes on, hanging from the porch light cover latch by a length of twine that had been fashioned into a tiny noose around its plastic neck. Its neck had been wrenched back at an awkward angle. Safety-pinned to the twine was a piece of paper folded into quarters.

Harvey quickly circled the house, .38 in his hand, but saw no other signs of vandalism or forced entry. When he got back to the porch, Moss was still standing on the stoop, looking at the Ken doll.

"Goddamn motherfuckers."

"Someone didn't hear the streak's over," Harvey said.

But the note, once he'd unpinned and gingerly unfolded it, removed any doubt that its author had heard about Cooley's hitless game last night. Like the note that accompanied the lawn jockey, it consisted of letters cut from magazines and glued to the page.

ShAmE AboUT thE STReAk.
NoW waTcH YOUr aSs OR it wILL bE
an unSoLVeD rACe CRime.

Harvey cut the Ken doll down with his pocket knife, and they went inside, Harvey holding the doll by the very end of the rope. He put it on the living room coffee table, where it lay on its back as though awaiting a miniature autopsy.

"Somebody's fucking with me," Moss said, slumping on the sofa while Harvey paced.

"This is the same guy who sent you the lawn jockey." He held the note by the edges and studied it as he walked the floor.

"I can see that."

"Why does he say 'unsolved race crime'?"

"I don't know."

"It's the only thing in the note where there's any traction."

"Damn," Moss said. "He's got to be talking about GURCC."

"What's that?"

"The Georgia Unsolved Race Crimes Clearinghouse. GURCC. Bunch of lawyers and investigators in Atlanta who try to reopen and prosecute old race crime cases."

"Yeah, I know about them," Harvey said. "Murder and rape cases. No statute of limitations. What's it got to do with you?"

"One of my childhood friends from Alabama—Charlie Fathon—he became a lawyer for them last year just out of law school, and he asked me to get involved over the winter."

"Doing what?"

"Oh, the usual shit. Lending my name to their fund-raising campaigns. I dropped some cash on them. They've been talking to me about being their spokesman. Doing some speaking for them. You know, 'cause of my granddaddy and all, I've got some credibility. I hate to put it that way, but there it is."

"Moss, why haven't you mentioned it to me before?"

"It never occurred to me the threats had anything to do with it."

"C'mon, Moss, you're the object of racial threats, and you're involved in a race organization—"

"Now don't get in my face about it," he snapped. "I don't know what's going on any more than you do. I thought it was the damn streak, just like you."

"What I don't get is that this is the first I've heard of you and GURCC. The press doesn't mention it."

"I keep it low. I don't like these rich motherfuckers who go around saying, 'Look at me, I'm giving to this, giving to that.'"

"But this asshole knows about you and GURCC."

"It's public information. I just don't blow my horn about it. But my name's there on the mailings and the ads." He rubbed his face with both palms, then dropped them. "Let me ask you something: If this is the same guy who wrote the note about the streak, why's he on a different page now?"

"What if it's the page he's always been on? What if the first note was just a smoke screen?"

"What if it's just some crazed motherfucker toying with me? What if next time I get a note telling me to lay off the goddamn stuffies at Hemenway's?"

"Right now, we got this." Harvey finally sat opposite Moss. "Why would he want you to cut your ties with GURCC?"

"I have no goddamn idea!"

"You got any literature from GURCC I can look at?"

"He's not interested in GURCC! He's just some goddamn motherfuckin' stalker!"

"I'd like to look at it anyway," Harvey said softly.

"All right. Hold on. Maybe I got some upstairs." Cooley stalked off toward the stairs. At the foot of them he turned and said, "I want those pieces back."

"We'll get them back," Harvey replied.

While Cooley was upstairs, Harvey took out his pen and notebook and wrote down on a fresh leaf: "DiMaggio evades apprehension. Do nothing in greatest game. Escape retribution." What was going on? It *had* to be the same person, but the language was different. The first note was stilted, telegraphic, the second conversational. Where the first was an all-purpose warning to lay off DiMaggio's record, the second pointed to a specific association of Moss's. Harvey felt the man meant business with this new note. Now, in retrospect, the first time around he just seemed to be playing a game. A game, Harvey thought, studying the first note again, breaking it down. . . .

He reached for his cell phone and called Marshall Levy.

"Where are you?" Harvey said.

"I'm at home. Where are you?"

"I'm at Moss's house, and we've got a problem."

"I thought our problem was over."

"I'm afraid it might just be starting."

"I'm not happy hearing this, Harvey."

"I didn't write the script, Marshall."

"What's going on?"

Harvey told him about the Ken doll lynching and the note.

"I didn't know about this GURCC," Marshall said.

"Neither did I. We need to meet. You, Felix, Moss, and me."

"When?"

"Before the game."

"All right. Come to the skybox at eleven-thirty. Cool okay?"

"Pissed. You'd be pissed too."

Harvey went to Cooley's kitchen and found a Ziploc bag. He dropped the Ken doll into it, and when he came back to the living room, Moss was there looking at the doll in Harvey's hand with an expression suggesting that what Moss saw in the bag was not just the most recent token of some stranger's hate, but a relic of generations of hate leading back to his granddaddy and before.

"All I could find was this," Moss said in a flat voice, holding some papers folded into thirds. "Here." He thrust it at Harvey.

It was a slickly produced four-page direct-mail fund-raising solicitation from GURCC. He skimmed it: "So we need your help if we are to continue our efforts to reopen these cases, arrest and convict these criminals, still at large. . . . Even in a democracy, justice has a price tag. . . . We accept no public funds, no fees from monetary jury awards. . . . some of the most experienced investigators and lawyers in America. . . . Last year saw us bring two men to justice thirty-two years after they bombed a black-owned motel in Jackson, Mississippi, killing a housekeeper."

There, on the third page, was a photo of Moss Cooley's face with an adjacent bold-face quote from him: "'My own family has known what it is to lose someone to racial hatred and never even learn the murderers' names. The Georgia Unsolved Race Crimes Clearinghouse is the best shot we have at ensuring that those who kill out of racial hatred will not go scot-free.' —Moss Cooley of the Providence Jewels."

Harvey glanced at a block of text highlighting some of the race crimes the group was in the process of gathering evidence to reopen: "the rape and murder of sixteen-year-old Joella Barnes . . . the execution-style shooting death of Ephraim Woodson . . . the lynching of Edward Gomez and Allen James Spellman . . ." The atrocities raced by on the page. He folded the letter and put it in his jacket pocket.

"Let's go. We're meeting with Marshall and Felix at eleven-thirty."

"I don't know about any meeting."

"I just set it up, Moss. We've got to figure out what we're doing."

"I know what I'm doing. I'm out of this drama. I just want to play baseball."

15

A SMATTERING of Cleveland Indians and Providence Jewels dotted the field below Marshall's skybox office, running wind sprints and stretching beneath a hard blue sky. The office contained the same cast of characters as three nights ago, but instead of a headless lawn jockey on the desk between them, now it was Ken in the plastic bag, the note that came with it, and the fund-raising letter open to the page with Moss Cooley's picture on it. Robert, Marshall's skybox steward, had already brought the four of them fresh orange juice, coffee, croissants, Danish, and a selection of gourmet half sandwiches arranged in perfect concentric circles on a plastic tray.

"GURCC," Marshall was saying, smacking as he chewed a bite of roast beef on onion roll. "As a card-carrying liberal, I'm sure I'm on their mailing list. Probably even gave them some money. I had no idea you had a friend there, Cool. You know, I get so much goddamn stuff in the mail. Sometimes I think I'd like my epitaph to read: 'I'd rather be here than have to go through any more mail.' What do you think, Harvey?"

"I believe it's the lawn jockey guy, and we need to look a little deeper into it."

"What if the guy's just going to come up with one thing after another?" Felix asked.

"That's what Moss thinks," Harvey said.

"I think he's just going to keep going," Moss said. "One thing after another."

Harvey popped a pitted black olive in his mouth. "We can sit and wait for the next thing, but my guess is this asshole wants Moss to quit his association with the organization, and he wants him to do it for a reason."

"Which is?" Marshall said.

"Moss says he doesn't know," Harvey said.

Moss stood and slammed his fist on Marshall's desk. "For chrissakes, I *don't* know." Moss, his face clenched, appealed to Felix and Marshall. "Harvey over here seems to think I'm holding out on him."

"Look, Moss," Harvey said, "I believe you."

"Then why do you think it matters so much to someone out there if I'm involved with GURCC? That's why I think this guy's just yanking my chain. Why would it matter if I don't know anything?"

"I can't figure that part out."

Felix raised both palms abruptly, like a third-base coach holding a runner at third. "Professor," he said, "I'm a man of modest intellectual means. If Moss can't think of a reason why anyone would write him telling him to quit GURCC, except as part of a scattershot racist campaign against him, why should we pay special attention to it?"

"Look, here's what I'm saying," Harvey said. "The most significant threat that came Moss's way during the streak— the lawn jockey—comes from the same man who sent this." He gestured at the Ken doll. "The man is serious, and the issue's not a black man overtaking Joe DiMaggio. The streak's over, but he's still at it. I don't think the lawn jockey was about the streak at all."

Owner Marshall Levy stirred. "What about the note that came with it?"

Harvey opened his notebook to the leaf on which he'd written "DiMaggio evades apprehension. Do nothing in greatest game. Escape retribution." He held up the notebook for the other three men to see. "This is what the note said, right?"

"What's your point?" Marshall said. "The note basically says for Cool to stop his own hitting streak or else."

"That's what it *says*." Harvey took out his pen and, reaching over the top of the notebook page like a first-grade teacher showing her class a picture book, circled the first letter of each word. "Here's the message, though."

"'Dead nigger,'" Moss said. "When did you figure that out?"

"At your place. I don't know, but I figured the same guy, different-style notes. Made me wonder why the first one was so strange. So I started playing with it, and I got 'dead nigger.' First the words 'dead nigger,' then the dead nigger Ken doll."

"What's next, full-size inflatable dead nigger?" Moss said, not laughing.

Harvey looked at Marshall and Felix. "Look, we're dealing with a smart crazy person. He likes to play games. We just don't know how serious the game is."

"Question," Felix said. "If the real issue is GURCC, why didn't the man just come out and say it the first time? Why waste any time at all with a lawn jockey and pretend it's only the streak?"

"I don't know. Maybe he was trying to obscure his real objective. Not draw too much attention to it."

"Don't overthink it, Professor," Marshall Levy said.

"Why don't we wait to see what else we get from the guy?" Felix Shalhoub said.

Marshall nodded. "I agree. Let's wait. But, Harvey, I'd like you to look after Cool until further notice. You might as well keep your safe house for a little while. I'm paying for it, anyway. Meanwhile, can we keep Cool's house under surveillance for a few days?"

Harvey sighed. "I know a guy I can put in Moss's house with a gun and a camera with a telephoto lens." He was thinking of Linderman senior. "But I don't think you're taking this seriously enough."

"What do you propose?" Marshall asked, polishing his glasses on his tie. "Bring in the cops?"

Harvey looked at Cooley. "Moss?"

Moss, who hadn't touched any food, took a tiny sip of orange juice. "Would it be all right with y'all if I went back to playing baseball?"

"Sounds good to me," Felix added.

Cooley nodded. "I've had it with this motherfuckin' nonsense. I'll cut my goddamn ties with GURCC and get back to playin' some ball."

"Give in?" Harvey said. He had thought that history—the larger playing field— mattered to Moss.

"This crazy-ass wants me to break my ties? Fine." Moss turned to Felix. "Let's put out a press release saying I've ended my relationship with GURCC, that I'm not their spokesman, whatever. We'll get it in the papers where this asshole can see it," Moss went on, "and that'll be that. If the guy's agenda is GURCC, as you say it is, Harvey, then we won't hear from him again. If it's not his agenda, we'll hear from him on some other motherfuckin' subject."

"What reason are we going to give for your severing your relationship with GURCC?" Marshall asked.

"Why not tell them the truth?" Felix suggested. "Then they'll print it. Hell, it'll be all over ESPN. Because of an anonymous death threat to Moss Cooley urging him to sever his relationship with GURCC, Mr. Cooley has decided to end his association with the civil rights organization. He was slated to become GURCC's national spokesman. Etcetera, etcetera."

"Wait a minute," Harvey said. "You want to advertise that you're the subject of a death threat, go ahead. Then we got the cops and the feds all over us for more information. You want that, Moss?"

"No."

"How else do we let this guy know Moss is not in bed with GURCC anymore?" Marshall asked, helping himself to a tuna salad on whole wheat.

"Give it to Bob Lassiter of the *Providence Journal*," Harvey suggested. "Give him an exclusive, but don't mention the death threat. Just say you're quitting GURCC 'for personal reasons.' If you mention the jockey or the doll, you run the risk of either encouraging or antagonizing the guy. This way, it's really just a private communication between Moss and this asshole."

"I like it," Felix said. "Give the old scribbler an exclusive."

"What if the guy doesn't see it?" Marshall asked.

"He'll see it," Harvey said. "He lives here. Or near here. I don't think the guy drove long-distance to deliver sixty pounds of lawn jockey. In any case, if you give the story to Lassiter, it'll be picked up. It'll still end up on ESPN. If Moss picks his nose, it'll end up on ESPN. What do you think, Moss?"

Cooley thought about it for a moment, his right hand playing with one of the gold rings on his left. "But let me talk to Lassiter myself after the game. I'll keep it low, mix it in with some other quotes about the end of the streak."

"Go for it," Marshall said.

"Make it clear I'm only doing this because of my schedule or other obligations."

"Good," said Felix..

Moss stood. "I better suit up."

"Sorry about the streak, Cool," Marshall said, standing.

"My mama said all good things come to an end."

Felix stood as well. "Rusansky pitched a whale of a game. Otherwise you'd still be chasing the Clipper."

✦

Harvey accompanied Moss down to the clubhouse in silence.

"It's the best thing," Moss said to him finally as they got off the elevator.

"You have to do what's comfortable," Harvey replied. "But you should call your friend Charlie at GURCC and tell him what's going on."

"I plan to." He paused in the concrete corridor and faced Harvey. "I know you think there's more to this, and maybe there is, but I'm going to give the man what he wants, and maybe he'll go away satisfied. In the meantime, I want to help the team win a pennant. For now, I'll let *that* be my good works."

In the clubhouse, Moss's teammates delivered their death-of-the-streak condolences with silent high-fives and pats on the fanny. As he watched Moss move through the clubhouse, collecting his due, Harvey thought, First prize— baseball immortality; second prize—the team's equipment manager slaps you on the butt.

"You'll get 'em next time," Monkman said, although everyone knew what the odds were that Cooley—or anybody, for that matter—would ever have a streak like this again.

"Hey, Blissberg!" It was Andy Cubberly across the way, folding a stick of Wrigley's into his mouth. "Come over here and motivate me. My average has dropped twenty-two points in the last three weeks."

Harvey adopted a smile. "Don't worry. Moss has been using up everybody else's hits for the last two months, and now he's going to give them back."

"Yeah, I'm planning on going hitless for the rest of the year," Cooley said. "That hittin' thang just wasn't doin' it for me."

Ray Costa, the light-hitting catcher, deadpanned, "Boy, do I know how boring those hits can get."

Harvey wandered off toward the dining area and helped

himself to a glass of ginger ale from the soda fountain dispenser. As he sipped it, watching the ballplayers pick at the pregame spread or sneak a look at ESPN's Sports Center on the TV mounted high on the wall, Harvey felt his mood darken. It was a visceral sensation, as if he were watching a massive cloud front move into the Northeast on a Weather Channel radar map. Except he was the Northeast, and the cloud formation was a massive feeling of frustration, incompleteness, and confusion. With Cooley's streak over, the case was abandoning him before he was ready to abandon it. It was possible he had never been this flummoxed by a case before. A headless lawn jockey and a black Ken doll, an acrostic and then the note about GURCC—it was like a dream full of strange, elaborate symbols. How could there not be a method somewhere to this madness? Was the man working up to something, or had he already passed it?

Harvey escaped the clubhouse, hungry for fresh air, and wandered into the players' parking lot, a gleaming, glinting field of luxury cars. He called retired Providence police detective lieutenant Linderman.

"The time has come for me to fill you in," Harvey said.

"The least you can do for the guy who got your pistol permit processed so quickly."

Harvey told him about Cooley, the jockey, and the Ken doll. Then he offered Linderman two bills a day to make himself at home in Moss Cooley's Cranston house for a few days.

"I accept."

"But keep it under your hat," Harvey said.

"I don't have a hat."

"C'mon, Linderman, I've already had a run-in with your nephew."

"Joshua."

"Who found out from a friend what I was doing. I swore him to secrecy in exchange for a piece of whatever action comes out of this."

"It wasn't me."

"I know."

"Anyway, I appreciate the opportunity. I can use the bucks."

"I can't promise you much action. This guy's behavior makes no sense to me. But he has made two visits to Cooley's house and he might make a third. I want photos if he does."

Off the phone, Harvey blinked in the glare of the sun bouncing off all the high-priced automobile hoods. He breathed deeply a few times. He would do as Marshall asked, keep Moss company for a while longer, and hope that his tormentor made another move or backed off forever. But Moss's tormentor was now Harvey's too. To follow Moss Cooley around for a few days and then slink home, without answers, feeling useless—that was intolerable. The assignment that had given his amorphous existence some shape, given him a taste of usefulness, now felt demeaning. He had not left the dubious comforts of his Cambridge sofa for this.

16

WITH the prop of meaningful work removed, Harvey resumed his life on the sofa.

The reprieve that had been his week in Providence was over. The GURCC item had appeared in Lassiter's *Providence Journal* column on Sunday morning, and by Sunday night it had entered the nation's bloodstream of sports minutia, showing up as a brief item on ESPN. Harvey had stayed with Moss in the Exeter house for three more nights, without incident. Linderman had stayed at Moss's Cranston house for three nights, again without incident. The Jewels' home stand ended, with the Jewels taking two of three from the Tigers. When the Jewels left on a thirteen-game road trip to New York, Chicago, Toronto, and Tampa Bay, Harvey returned to Cambridge with a bad feeling and a $14,500 check from Marshall Levy for services rendered.

It was like coming out of the woods without the ball. Without knowing if there even *was* a ball lost in the woods.

All he had come away with, really, was Cubberly, and that wasn't much. A history of racist activity, a creepy rented house, plus two stupid base-running plays might provide some bricks for a case against him, but where was the mortar? On his last night in Providence Harvey had tailed Cubberly after the game, followed the outfielder as he walked from the ballpark to a waterfront bar in Fox Point, near one of the hurricane barriers, two garagelike concrete-and-metal structures out of which metal walls were prepared to slide shut during the next hurricane to block the street and arrest the kind of flooding that had proved so disastrous in 1938. Cubberly sat at the bar, unrecognized, drinking draft beers and trying to lure college girls into conversation. After an hour or so of this halfhearted courtship he returned to his Jeep Cherokee and went home to his depressing Tudor in Wayland Square.

It was Friday now, ten days since Felix Shalhoub had first called. Mickey had come back to town for a day and a half and left again, flying off to St. Louis for "a Cards-Pirates tiff." Some tenderness had passed between them, inexplicable, like the sudden remission of a disease. Their relationship just seemed to go on, a strange mix of inertia and destiny.

He watercolored in the afternoon, completing a passable portrait of a neighbor's Victorian house in strict late-day shadows. Then he persuaded his old mentor Jerry Bellaggio to let him buy dinner at Socrate's Newtown Grill, an old haunt in Porter Square. Over linguini with white clam sauce, Harvey described in detail the lawn jockey and Ken doll incidents and the two notes.

"There's a confusing lack of pattern," Bellaggio said, his portable oxygen unit sitting discreetly next to him in the wooden booth. "Almost deliberately so. A deliberate smoke-screen, perhaps."

"But for what?"

"If I had to choose, Harv, I'd say the first act was a smoke-screen for the second."

"That the general threat—to stop the hitting streak—is a screen for the specific one—cutting off his relationship with this group?"

"Yes."

"Jerry, that presupposes that the hitting streak came along at just the right time to provide a smokescreen."

"Fine. So it did. If I'm right, and there hadn't been a hitting streak to provide cover for his true business, he would've used something else."

"Like what?" Harvey asked.

"What else you got? Where else is Cooley vulnerable to racist attack?"

"He's got a white girlfriend."

"There you go."

"But this guy doesn't seem to know it."

"If he knew it, he would've used it." Jerry pointed a forkful of chicken parmesan at Harvey. "Instead he had the streak. Here's the conjecture, Harv: By using the lawn jockey, the guy wanted to establish himself as a guy who means business, lending force to any later threat or demand, which would be his real demand."

"You really think this?"

"Let's say I do. Then I'd want to know more about his relationship with GURCC."

"Cooley couldn't think of any reason why his involvement with GURCC would be a specific problem for anyone. He says he's only been lending them his name. And making financial contributions."

"This chicken is delicious, Harv. Want a bite?"

"No, thanks."

"Look, I could be all wet. Surely Cooley's self-interest would prevent him from concealing anything."

"You would think."

"Just the two threats, huh?"

"That's it."

Jerry chewed thoughtfully. "If GURCC was the point, and the guy's really clever, he'll do something else, an ex post facto smokescreen. Really confuse the hell out of Cooley."

"On the other hand, another threat could be taken as evidence that the guy *has* no specific message other than racial hate."

"This is a tough one, Harv."

"Well, I'm relieved to know you think it's a tough one, and it's not just that I'm out of practice."

"How worried are you about Cooley's safety?"

"I don't know. The team's on a road trip now, so I'm trying to relax about it. Anyway, the owner and general manager took me off the case. It's their problem now."

"Is it?" Jerry said, concentrating on spooling some pasta marinara around his fork.

"No," Harvey said ruefully. "Of course not. You know I don't let go of things that easily."

Jerry smiled, his gray face brightening a bit. "That's why I thought you'd make a good private investigator fifteen years ago."

"But I did let go. Four years ago I let go of investigating and became a motivational speaker."

"You thought you'd try living life as an optimist, huh?"

Harvey smiled.

"Thought you'd try being a cheerleader instead of a player, huh?"

"Okay, okay."

"You can run from your melancholy, Harv, but you can't hide."

"That'll be enough, Jerry."

When he got home, Harvey went to his study, where he'd been keeping the headless lawn jockey. He lifted it out of its box and set it on his big rolltop desk. He put the grinning, deferential head next to it.

When his cell phone started up with "Take Me Out to the Ball Game," he fumbled the phone out of his pocket and brought it to his ear.

"Bagel Boy?"

"Moss. Hey, what's going on?"

"I'm still on his list."

"What happened?" Harvey walked into the living room and sat on the sofa.

"There was a message waiting for me at the hotel when I got back tonight after the game."

"You're sure it's from him?"

"Same cutout letters. It says, 'You better not be making no Fudge Ripple Babies.'"

"No Fudge Ripple babies?" Now their man was affecting bad grammar.

"Down South, that's what they call 'em—half-black, half-white babies."

"He's figured out who your girlfriend is."

"He's in New York."

"The letter wasn't mailed?"

"It was left for me."

"Where are you?"

"Marriott Marquis."

"Are you in your room?"

"Yeah."

"I want you to go down to the front desk and talk to the desk clerk who handed you the letter. See if he or she remembers who left it for you."

"I'll try, but there was a bunch of messages waiting for me."

"Just give it a shot. Did you call Cherry Ann yet?"

"You think I should?"

"Hell, yeah."

"She'd be at the club right now."

"Can't you call her there?"

"I can try. I don't want to scare her."

"You don't want anything to happen to her, either. See if she can stay with a friend and tell her to call me. Let's play it safe."

"Wait till I get my hands on this motherfucker."

"You predicted we'd hear from him on some other subject. And now it's happened. Listen—don't talk about this with anybody, okay. Except for Marshall and Felix."

"They're in Providence."

"I'll call Marshall at home," Harvey said. "See what he wants to do. Now get hold of Cherry Ann and then call me back either way after you've talked to the desk clerk. And stay in your room."

"Me and my Spectravision."

"By the way, Moss, did you ever call your friend Charlie Fathon?"

"Yeah, I called him and told him about the note and that when this thing was resolved, I'd be GURCC's boy again."

"Did he have any ideas?"

"No."

"Good." Maybe it *was* a meaningless, scattershot campaign. Except that he'd gone to the trouble, apparently, of identifying Cherry Ann. "Incidentally, how'd you do tonight?"

"We lost, three-one."

"And you?"

"Zip-for-four. I had no focus."

The rest of the night was a flurry of phone calls. First, to owner Marshall Levy, who rehired Harvey to bodyguard Moss on the road trip until further notice. Next, from Moss, who had had no luck at the front desk. None of the three clerks he spoke to had any recollection of who might have left *any* of the dozens of letters for hotel guests that evening. There had been, the clerks all agreed, no unusual transactions at the desk, no suspicious characters. One told Moss that letters and messages for guests were sometimes just left on the front desk. There was a brief, angry call from Cherry Ann Smoler, letting Harvey know that she didn't appreciate being caught up in the continuing intrigue, as if he were responsible for it, and that she would be staying with a friend named Dawn on the East Side. Then he left a message for Mickey on her voice mail, letting her know he was headed for New York in the morning.

Shortly after eleven P.M., as Harvey was packing his bags, the phone rang one last time.

"Is that you, Blissboig?" a voice barked in a Brooklyn accent.

"Arnold?" Harvey said.

Arnold Slavin, civil rights lawyer, activist, litigator, former all-Brooklyn high school basketball star, was one of those guys who used his courtroom voice whenever possible. It was part of a general strategy to browbeat others into submission. To him, every conversation was a contest that could have only one winner. And that would be him. You came away from a conversation with Arnold feeling psychologically manhandled. Not that he didn't use humor to distract you from the pummeling. Arnold once greeted Harvey at a restaurant in Manhattan by saying, "I can't tell you how good you look now that you've put on a little extra weight."

"You're not sleeping, are ya?" Arnold said now. "You're not in the middle of making love to my daughter, are ya?"

"No and no. Mickey's in St. Louis tonight, doing the game."

"It's not her I want, anyway. She told me about the job you've been doing for Moss Cooley."

"You know, I keep telling—"

"You don't think I can keep a secret? You find the slimeball yet?"

"No."

"Guy left Cooley a lawn jockey?"

"That's right."

"Without a head?"

"That's right. The head came later."

"Well, now that his streak's been stopped, I don't know if

you'll be interested, but I'm convinced it must've resonated for her."

"Resonated? What resonated?"

"The lawn jockey without a head," Arnold Slavin said. "You know, sitting around the dinner table in the sixties, she heard a lot of interesting stuff."

"Like what, Arnold?"

"You know, Harvey, the unconscious mind stores all sorts of impressions that can resonate years later with something that crosses your path."

"I'm aware of that."

"And that's why I think she mentioned the lawn jockey to me. She was only six or seven when I represented those SNCC boys after their malicious arrest on bogus state anti-boycott laws. Imagine the impression that would make on a little girl."

"I still don't know what you're talking about."

"Back in the sixties, Harvey, at least when I was close to the situation, Klansmen and their sympathizers used to try to intimidate blacks by spray-painting 'KKK' on church doors or throwing acid on their cars or just driving around nigger knockin'—leaning out the window and whipping them with a detached car radio antenna. But there was one Ku Klux Klan klavern outside of Atlanta—the Wyckoff Klavern, if I remember correctly—whose members preferred a more metaphorical twist. They'd leave the decapitated head of a lawn jockey on the front seat of a car, or on the doorstep of the local preacher's house. And that's the only other instance of decapitated lawn jockeys I know of."

"You're sure about this, Arnold?"

"Don't tamper with my integrity, Harvey. I have to believe that your girlfriend there must've picked that up at the dinner table when she was still playing with Barbie dolls, and that's what I mean when I say it resonated."

"This is the only instance you know of involving decapitated lawn jockey heads?"

"What did I just say, Harvey?"

"All right, Arnold. Thank you. I believe you've done me a big favor."

"Now do me a big favor and make an honest woman out of her, Blissboig. Don't you think fifteen years is enough pussyfooting around?"

When he got off the phone, Harvey looked into his dark study through the open door and saw the lawn jockey, its alienated head smiling at him in the blue light of the moon pouring in through the study window. Harvey smiled back. His man had made his first mistake. He had spoken in a dead language from the past, and Harvey had found someone who spoke it too.

17

CHARLIE Fathon of GURCC had a slow, plush drawl that made him sound much older than his childhood friend Moss Cooley. Harvey felt as if someone were pouring sorghum syrup over his head.

"No, suh," Fathon said when Harvey reached him at GURCC's offices on Saturday morning, "Maurice only enlightened me in a most general way as to the other incidents. He called mostly about the note demanding that he suspend his public relationship with us. I don't believe you have to fight every battle, so I told him not to think twice about doing what was right for him and that I was sure the time would come again for him to lend us his spiritual help." Fathon emphasized "spiritual" in a way that implied that Moss planned to continue his financial support.

As Harvey told him about the lawn jockey and his conversation the previous night with Arnold Slavin, Fathon kept up a steady, soothing stream of "uh-huhs." "I can't help thinking," Harvey concluded, "that this all has something to do with Moss's association with GURCC. Problem is, Moss can't

think of why he'd be a threat to anyone. Does Moss know
something he's not supposed to as a result of his association
with GURCC?"

"I can tell you that he's familiar with some of the cases
we're investigating. I went over some of the high-profile cases
with him and his friend, so that he could speak publicly about
our work here with some degree of intelligence."

"What friend?"

"Maurice's lady friend. As cute as a speckled pup. But
that'd be true of all Maurice's lady friends. I can still see him
holding hands with May Alice Hughes, the prettiest girl in
second grade."

"Was she a young white woman?"

"Yes, but I can't recall her name to my mind at the
moment."

"Cherry Ann."

"That's the one. Studying to be a chef. Why, Claude Reed—
he's the young man who answers our phones—Claude couldn't
stop talking about her for days. Between Cherry Ann and meeting the great Moss Cooley, I thought we were going to have to
take Claude out back and hose him down." Fathon laughed a
dark, rich laugh.

"When was this?"

"Oh, maybe three weeks ago. Maurice had a day off, and
bless his heart, he flew in with Cherry Ann. I don't get to see
that boy enough anymore. All I get to do is watch him swing
that stick on TV."

Three weeks ago placed the visit more than a week before
the lawn jockey showed up at The Jewel Box. "Did they come
to your offices?"

"Yes. I introduced Maurice to everyone, he signed a
mess of autographs and chatted with the staff, and then
we sat down, and I showed him some of the case files. I
don't know if you happen to know about Maurice's own
grandaddy."

"I do."

"Then you know that his interest in seeing justice done is not abstract. It has a personal nature."

"What sort of cases did you discuss with him?"

"As I recall, the two or three cases we're concentrating on at the moment. I guess I was showing off a bit for him. Have to let Maurice know he's not the only one who'd done something with his life. So I showed him a little bit about some of the cases that've moved up our ladder. You know, every time we successfully prosecute one of these old cases, the others move up a rung. Now we're focusing on Joella Barnes, a teenager raped and murdered in nineteen eighty-one in Florida, where we've received new information from one inmate that another has been boasting about her murder. Then we're busier than a swarm of dog peter gnats working on the unsolved lynching of two black men, itinerants, Gomez and Spellman, back in 'seventy-six. That case wasn't just cold, it was frozen solid, until, once again, a fellow already in prison on assault and battery charges began reminiscing about some fun he had with a couple of nigger boys once near Huntsville, and after that we were able to place the gentleman in the employ of a machinist shop in the area at the time of the lynching."

"So these are both fairly high-profile cases at this point."

"I think just about any article you read these days about our work would include references to the Barnes case and the Gomez/Spelling lynching."

"Is it possible that Moss possesses any unique information that could contribute to the arrest or prosecution of your suspects?"

"Mr. Blissberg, I think it would be safe to say that whatever information Maurice has about these cases, he learned directly from us."

"What about other cases GURCC is involved in investigating where Moss has brought you any incriminating information about a suspect? Knowingly or unknowingly."

"I feel confident in saying that Maurice's role with us has

been limited to spiritual and financial support, and also as a student of the sad record of unsolved race crimes."

"Anything else happen when Moss and Cherry Ann were down there? Did they see anybody else?"

"No, suh. Not while I was with them. Maurice doesn't like to spend more time out in public than he has to. I picked them up at the airport and took them back to their hotel, and I believe they flew out the next morning. I believe he was rejoining his team in Texas, and she was flying home to Providence. What they did on their own time I have no idea, sir."

"Who was at your offices when Moss was there?"

"Like I said, the staff was there. Not all of them, of course. Some of the investigators were out, and Malcolm— our director—was away on business. And we had a fellow here, a writer, doing an article about us for a magazine."

"What magazine was that?"

"One of those New York City magazines—I believe it was called *Talk*. *Talk* magazine, if I can recall it to my mind correctly. He was here around that time, on and off, interviewing folks and taking notes. We always seem to have a reporter lurking around. The price of fame."

Harvey picked up the jockey's head off his desk and weighed it in his palm. "I suppose his article hasn't appeared yet. *Talk*'s a monthly."

"No, sir. And I believe this fellow was just beginning his research."

"Do you remember his name?"

"Had an unusual last name. I know I have it written down somewhere in my appointment book. Let me go back a few weeks. I believe he works out of Athens. That's about a hundred miles east of here. Here it is. Clay Chirmside."

"Churnside?"

"Chirm, with an i-r-m. Clay Chirmside."

"Mind if I take his number down?" Harvey wrote it in his

leather looseleaf notebook. "Mr. Fathon, do you have any other ideas about who might be harassing Maurice?"

"I'm sorry, suh."

"I have to admit, it's something of a mystery to me."

"Well, as one truth seeker to another," Fathon said, "I do understand the frustration of it. The world's never a bigger and more crowded place than when you're looking for the evil in it. It's as hard as picking fly shit out of black pepper."

"Moss, goddamn you," Harvey said when he reached Cooley at the New York Marriott Marquis, "is there some reason you never bothered to tell me you flew down to Atlanta with Cherry Ann to spend a day at GURCC?"

"Yeah, there's a reason, and the reason is that what I do every minute of my life is not always any of your business."

"Jesus, Moss, I'm on your side! You didn't get the lawn jockey until after your visit to GURCC. Did anything unusual happen when you were at GURCC?"

"Not if you don't count some young dude working there who kept hanging around drooling over Cherry Ann. I finally had to ask him if he didn't have some work to finish before the end of the day."

Harvey looked at the notes from his conversation with Fathon. "That must've been Claude Reed. Your friend Charlie mentioned the impression both you and Cherry Ann made on him. Did you give any interviews while you were there? Charlie also said a magazine writer was there researching an article about GURCC. Guy named Clay Chirmside."

Moss paused to think. "I remember him. A long face, like a bloodhound. I think he asked me for a quote or two."

"What did you tell him?"

"Same old bullshit, no doubt. What a good cause GURCC was, the importance of the struggle for racial equality."

"Was he aware you were going to be GURCC's spokesman?"

"I believe that's how Charlie introduced me to just about everybody down there."

"Besides going over some of the case files and chatting with the staff, Moss, did you do anything else down there?"

"Charlie had me sit down with their fund-raising and public-relations ladies. We talked about how they might put me to good use. It was a preliminary discussion."

"How long were you in Atlanta?"

"We flew in on a Thursday morning, and flew out separately the next morning."

"And Thursday night?"

"Cherry Ann and I ate some seafood at a place in Buckhead and hit the sack early."

"Listen, Moss. I'm going to get someone else to look after you in New York."

"Why?"

"I'm going down South."

"But New York's where I am."

"Moss, I'm going to call Marshall and tell him I'd like to put Paul Zarg on you, if he's available. He's a very capable private security man in Manhattan."

"You're blowing me off."

"To the contrary, Moss, to the contrary."

Marshall Levy said, "I expected you to finish the job."

"I thought the job was finished in your mind, Marshall."

"That was before he got this last note at the hotel."

"Well, I plan to finish this the best way I know how. Paul Zarg will take care of Moss. I'm following the bread crumbs back to Atlanta."

"What's there?"

"I won't know until I sniff around. I found out that decapitated lawn jockeys were a Klan thing back in the sixties."

"Who told you that?"

"Someone who was there."

"Harvey, I'm not writing you a blank check to subsidize your sniffing."

"I don't expect you to. Give me a few days to find out who the hell is stalking Moss."

"I hired you to bodyguard Moss. I've got to protect my assets."

"The truth's an asset, too."

"There may *be* no truth, Harvey, and you know it."

"But if there is, I don't want to be the guy who had his back turned."

He dialed Cherry Ann Smoler's cell phone.

"It's Harvey Blissberg. You all right?"

"I've been better. Hold on a sec. I'm just making lunch, and I don't know where my friend keeps her silverware." He heard a brief clattering of cutlery, then: "Okay."

"What happened when Moss took you down to Atlanta to visit GURCC?"

"GURCC?"

"The Georgia Unsolved Race Crimes Clearinghouse."

"Oh. That. I don't know, it was a chance to get away with Moss for a little while. Be alone."

"But what happened at the offices of GURCC?"

"They talked to Moss. They showed us some stuff. It was an education. I'd never seen photos like that in my life."

"What photos?"

"All different cases. Police photos from all these horrible crimes. I just remembered something."

"What?"

"Hold on, I need to get a napkin." Then: "Okay."

"What happened?"

"There was a lynching photo."

"Gomez and Spellman?" Harvey asked.

"Who's that?"

"Two guys lynched together back in nineteen-seventy-six."

"No, this was one guy. A black guy hanging from a tree branch. And standing in front of him hanging there was a white guy looking at the camera. No, there were two photos. In the other, another white guy was standing there. But I'm talking about just one of them."

"Yes?" Harvey said when she paused.

"He looked familiar to me."

Harvey's scalp tingled. "Who was he?"

"I don't know. Later I thought I must've seen him, maybe at the club."

"You're kidding," Harvey said. "But when was the photo taken?"

"A long time ago."

"Then how could you recognize the guy?"

"I didn't say I recognized him. I said he looked familiar. It was the look in his eyes. I told you that's what I do. I watch men watching me. I watch their eyes. And there was something about the eyes of one of the guys in the photo. I remember turning to Moss and saying, 'I feel like I've seen this guy.' And Moss said, 'Don't be ridiculous, this photo's thirty years old,' or whatever. And then I forgot about it. Until now."

"You still feel you might have seen the guy in the photo?"

"I don't know. I really don't know. If I saw the guy again, I might know for sure."

"But you haven't?"

"No."

"Was anybody at the table with you at the time besides Moss? Anybody hear you say that?"

"No, but there were a lot of people around the office."

"Moss's friend Charlie told me there was a guy who worked there who kept hanging around you."

"Oh, yeah. Creepy Claude."

"Did Claude hear you say the guy in the photo looked familiar?"

"I don't know. He might have. And there was another guy."

"A magazine reporter?"

"Maybe. He had a notebook, and he kept trying to get quotes for his story from Moss. I remember he had on nice cowboy boots."

"Long face?"

"Yeah, and blue eyes. Kind of dead blue eyes. The eyes of a Vietnam vet or a heavy drinker or something."

"Could he have heard you say the guy in the photo looked familiar?"

"Might have."

"The guy you think you recognized—what was he wearing?"

"A work shirt, I think, and a straw cowboy hat."

When he got off the phone with Cherry Ann, Harvey's stomach was churning. He went to the kitchen and got a glass of seltzer. For an instant, pouring the seltzer into a glass, he thought he heard his and Mickey's two Siamese brother cats, Duane and Bubba, meowing sharply in the utility room, and he turned his head, expecting to see them prance through the doorway the way they did at the first sound of a can opener biting into the lid of a Friskies Turkey & Giblets Dinner. But they had been dead for years. Just middle age playing another trick on him.

He returned to his study with the seltzer and called the offices of *Talk* magazine in New York City. A recorded message announced that the offices were closed for the weekend. So he drove into Harvard Square for a copy, brought it back to his study, and opened to the masthead. The name of the managing editor was an uncommon one: Kelly Topler.

There was only one in the Manhattan phone directory, and he was home.

"Sorry to bother you at home, Mr. Topler, but my name's Harvey Blissberg, and I've been contacted by a writer who wants to interview me for an article he says he's writing for you about the Georgia Unsolved Race Crimes Clearinghouse. I'm just double-checking to make sure you actually assigned him such a piece. His name is Clay Chirmside."

"Clay what?"

"Chirmside," Harvey said, enunciating.

"Writing a piece for us about what?"

Harvey told him again.

"We haven't assigned any article on the Georgia Unsolved Race Crimes Clearinghouse. I have no idea who this guy is."

"Could somebody else have assigned the article without your knowing it?"

"If it's been assigned, I know about it."

"Thanks," Harvey said, putting the phone down. He picked up the jockey's head and ran his fingers over its farcical features. He gazed out his study window at his cute Cambridge neighborhood, full of stucco and pastel-painted clapboard and children's toys littering the yards, the cozy academic cocoon where he and Mickey had chosen to settle.

There was a ball in the woods, and Harvey was going to go get it.

18

CHARLIE Fathon was a short, solemn-looking black man in a crisp white shirt and neatly barbered hair. He had a rooster's jutting chest and a withered leg he had to hoist ahead of his good one when he walked down the corridor of the GURCC offices on Saturday night to meet Harvey. Somehow Harvey could have predicted that Moss Cooley, the sensitive slugger, would befriend his grammar school class's cripple.

Life had taught Fathon the virtues of a booming voice and pugnacious bearing. "Welcome to our humble abode," he rumbled in his baritone, taking Harvey's hand in a crushing grip.

"Thanks for keeping the store open for me." Outside the offices, a warren of rooms over an Indian restaurant in Little Five Points, traffic hissed by on Euclid Avenue.

"No problem," Fathon said, "and I apologize for the rain. Interesting case, though, the one you want to look at. Just came through our door recently. Come with me."

Harvey followed Fathon down the corridor, whose walls

were decorated with framed newspaper clippings of GURCC's successes: "Atlanta Legal Group Wins $5M Civil Rights Award for Victim of '84 Racial Assault"; "Carson Convicted for Rape of Black Teen in Reopened Case"; "Klansmen Sentenced for 1991 Temple Fire."

"Our Wall of Acclaim," Fathon said, gesturing at the headlines as he limped ahead of Harvey. "And their Wall of Shame."

Every case started as a huge empty space, a hangar filled with silence and clutter. You found the door to a room, bigger than you'd like but much smaller than a hangar, and in it you might find the door to a somewhat smaller room, and finally, with luck, to the hallway that narrowed inexorably to the truth cowering at the end of it. Harvey now had the feeling he might be walking in that hallway.

Fathon turned into a doorway and flipped on the light, illuminating a colorless, windowless room lined with tall fireproof metal file cabinets. In the middle was a long Formica table, and on it were piles of manila folders, accordian files, phone directories, and loose papers.

"Have a seat," Fathon said. "So you used to play baseball?"

"I did."

"And now you're a private investigator."

"I am."

"That's an odd combination."

"I'm an odd person."

"Life has a way of reducing us to our oddities, doesn't it? It's a distillation process."

"You're young to be knowing that."

"Cripples start out odd. It's harder for us to maintain the illusion of normalcy. Now, if I've pulled the right file, the one Maurice's lady friend was telling you about, you have to keep in mind how rare lynchings have been for the last seventy years. You don't mind a little perspective, do you?"

"Always grateful for it."

"I do love a captive audience. Between the end of Reconstruction and the beginning of the Great Depression—that's almost fifty years—there were almost three thousand lynchings recorded in this country, more than eighty percent of them blacks. Some academics claim there were over three thousand lynchings by the year nineteen-eighteen, but let's go with the lower number—just under three thousand by the nineteen-thirties. And, while I'm at it, let me ask you how many people you think were ever convicted of any crime associated with a lynching between the years of eighteen-eighty and nineteen-oh-five."

"None?"

"Bingo. As you know, they lynched one of yours right here in Five Points—Leo Frank, in nineteen-fifteen, convicted two years before of murdering a Mary Phagan here at the pencil factory he managed for his uncle in New York. Convicted him on the perjured testimony, ironically, of the black man who most likely *was* the murderer. Those were the days when one drop of black blood, and you were as good as a nigger. The hatred of the black man shifted to hatred of white niggers, the *unseen* enemy, those who looked white but were thought to be black *inside*. And Leo Frank was ground up in the wheels of that new logic. His lynching got more press than any hundred black lynchings, although they used to advertise a lot of black lynchings in the local newspapers, just as they might a circus or a traveling Shakespeare theater company. Talk about the complicity of local law enforcement."

He shook his head when a manila folder he yanked from under a pile turned out not to be the one he was looking for. "Now I don't know why this happens to be in my head, but I do recall seeing an old clip of some lynching coverage in the *Arkansas Gazette* in which it was noted that the lynching was 'conducted in a quiet fashion,' as if the issue was the comportment of the murderers. 'Conducted in a quiet fashion.' That's like complimenting the Nazis for having their shirts tucked in. Fascinating, isn't it? In the annals of man, of course, I'm talking"—he snapped his fingers—"*that* long ago. But there it is. You do know that it was customary to take souvenir photos of lynchings?"

"Moss showed me the one of his grandfather."

"And that the body was often dismembered and parts of it—the genitals, fingers, toes, and pieces of the major organs—sold as souvenirs? You ask most people what lynching is, and they'll tell you a vigilante mob hanging, when in fact lynching often didn't involve hanging at all, but the torturing and burning of a human body. And for what? The charges ranged from acting suspiciously and using inflammatory language to entering a white woman's room. Or addressing her at all. I'm talking about Emmett Louis Till. Nineteen-fifty-five. His mama insisted on an open casket so the world could see what they had done to that poor boy. His head didn't even look like a head anymore." Harvey could easily see Fathon wooing a jury—chest thrust out, baritone booming, punctuating his summation with a flourish of that withered leg.

He began pawing through folders. "I got it out for you a few hours ago, and already I don't know what I did with it. I have no idea how I got through law school with my pathetic organizational skills. Do you know where the term 'lynching' comes from? I'm not even going to wait for an answer. Colonel Charles Lynch, a Virginia plantation owner and veteran of the Revolutionary War, took to punishing miscreants after the war—Tories, mostly—by holding court on his land and then tying the defendant to a tree in his front yard and beating him. Without an ounce of legal jurisdiction. It was only in the latter half of the nineteenth century that the phenomenon, now bearing his name, came to include such improvements as burning and hanging. But I began by telling you how rare they are nowadays."

He resumed looking for the file, saying, "Between Reconstruction and the Great Depression we're talking about one lynching a week, every week, for fifty years. Now in the entire decade of the nineteen-thirties there were only eighty or ninety, and since then there've been just a handful. Most recently, as you know, the dragging to death of Jerome Byrd in nineteen-ninety-eight. Well, now, here we go."

He waved a legal-size manila folder over his head in triumph. "November. Nineteen-seventy-one. Snellville, Georgia. A twenty-four-year-old black man named Isaac Pettibone, who worked in the local sporting goods store, was found lynched from a tree in the piney woods outside of town by two hunters." Fathon was reciting from memory, the closed folder still clenched in his hand. "The sheriff's department conducted an investigation and discovered that Mr. Pettibone, a reliable worker and as I recall quite an athlete himself, had been promoted from stock boy to sales clerk at the store, the first black clerk ever at the store, and that he had immediately run into some difficulty with a white colleague, a clerk by the name of Felker. Ed Felker was also in his twenties and, as luck would have it, the son of a good ole boy named Thomas Felker, who a few years before had been the Exalted Cyclops of the Snellville Klavern of the Ku Klux Klan. Well, he *must've* been a cyclops, because he didn't see too well. Ran his car off the road one night, flipped over, and paralyzed himself from the waist down. Of course, his blood alcohol level might also have had something to do with it. In any case, his son Ed, who seemed to have inherited his father's love of whiskey and hatred of the black man, didn't like it when Isaac Pettibone was promoted at the store. There were words between them, apparently a bit of a flare-up in front of some white customers. Isaac probably held his own with Felker."

Now Charlie Fathon sat down across the table from Harvey, who was mesmerized both by Fathon's command of the facts and the seamlessness of his presentation. "The sheriff's people didn't have any trouble turning up this much, of course, but they also turned up another coworker at the store to whom Ed Felker had said something to the effect that he was 'going to get that nigger.' Plus his only alibi was his wife, whose claim that Ed was at home with her all night lacked both enthusiasm and credibility, given that another interview, with one of the wife's friends, had established that the wife complained often that Ed spent most evenings out of the house. The time of Mr. Pettitbone's death, by the way, was set at between ten and midnight."

Fathon now opened the folder in front of him, and Harvey saw a few newspaper clippings on top. "But what really did Ed in," Fathon continued, "was the fact that he neglected to dispose of the wool plaid hunting jacket he wore the night of the lynching. In fact, he put it right back on a peg by the door of the trailer he shared with his wife. Which was a terrible error on his part, because the sheriff's men, God bless them, found some fibers on Mr. Pettibone's pant cuffs—his feet, of course, were bound—that perfectly matched the wool fibers of that jacket. And *that*, even in Georgia, where the chances of convicting a white for killing a black were still about the same as finding a Swiss watch in a bowl of cheese grits, was enough to do Ed Felker in.

"The DA actually offered to bargain with Ed Felker if he would be so kind as to name any others who were involved, since it's unlikely that one man alone could subdue and hang another. However, loyalty to friends, if not to the law, was one virtue that Felker did possess in some abundance, and he refused to name anyone else. In the end he was convicted of murder in the second degree—thank God for the movement!—and went to prison for the next twenty-five years or so. He was released a few years ago and tried to get back together with his wife, who had never remarried, although I understand she had plenty of boyfriends. She wasn't having any of that conjugal stuff, though, and in any case, in an act of divine justice in my view, he contracted lung cancer and was dead within eighteen months of his release."

"And you're handling the case because you're determined to find his accomplices?" Harvey asked.

Fathon wagged his head. "Until recently the Pettibone case wasn't on our radar screen. And the fact is that we're not even actively pursuing it now. After all, there was an arrest, a conviction, and a long prison sentence, and on the theory that half a loaf is better than none, the case came to be widely considered closed a long time ago. Triage, Mr. Blissberg. So many homicidal bigots, so little time. We have to concentrate on those cases where (a) there is new information and (b) there have been no arrests in the past, or arrests and no convictions."

"Then why do you even have a file?"

"Well, now, that's an interesting little story. Some months after Ed's death, his wife was sorting through his papers. Lo and behold, there in a locked box with some of her early love letters to him and some insurance papers, in a sealed envelope, were two black-and-white snapshots that are now in a safe here. These are the eight-by-ten glossies we made from them."

Fathon handed them to Harvey. The first showed a bareheaded young man in his twenties wearing a plaid flannel hunting jacket. His hands were stuck in his pants pockets, almost sheepishly, and the faintest of smiles played on his lips as he looked into the camera lens. It was as if some secret pride had barely won out over his natural disinclination to be photographed. Behind him and over his left shoulder the source of this pride, Isaac Pettibone, dressed in soiled and bloody clothes, bound hand and foot, dangled limply from a pine limb by his now unnaturally long neck.

"That's ole Ed Felker there," Fathon said. "No doubt about that."

Harvey looked at the second photo, almost a duplicate of the first. Same basic composition, same black man hanging in the background, but Felker had been replaced, presumably by the man who had taken his picture. This young man, in a work shirt and straw cowboy hat tipped back on his head, just as Cherry Ann had remembered, was a little stockier than the first and less coy about looking into the camera. In his eyes there was no trace of ambivalence; instead, as Harvey read his expression, there was a tincture of defiance, as if to say, "Yeah, I killed a nigger. You want to make something of it?" There was nothing much to say about his face, with its incipient jowliness and dark sideburns. The South was full of these fleshy, good old Anglo-Saxon boys.

"What do you know about him?" Harvey asked.

"Nothing. Didn't even know he existed until a few weeks ago. I just can't get over the fact they took each other's picture, like they were paying homage to an earlier age, creating their own incriminating souvenirs. Like they were signing their names to the job."

"Who do you think developed these?"

"I suspect one of these fellows did. The original prints were obviously tray-processed. They weren't fixed properly, judging from the brown spots. And the matte finish suggests they were air dried."

Harvey studied the second photo, wondering what—and who—Cherry Ann had seen in it. "So Ed Felker's wife found these. How'd they end up in your hands?"

"The newspaper up in Marietta did a little story on her discovery. Can't say what Connie Felker's motives were, talking about it, but she did, there was no love lost between her and old Ed, and one of our investigators ran across the piece—picture of her holding up the two photos and all—and we approached her to give us the photos in the interests of justice. She told us she wasn't sure what she was going to do with them, that she already had a local private collector offering her a lot of money for them, but she hadn't decided what to do. Well, then I went up to Marietta to sweeten her tea a little. So I told Connie that if she'd donate the photos to GURCC, why, I'd make sure she was properly compensated. And she couldn't see anything wrong with that." He smiled at Harvey. "We can't be above a little quid pro quo now and then, can we?

"Now we showed that photograph around"—he laid a dark forefinger on the young man in the straw cowboy hat—"and, of course, a lot of people saw the photo in the *Constitution*, and the fact is that no one has any idea who he is. And Ed Felker is in his grave. And we went on about our business. Now you call me yesterday to say that Maurice's lady friend thought she recognized him. Where'd she think she knew him from?"

"She just had a feeling. I'd like to send a copy to her. See if it'll jog her memory."

"There's a Kinko's not far from here. Open all night."

"I'd also like to study that file, if I may."

"There's not much in it, but I don't see why you can't have it overnight. There's a copy of the sheriff's report, but no trial transcript." He handed the file to Harvey. "You got a place to stay tonight, Mr. Blissberg?"

"I thought maybe you could recommend a cheap motel."

"I can recommend a cheap sofabed, if you don't mind clutter."

"I couldn't impose."

"You didn't. I offered. C'mon, after Kinko's we'll run by the Varsity for some onion rings."

"All right, I accept. On one condition."

"What's that?"

"You start calling me Harvey. By the way, is Snellville, Georgia, near Wyckoff?"

"Wyckoff?" Fathon said. "You mean, the home of the headless lawn jockeys? It's maybe twenty miles away."

"I'm just thinking," Harvey said.

"I know what you're thinking," Fathon said, turning off the light in the room and ushering Harvey back into the hallway. "You're thinking that the fellow who's after Maurice is the one in that photo there. That he thinks Maurice and his lady friend are onto him after all these years."

"I know it sounds improbable."

"The improbable doesn't scare me, Harvey. I've only been a lawyer for five years, but I've already seen a few cases broken wide open by a fluke. But, tell me—how do you suppose that this fellow found out that Maurice and his lady friend were even looking at the photo?"

"I have a thought about that," Harvey said as Fathon flipped off the lights in the rest of the offices of the Georgia Unsolved Race Crimes Clearinghouse. "I'll let you know if I'm right."

19

B Y noon the next day, Sunday, Harvey rolled into Athens, Georgia, in his rented Pontiac Grand Am. He felt the rush of heightened awareness, a tingle of worldliness, that came on him whenever he entered an unfamiliar town. Everything assumed a cinematic clarity. Even the gas station attendant who gave him directions to Clay Chirmside's street seemed as vivid as a veteran character actor. Harvey almost complimented him on his accent.

Before he left Charlie Fathon's, he had made four phone calls. He'd made sure Moss was all right in New York and that Cherry Ann Smoler was safe in Providence and would be at her friend's the next day to receive the overnighted copy of the photograph. Then he reached Mickey in her Pittsburgh hotel, where she was working "a big Pirates-Diamondbacks clash" that evening.

"Whatcha doing?" he asked.

"Reading a book review from the *London Review of Books* on the Internet. Want to hear something interesting?"

"Sure."

"The slug has a penis that's seven times the length of its body."

One could do worse, Harvey thought, than share life with a sports reporter who read the *London Review of Books* on-line, although perhaps one could do better than share life with a person who found the most interesting thing in it a passage about slug penises.

"They often get knotted up with other slug penises," she said.

"I hate when that happens."

"The only way for them to get free is for one slug to bite off his own penis at the base."

"Couldn't he nibble off just enough to get untangled?"

"Here's the best part," she said. "The self-castrated slug immediately becomes a female."

"Would that it were so easy."

"What are *you* doing?"

"Getting ready to drive off to Athens, Georgia, to talk to someone who's pretending to be a journalist."

"Oh," she said "Just like me."

The fourth call was to make sure that Clay Chirmside was in town.

"Mr. Chirmside?" he said from Fathon's disheveled apartment.

"Speaking." *Spuheekun*, it came out. A deep drawl.

"Are you the one writing the article about GURCC?"

"Who told you that?"

"Mr. Chirmside, my name is Harvey. I used to work at GURCC, and I've got some information about the organization that might interest you. I'll swing by this afternoon." And Harvey hung up, hoping that would be enough to hold him.

Chirmside's house was a red brick bungalow on a working-class suburban street with a new Ford pickup in the driveway. Its lone bumper sticker said, "If at First You Don't Secede, Try Try Again." The cement urns on either side of the front steps gushed ferns. When Harvey got out of his air-conditioned car, the humidity whacked him in the face like a hot pillow. Before he had taken three steps, the bungalow's screen door opened.

Chirmside came down the steps in a brown T-shirt and gray slacks. Harvey squinted at him in the bright sun. He was a tall middle-aged man with thin sandy hair through which his sun-reddened scalp showed on top. Gravity was doing a job on him: the flesh on his face had fallen around his mouth like the jowls of a hound dog, giving him an expression of angry fatigue, and his stomach ballooned over his belt. Despite his muscular freckled forearms, the seeds of his premature old age were already sprouting. Lush tufts of hair were growing in the depression at the bottom of his ears.

"Something I can do for you?" he said, frisking Harvey with his eyes, evaluating the fall of Harvey's shirt, checking for pocket bulges.

"Clay Chirmside?"

"You got him."

"I called you before about GURCC. I'm Harvey Johnson."

"Who told you I was writing an article?"

"Well, you spent some time at the office a couple of weeks ago. You told folks you were writing an article for *Talk* magazine."

"What if I was?"

"That's a pretty prestigious periodical."

Chirmside screwed up his eyes. "Something wrong with that?"

"It seems they never heard of you."

"How would you know?"

"I spoke to the managing editor yesterday."

"I don't know about any managing editor. He wouldn't know me from Adam."

"Were you dealing with someone else then?"

"Another editor."

"Whose name is?" Harvey said, feeling Chirmside's anger come off him in waves. Curiosity and confusion were the only things holding the jowly man back.

"Jim."

"Jim who?"

"Jim Parker."

"Let's see now," Harvey said, plucking his current copy of *Talk* out of his back pocket. It was already folded back to the masthead page. "No, I don't see any Jim Parker on the masthead. You sure you got the name right?"

"Listen here, Mr. Johnson," Chirmside said, bits of cheesy spittle collecting in the corners of his mouth. "I don't much like you waltzing into my driveway and calling me a liar. Suppose you tell me exactly what your business is before I kick your Yankee ass out of here. And I guaran-damn-tee you I'll do it."

"Clay, I don't believe I've ever been bodily threatened by a freelance writer before."

Chirmside turned his head and spat on his own lawn. "I'm waiting."

"My friends at GURCC asked me to check you out. I'm a private investigator. Clay, what were you doing at GURCC?"

"Why don't you tell me why you wanna know so bad?" He spat on his lawn again.

Harvey sized him up and went for it. "Clay, if I thought you were the kind of man who could be bought, I'd try to pay you for the information."

He looked at Harvey for a full five seconds. "What kind of money are we talking about?"

Hot damn, Harvey thought—we've got a winner. "What kind of money is worth talking about in your opinion?"

"I'm not interested if it don't have three zeroes."

"Maybe we could continue this negotiation on your front porch. It's hot out here."

Harvey preceded Chirmside into the shade of the porch. Harvey sat on an aluminum chair. Chirmside leaned against the outer brick wall, lighting a Marlboro Light with an irritable flip of his chrome Zippo.

"Here's what I want for my thousand bucks," Harvey said.

"I want to know what you were doing at GURCC and who hired you."

"I want a sneak preview of the dough."

Harvey reached into his front pants pocket and produced a folded wad of crisp ATM bills. He fanned them out—five one-hundred-dollar bills and twenty-five twenties.

Chirmside held out his hand and said, "Give it to me."

"Easy, Clay. Where are your manners?"

"Please."

"Now you're talking." Harvey counted out the five hundreds and handed them over. "Start at the beginning."

Chirmside folded the bills and slid them into the pocket of his gray slacks. Then he inhaled half an inch of his Marlboro and said through the smoke, "A guy called me a few weeks ago to buy two photographs for him."

"What guy?"

"He didn't say, and I still don't know."

"I don't think you're telling me the truth."

"Now, listen, you're gonna get your money's worth before I'm through, but you're not gonna learn the guy's name, 'cause I don't know it myself." The money had already changed him, softened his manner. "If you wanted the photos this fella wanted, you wouldn't give your name, either."

"Because they were photos of a lynching?"

Chirmside's sandy eyebrows jumped. "Well, now."

"So you posed as a collector and made Connie Felker an offer for them."

"Now you're not letting me earn my money." He leaned down and put his cigarette out in one of the cement urns.

"She said she'd think about it, didn't she? Then she went with a better offer. She gave them to GURCC."

"She just gave 'em away."

"Then what happened?"

"Then I told the guy the next time he called that GURCC got the photos, and he told me to pretend I was a reporter and go there and see what I could do."

"See if you could 'acquire' the photos?"

"Sumpin' like that. Find out what they intended to do about them."

"If they were going to investigate. Is that it?"

"Sumpin' like that."

"He wanted you to steal the pictures, didn't he?"

Chirmside nodded once.

"And did you?"

"Couldn't do it. I tried. One day when I was there, they had that ballplayer there, the one with the big hitting streak."

"Moss Cooley."

"Right. And his girlfriend was there with him. And that crippled nigger fellow works there that's his friend—"

"Charlie Fathon."

"Right, he was showing them some case files, and I said, 'Boy, why not show 'em them photos you just got from that old Ed Felker business?' So Charlie Fathon showed them the two photos, and I was hoping I'd have me a chance to steal them and make some extra money, but Moss Cooley and his girlfriend never let 'em out of their sight."

It hadn't occurred to him that the originals were locked away and that he'd only be stealing copies. "Why'd the man want the photos, anyway?"

"Damned if I know. For the amount of money he was paying me, I didn't want to ask any questions."

"Anything else happen while you were at GURCC?"

"Well, that's when I overheard Moss Cooley and his girlfriend talking about how the man in the photo looked familiar."

So Chirmside assumed that they *both* recognized the man, whereas Cherry Ann had told Harvey that it was only she who did—and that Moss in fact had chided her for thinking she would know a man from a thirty-year-old photo. "You're not talking about the picture of Felker, are you?" Harvey said.

Chirmside shook his head. "Other one."

"Which is a photo of what?"

"Another guy standing in front of the hanging man."

"What's his name?"

"Damned if I know."

"So tell me why you think you were hired to get those photos for the man?"

"I told you I don't know."

"Do you think it's because he might be protecting the man in the photo?"

Chirmside shrugged. "Got me."

"Because he *is* the man in the photo?"

"Got me again, Harvey Johnson."

"Because there was only one arrest in that case: Ed Felker. That other man's never been identified. And until the little newspaper story appeared a while back about Connie Felker and the two photos, no one knew who else might've been involved in the lynching of Isaac Pettibone. Isn't that right?"

"Hell, you're the one with all the answers. I've got half a mind to give you back, say, twenty dollars of your money." He laughed mechanically, like someone who had learned how from a manual.

"So you told the man who hired you that Moss Cooley and his girlfriend thought she recognized the man in the photo? The one in the straw cowboy hat?"

"That's right."

"Did the man also ask you to find out if GURCC was going to try to reopen the Felker case and identify the second man?"

"I found out that, no, they weren't fixing to do that."

"Did he ask you for the name of Moss Cooley's girlfriend?"

"Yes, sir. I tried to get her last name, pretending I was going to put her in my article, and Mr. Cooley, sir, he asked me in no uncertain terms not to mention either of them in my article and stopped me from getting her name. I did try to describe her best I could to the man who hired me."

Harvey counted out ten twenties and handed them to Chirmside. "Did the man give you a phone number to call when you wanted to get in touch with him?"

"No, sir. He just told me to wait for his calls."

"You don't have caller ID?"

"No, sir."

"What did he sound like?"

"Nothing special."

"Did he have an accent?"

"None that I could tell. Maybe midwestern. I'm not real good on accents."

"How did he pay you, Clay?"

"He sent me cash in them padded bags through the regular mail without a return address."

"How many installments?"

"Two."

"Can I see those bags?"

"They're long gone."

"Where were they postmarked?"

"Don't rightly recall." He lifted his chin and closed his eyes. "Not too far away, is my recollection."

"Don't tell me you don't remember the postmarks, Clay. You had to be mighty curious at that point."

"Maybe it was some place in Tennessee."

Harvey reluctantly counted out ten more twenties. Chirmside's hand shot out like a trained monkey's and took the money. Harvey held the last five twenties up by his ear and made it shake.

"Now, for the last hundred dollars, Clay, I want to know how this man come to hire you to do this job."

"It just so happens I do a little private investigation work myself."

"Why you?"

"I guess it's my reputation," he said with a smile. "Word of mouth. Man of a thousand disguises."

Right, Harvey thought to himself. More like a man of two

disguises—dumb and dumber—even if he had managed to fool the folks at GURCC. "So you do a lot of this sort of work?"

"Like I say, I'm a private investigator."

"Then how come the side of your pickup says 'Chirmside Paving and Resurfacing'?"

"Got to make ends meet," he replied without missing a beat. "You know how it is."

"You got a license to be a private investigator, Clay?"

"No, sir. I'm not that kind."

"You advertise?"

"Don't need to."

"I'll bet you have to beat the customers away with a broom." Harvey laid the last bills in Chirmside's hand.

"Is that it?" Chirmside walked toward the porch steps. "I hope I've been a help."

"You've been an enormous help," Harvey said, descending the steps ahead of Chirmside. "I appreciate your candor."

"I don't know what that is, but I'm glad you appreciate it."

Harvey drove off, thinking that you had to hand it to the civil rights movement. It had helped make possible both Charlie Fathon, who became what his father probably never even dreamed of, and Ed Felker, who became everything his father had dreamed of, and more.

20

O<small>N</small> the outskirts of Athens, Harvey found a buffet lunch joint and waited in line for his meat-and-three. He took his tray—chicken-fried steak with sawmill gravy, collards, black-eyed peas, stewed yellow squash, corn bread, and sweetened ice tea—to a chipped table in the corner under the air conditioner and began telling himself what he thought he knew.

First, that the man he was looking for was the man in the photo—possibly his son. After thirty years, a home-processed photo had jumped out of a Georgia lockbox, threatening to deliver him from his anonymity. He thought both Cooley and his girlfriend were in a position to identify him.

Harvey sprinkled everything on his plate with a homemade pepper sauce, then speared a corner of meat, loaded the back of the fork with greens, chewed it with an audible hum of pleasure, and washed it down with tea.

If the man hadn't directly intimidated Cherry Ann, it was only because he didn't know who she was. If he already knew her, then learning her first name—a highly unusual one—from Chirmside would have been enough to identify her.

Harvey bit into the corn bread and shoveled forkfuls of smoky peas and squash into his mouth.

If the man didn't know Cherry Ann, then he must have thought that Cherry Ann knew him. Cherry Ann lived in Providence. Therefore, it was most likely that she had seen him there. Therefore, it was likely that the man lived in or around Providence. Cherry Ann herself thought she might have seen him at the club, where a man's gluttonous eyes were sure to make more of an impression on her than elsewhere.

Now another wedge of chicken-fried steak, on which Harvey balanced some black-eyed peas before loading it into his mouth. Chirmside had made him ravenous. He drained the rest of his twenty-four-ounce plastic tumbler of tea, and by the time he put the empty glass back on the table, a waitress with pretty wide-set green eyes refilled it from a pitcher. It was as if she'd been hovering, waiting for customers' glasses to be emptied. Harvey realized that's just what she'd been doing.

How hard would it be for the man to discover Cherry Ann's identity, even given Moss's and her secrecy about their involvement? Once he knew it—and it appeared he did—he would try to neutralize her.

In any case, the man was in New York now, leaving Moss a note at the Marriott Marquis.

Harvey sucked up some squash, then ground a piece of steak between his molars.

And he knew where Moss Cooley lived in Cranston.

Andy Cubberly was too young to be the man in the photo, even if he resembled him, which he didn't. And although Cubberly came from Clawson, South Carolina, which Harvey knew now was less than seventy miles from Snellville and Wyckoff, Georgia, Harvey could find no mention of any Cubberly among the witnesses or suspects in the sheriff's report on the Pettibone case.

A huge man in bib overalls at the neighboring table cast Harvey a skeptical glance that suggested he didn't belong there. A little flame of self-consciousness inside Harvey flared up, and he hunched over his food, eager to finish.

Terry Cavanaugh, the manager? Harvey wondered as he dabbed his mouth with a paper napkin and headed for the cashier, a lady whose face was thirty years older than her hair. Cavanaugh was old enough, but he grew up in New Britain, Connecticut.

It took a phone call to Fathon for directions, and well over an hour on the road, to find Connie Felker's house on the town line between Smyrna and Marietta just northwest of Atlanta. Harvey called ahead on his cell phone to say that Charlie Fathon had suggested she might answer some questions for research he was conducting on behalf of GURCC. She agreed, saying, "Anything for those nice people. I'm so glad I did the right thing."

Harvey found her white-and-tan one-story ranch house in a neighborhood of similarly modest houses dating back to the 1950s or '60s, parked in the driveway behind a dark blue Buick Le Sabre, and knocked on the aluminum door.

When the door opened, it revealed a short, busty woman in her fifties whose face, though finely lined, was still once-pretty beneath a mass of frosted swirls. Her turquoise cotton top said "LOVE" on it in silver sequins. She looked like someone who'd had her share of fun, and expected more any minute.

"Connie Felker?"

She held out a tiny hand and took Harvey's. "It's Connie Rush now. My maiden name." *Muhayden nime.*

"I'm Harvey Blissberg."

Two tiny brown dogs erupted from the back of the house and bustled toward him like motorized mop heads.

"Queenie! Prince!" she said, glowering at them, and they

took refuge behind her. "Ignore those two, or you'll be picking hairs off your pants for a week. They never met a lap they didn't like."

"They couldn't be cuter."

"Blissberg," she said, now ushering him inside. "Now that's a Jewish name, isn't it?"

"As a matter of fact, it is."

"I thought so." As if she had found him out. "How come you're not wearing one of those cute little beanies?"

"A yarmulke?"

"Looks like a coaster."

"It's usually just very religious Jews who wear them all the time."

"Well, I'll tell you, I don't believe everything they say about your people. I buy my meat from a Jew butcher in town, and I've never had any reason to complain."

"I'm glad to hear that."

"Barry Cohen," she said, leading him into the tidy living room.

"You give him my best," Harvey said.

The living room was filled with comforting touches like needlepoint pillows and a crocheted afghan draped over the back of the plaid sofa. It was the home of a woman who has reached a certain stage of her life and only wants around her what she can trust: familiar objects, order, and a limited serenity. Harvey wondered if it was her way of dissociating herself from the ugliness into which she had once married.

When Harvey settled onto the sofa, Queenie and Prince arranged themselves near his feet like a pair of bushy eyebrows. To avoid exciting them, he averted his eyes, which fell on a framed photo on the coffee table of Connie Rush, looking only a few years younger, standing by a lake with her arm around a smiling middle-aged man. He had a full beard and a full head of hair, and was decidedly not the man in the lynching photo.

"I know you probably don't want to delve into the past," Harvey said. He laid his old leather briefcase—a birthday present from Mickey many years before—on top of his thighs. An air conditioner over his shoulder sounded like it had emphysema.

She plopped into an armchair, saying, "Edward's dead"— as though those two words were all that needed to be said on the subject of the past and the putting of it in its place. "Can I get you something to drink? Hell can't be any hotter than Georgia in July."

"I'm fine. Thank you, ma'am—"

"Connie to you, young man."

"All right then, Connie, I'll get right to the point." Out of his briefcase he slid a Kinko's copy of the eight-by-ten and propped it up on his lap for Connie Felker to see. "I need to know who the man in this photograph is."

"I've been through this, dear. I don't know who he is."

"No idea?"

"If I knew, don't you think I would've told Charles Fathon at ˇGURCC? I gave them the damn photos, hoping *they'd* know who the other guy is."

Harvey nodded. "I assumed that, of course, but I wanted to ask you myself."

"Ed had a lot of associations in those days I knew nothing about. He'd go out most nights and run around with friends he'd never bring home and introduce me to. He had another life, and other women, for all I know." It sounded memorized, like a stump speech.

"As far as you know, who were his best friends?"

"The only ones I ever saw him with were two old high school pals, Dave Womack and Jimmy Schott."

The sheriff's report indicated they had both been interviewed during the investigation in 1971 and were either not talking or didn't know anything. They had strong alibis and were never under suspicion. "Where can I get hold of them now?" Harvey asked.

"Oh, I'd have no idea. My recollection is that they both left this area shortly after Ed's trial. When Ed went away, that changed life for them around here."

"Their families still around?"

"I imagine their folks are dead and buried by now. I don't know who's left."

Harvey despaired of finding Womack and Schott after all this time without a major effort, and he doubted they'd have any more to say than they did before.

"Connie, does the name Cubberly mean anything to you?"

She thought for only a second before shaking her head. "Sorry."

"Can I ask you why you provided an alibi for Ed on the night of the lynching?"

"Why the hell not?" she said. "He was my husband, after all, and he asked me to, and in those days I did what he asked. If I didn't, he'd pop me one."

"He'd hit you?"

"Sure as you're sitting right there."

"Was he active in the Klan at the time?"

"Well, his daddy had been the Exalted Cyclops of the Snellville Klavern until about a year before we were married, when he had a bad accident and lost the use of his legs, so Ed was brought up in that environment. But was he active during the first two years of our marriage before that thing he went and did? Yes, I'm sure he was, but I never knew to what extent."

"The sheriff's report included an undercover cop's statement saying Ed had a spotty attendance record at Snellville Klavern meetings." He was probably one of those rednecks who operated in the shadowy world between the law and official Klan activities.

"I wouldn't know about that," Connie Rush said.

"Would you know—can you remember if Ed seemed to you at the time to need to prove anything to anybody?"

"I wouldn't know about that, young man. Ed usually didn't say boo to me."

"Did he mention to you at the time that Isaac Pettibone had been promoted at the store?"

"I believe he did."

"Was he upset about it?"

"Well," Connie said, picking at the fabric on the arm of the chair, "I don't believe that I ever told this to the sheriff's people at the time, but he did complain about it and—I'm using his words now—he said some nigger at work was being made a salesman and making almost as much as he did."

"Did he say that other whites at the store were upset?"

"Not specifically, but you can probably bet they were."

"You remember the names of his coworkers, besides Isaac Pettibone?"

"No, dear. And I don't believe Allison Brothers is still in business."

"It's not," Harvey said. "It went out of business in nineteen-seventy-nine."

"Well, I know the sheriff's people talked to everyone who worked at the store."

"That's right, they did," Harvey said, looking up now at the photo on the wall. "Who's that with you in the picture?"

"That's my friend Reggie. He's shaved that beard off. I told him he looked like a dust ball with teeth. He's a good-looking man, and I wanted folks to know that."

"What's he do for a living?"

"You just don't stop asking questions, young man, do you?"

"Connie," he said, "it's a little like eating those smoked almonds for me. Once I get going, I can't stop."

She smiled. Harvey was surprised at how nice her teeth were, and they weren't false ones. "Anyway, he owns a couple of service stations."

"Was that picture taken around here?"

"At my lake house."

"Where's that?"

"Oh, it's just a little bitty cottage about fifteen miles from here. I should be there right now in this heat, but I had some errands to run."

"Well, I'm sure glad I caught you in."

"I don't think I've told you anything you didn't already know, dear."

"You'd be surprised."

"Are you sure I can't fix you some iced tea?" She braced her hands on the arms of the chair.

"I'm sure."

She lowered herself back in the chair, disappointed.

"Anyway, your kids must enjoy having a place on the lake," he said.

"I don't have any children."

"No?"

"No. After the business with Ed, I didn't feel like doing anything with a man, least of all making a baby. And then the time just got away from me, and I never did find the man I wanted to have children with until it was too late. Reggie's got a couple of boys in their twenties, though, and they come down to the lake to ski quite a bit."

"Reggie keeps a boat there, does he?"

"The boat's mine."

"Then you've done all right, haven't you?"

"Things sometimes work out all right, don't they? The good Lord sees to it."

"Yes, indeed," Harvey said, slipping the photo back in his briefcase, latching it, and rising slowly from his chair. "I can imagine that after a long week of work it's great to head out to the lake for the weekend."

Connie Rush rose too, saying, "I retired a few years ago."

"You did?" Harvey poured on the incredulity. "Connie, you don't look anywhere near old enough to even be thinking about retiring."

"I put my time in."

"Where was that?"

She put her little hands on her hips. "Well, dear, I sold notions at the Snellville five-and-dime, I set hair in three counties, and for a while I had my own gift shop."

"Good Lord, you've been busy." He walked toward the front door ahead of Connie Rush, past a wall-mounted shelf of china dogs. Connie's two real ones leaped into action, taunting Harvey's shoes.

"Queenie! Prince! Shoo!"

"Why did you give the photos to the Georgia Unsolved Race Crimes Clearinghouse?" he asked her at the door.

"I'm trying to get washed in the blood of the lamb. I can't believe I married that man. The things we do when we're young."

"It takes us a long time to learn about life."

"You said it."

"You know, you have the prettiest smile."

"Honey, you're too young and good-looking to be interested in me, so I'll just take that as the innocent compliment I guess it's intended to be."

Harvey pulled off the road a few miles from Connie Rush's place and dialed the number of Southern Bell. After fighting off five or six recorded instructions, he got a human being on the other end of the line and said, "I've lost my phone bill and wondered if you could tell me what the payment due date is on it. The name's Chirmside. Clay Chirmside." He spelled it and gave Chirmside's home number.

"Payment's due on August one. Seventy-seven dollars and ninety-four cents."

"So I'm up to date on my payments?"

"You're showing no previous balance."

"One more thing. I can't remember if my long-distance charges are included on your bill."

"Yes, sir."

"Because my son made a call or two that I want him to pay for out of his own pocket. Can you tell me just looking at the screen there if he's been calling New England? You know these kids."

"I can't access that information, but I'll be happy to send a duplicate bill to your house."

"How about faxing me a copy at work?" He fumbled for Fathon's business card in his pocket.

"No, I'm afraid I can't do that, but if I send you a duplicate, you should get it in a couple of days."

"No, that's all right. Thanks much."

"You have a good day now."

Next he called the Athens town hall, posing as a new resident, and found out that garbage pickup day was Thursday. It was now Sunday, July 28. Thursday would be August 1. Assuming that Clay Chirmside paid his telephone bill on time and that, like most earthlings, he no longer bothered to keep his itemized phone bills, Wednesday night would be a good night to be in the vicinity of 1719 Crosby Road in Athens, Georgia.

Then he called Fathon.

"Charlie?" Harvey said when Fathon picked up the phone at his house. "Or Charles, as Connie likes to call you."

"How'd it go?"

"People lie to me left and right."

"That bad?"

"But one thing I know is that Clay Chirmside isn't writing a piece for *Talk* magazine, or any magazine for that matter."

"You're shittin' me."

"You ought to run a simple check on these freelancers, Charlie. I don't mean to chastise you."

"Well, shit, I feel like a dentist with bad teeth. None of us thought anything about it. Writers come through here all the time. What was he doing?"

"Trying to steal the picture of the other fellow in the Pettibone case. Says a mysterious man hired him anonymously over the phone, never gave his name, paid him in cash by mail. Chirmside can't remember the postmark."

"Goddamn. How'd you get *that* much out of him?"

"Five hundreds and twenty-five twenties."

"That's a lot of money."

"Not if you're interested in finding the guy in the photo. Are you?"

"Well, when you told me Maurice's lady friend thought he looked familiar, my interest went from virtually nothing to fairly lively. Now I think it's spiking."

"All right, then, I need a little favor. You ever do much sanitation work?"

"Sanitation work?"

"I need you or one of your people to collect a little garbage from Chirmside's curb this Wednesday night."

"You think one of his lies is that he never called the man back?"

"I'm looking for area codes in Rhode Island, Boston, and southern Massachusetts, and maybe eastern Connecticut."

"I'll have to put one of the white boys on it."

"Yeah, of course. Now his phone bill is due on Thursday. Garbage gets picked up on his street Thursday morning, so he'll probably put it out Wednesday night, but I can't be sure. Could be an all-night stakeout. I'd do it myself, except I'm nervous about leaving Moss alone too long." If he flew out of Atlanta today, he could meet the team in Chicago for their Monday-Tuesday-Wednesday set against the White Sox.

"Nothing's going to happen to Maurice," Fathon said. It was halfway between a question and a statement of fact.

"Of course not. Charlie, can you also run the plates on the Buick Le Sabre in Connie's driveway? I want to make sure it's hers. I'd also be interested if there's a lien on it. I'd also be interested in whether she owns or rents her place in Smyrna." He gave Fathon the license plate number and her address. "Will you do that for me?"

"Hell, yeah. This is getting exciting."

"Well, don't go calling any press conferences, Charles. Listen, I'll probably be in Chicago for the next few days with the team. You've got my cell phone number, right?"

"That's not all I've got. You left your toothbrush on the sink this morning."

"Keep it," Harvey said, "as a token of my appreciation for your fine hospitality."

21

"L ET me shake the hand of the man who shook the hand of history."

Moss Cooley, who was waiting his turn in the batting cage at Comiskey Park before the opener Monday night against the White Sox, took Norman Blissberg's hand and said, "Thank you, man."

"Don't mind my brother if he's a little inappropriately poetic," Harvey said. "Too much academia." Their conversation was punctuated by the drumbeat of bats hitting batting practice pitches.

"Don't mind my brother if he's a little flip." Norm, almost fifty now, an inflated, nearsighted version of his little brother in an ill-fitting herringbone sport coat and a dark blue novelty tie bearing schematic drawings of demolished major-league baseball parks, touched his little rectangular eyeglasses. "Sometimes I don't think he shows the proper respect for the game—or the men who actually accomplish something in it."

"Norm, this is the last time I get *you* a field pass. From now on, you can sit home and watch the goddamn White Sox on TV."

Norm laughed. "C'mon, Harv, it weren't for you, I'd have no one to irritate." He gave a Gallic shrug for Cooley's benefit. "My son's in college, and my wife doesn't care anymore."

"It's nice when siblings can do things for each other," Harvey said, watching a group of Providence Jewels, including Cubberly, play pepper down the right-field line. After his thirty-six hours in Atlanta, baseball looked strange to him—more like the national distraction than its pastime.

Norm leaned closer to Moss. "Just tell me my baby brother's taking good care of you."

"I'm still here, aren't I?" Moss said, not looking at either of them, but surveying the sparsely populated stands. "Though your brother's friend in New York was a welcome change in bodyguards. This guy Zarg didn't talk so much."

"Moss, I had to get away from you for a day or two. Being around so much greatness was getting to me." Harvey's heart wasn't in the banter; he was on automatic pilot.

Moss cackled. "Exactly how I felt about being around so much mediocrity."

"You won't be saying that when I bust this case open."

"Poor Harvey," Norm muttered. "Never feels he gets enough credit."

"Now, now, boys," Moss said over his shoulder as Craig Venora stepped out of the batting cage and Moss moved in to take his cuts. "I hate to see grown men bicker."

Without an audience, Harvey and Norm dropped their timeworn routine.

"So," Norm said, "you're going to 'bust this case open'?"

"My old ex-FBI friend Jerry Bellaggio got me the name of the guy that the bureau uses for computer age-imaging. I sent him a print of the photo of the second lyncher. In a couple of days, maybe I'll have the picture of a man I recognize."

Harvey had let Norm take him out for an early dinner at

Greek Islands on Halsted before the game, so Norm was more or less up to speed.

They watched in mute admiration for a moment as Moss launched a shot over the 375-foot sign in left center.

"The man's a god," Norm said. "Jesus, I'd hate to be the ball when he's hitting."

"You're so goddamn literary, Norm."

"Incredible mechanics." Norm turned his head and spat copiously on the grass. Stepping onto a major-league ball field had a way of making grown men salivate. "You think Cooley's out of the woods?"

"I'm more worried about his girlfriend. She's the one who thought she'd seen the guy."

"Correct me if I'm wrong, Harv, but whoever it is can't stop the process now by stopping her, right?"

"It only matters what the guy thinks he can do. He may be desperate enough to want to do anything. Wouldn't you if you thought you were about to be plucked out of your life and thrown into prison for eternity?"

"What did you say she did for a living, this—what's her name?"

"Cherry Ann, and I didn't say. But she's a culinary school student in Providence. She moonlights as a stripper."

"Give me a break."

"And keep it to yourself."

"Moss Cooley dates a stripper?"

"She's not a trivial person, Norm."

"It's so corny. Although it's true I once had a Ph.D. candidate who worked as a dominatrix to pay her tuition."

"There you go. Anyway, I try not to pass judgment on other people's relationships. You'll notice I've never said one word about your twenty-five-year marriage to Linda."

"And I know my marriage is the poorer for it." Cooley launched another long-range missile into the left-field seats. "You're not worried about someone shooting Cooley from the stands?"

"No one's stupid enough to shoot someone in front of thirty thousand potential witnesses."

"Thirty thousand?" Norm said. "When's the last time the White Sox drew thirty thousand?"

Harvey laughed. "And we're not even going to be among them, Norm, because, as a special treat for you, I got press box passes for tonight."

"You do love me."

"Hey, Blissberg!" someone shouted behind him. Harvey turned and saw Andy Cubberly walking toward the cage with two bats in his hand.

"Hold that thought, Norm," Harvey said to his brother and met Cubberly about thirty feet from home plate in foul territory.

"Hey," Cubberly said, leaning on his bats. "We could've used you in New York."

"I took the weekend off. Anything happen in my absence?"

"I hit a triple."

"How about that?"

Cubberly chuckled. "How 'bout dat?" he repeated in Snoot Coffman's signature style. "By the way, Snoot was looking for you in Yankee Stadium after the game yesterday. I think he wanted you to be on his show again."

Harvey looked off toward home plate, where Moss hit a screamer down the left-field line and sauntered out of the cage. "Here in Chicago?"

"Go ask him yourself."

Twenty minutes before game time, Harvey and Norm climbed to the press box, where a dozen print reporters were already at their laptops and another dozen were feeding their faces at the complimentary buffet table.

"Is that food free?" Norm asked.

"I'm afraid it is."

His brother took a plate and approached a chafing dish filled with tortellini.

"Norm, didn't you just have braised lamb shanks an hour and a half ago?"

"That was someone else."

"Norm. If you had to pay for this food, would you be standing in line?"

"Don't be ridiculous, Harv. Studies show that the sight of complimentary buffet food causes the body to accelerate its digestive and metabolic processes, instantly causing secretions."

"Secretions?"

"Appetite-inducing secretions. I'm surprised you're not familiar with the work of Dr. Leonard Risotto." He piled some tortellini and a breast of roast chicken on his plate.

"You're pathetic, Norm."

"Nonetheless," he said, popping a tortellino into his mouth, "it beats peanuts and Crackerjack."

"And I don't care if you never come back."

"This is good," Norm said, chewing. "I think it's got mushrooms inside."

"Listen, you stand there and get fat while I do an errand."

Harvey made his way toward the series of enclosed broadcast booths at the far end of the press box, edging past the back row of baseball writers. Bob Lassiter of the *Providence Journal* was hunched over his Toshiba Satellite, thinning gray hair flecked with dandruff, as he pecked a sidebar—Harvey read it over his shoulder—about relief pitcher J. C. Jelsky's impending rotator cuff surgery. When Harvey tapped him on the back, Lassiter said, "One second," and finished typing the sentence before turning.

"Just wanted to say hi, Bob," Harvey said.

Lassiter twisted his body and shook Harvey's hand. He had an unlit Garcia y Vega jammed in the corner of his mouth. He was like something found in a time capsule marked "Beat Sports Reporter, circa 1962."

"Good to see you, Professor. I've been meaning to catch up with you. Maybe I could do a little story about one of the original Jewels returning to motivate his old team."

"We should make time for that, Bob."

Lassiter lowered his voice. "But I hear rumors."

"Oh yeah?"

"That you're here on an entirely different assignment."

"No kidding?"

"That Levy brought you in to baby-sit Moss."

"Who told you that?"

"Snoot Coffman. He says he found out that Moss may have gotten mixed up with the mob."

"I have no idea what he's talking about."

Lassiter lowered his voice to a hoarse whisper. "Snoot says he discovered that Moss has a nasty habit. A taste for female escorts. Two, three at a time that he likes to entertain in Cranston. Well, you know these services are all mobbed up. So Moss hurt one of the girls, then punched out some wise guy who objected. So Snoot says some mobsters have been threatening him and his girlfriend, and he found out through some connection of his own they're planning to teach Moss a lesson by getting to her."

"Oh, for chrissakes. When did he tell you this?" It was a little late in the day to be dealing with Snoot's rogue theories.

"Last night in New York."

"I can honestly say that the rumor is incorrect, and I hope you're not planning to run with any part of it."

"Okay, okay. Although it does help explain one thing."

"What's that?"

Lassiter yanked the wet dead cigar from the corner of his mouth and examined it as if its state of illumination were an issue. "Why Moss would end his relationship with that group in Atlanta."

"I don't see."

"Because who has time for charitable work when the mob's after you?"

Was it possible that the threat was coming from an entirely different direction? That Harvey had been looking in the wrong part of the woods? He quickly reviewed what he knew, or thought he knew, about Moss, and wondered whether the man who had neglected to tell him about his association with GURCC for so long also concealed a shameful secret about his recreational and sexual habits. With a sinking feeling, Harvey thought about the photo of Cherry Ann in Moss's cubicle. Wasn't a man who kept a nude photo of his girlfriend in his locker a man who might also be suffering from a kinky compulsion to party with multiple escorts? Had Harvey been overthinking it? After all, there was nothing yet to connect the man in the lynching photo at GURCC to anyone in Providence, nothing linking Clay Chirmside and his charade to either of the two warnings to Moss, except the curious coincidence of Chirmside's presence at GURCC the same day Moss and Cherry Ann came to visit. Could Chirmside's efforts to lay his hands on the lynching photos be unrelated to Moss's predicament?

"Listen, Bob," Harvey said, "it's completely fucking bogus."

"Now you sound to me like you doth protest too much."

Harvey felt his temper going. He jabbed a finger at Lassiter's rosacea-riddled face. "It's bogus, Bob. Stay away from it."

Lassiter pushed Harvey's finger aside. "So there *is* something going on?"

"Do I have your word, Bob?"

"Yes."

"Because if you cross me, I guarantee you that Moss will never talk to you again. That would be a hell of a handicap for you."

"I said yes, Professor."

"There's something going on."

"That's all you can tell me? I could use a scoop, Harvey," Lassiter said with sudden emotion. "I'm dying a slow death at the *Pro-Jo*. I'd like to get one of those commentator gigs at Fox or ESPN. Like Pete Gammons. A scoop would make me more attractive."

"Losing that stogie would make you more attractive."

"You'll let me have the story?"

"I'll give you a twenty-four hour jump on it. Fair enough?"

"Shake," Lassiter said with an eager brown smile, holding out his hand. "Maybe you could talk to Mickey Slavin for me, put in a good word at ESPN. I'll send you clips. I did a little television back in the seventies. . . ."

Harvey was gone, headed for the WRIX radio booth further down the press box, ready to confront Coffman. But through the Plexiglas he saw only WRIX radio color man Jack Sadler sitting at the desk with the *Chicago Tribune*'s Don Kollisch. They both wore headsets, and Sadler was asking Kollisch a question. Harvey waited impatiently, watching the Comiskey groundskeepers drag the infield fifty feet below, until Sadler went to a commercial and both men removed their headsets. Harvey knocked, and Sadler motioned him into the booth.

"If it isn't the Motivator," he said with a smile when Harvey stepped inside.

"Hi, Jack." Harvey nodded at Kollisch, whom he knew vaguely. "Where's Snoot?"

"He's not here," Sadler said. "But he wants you to call him."

"Where is he?"

"He had to go back to Providence. He had some sort of family emergency and flew back this morning."

"He did?"

"So I'm doing the play-by-play, and Don's going to play the role of me tonight. Snoot didn't know how to get hold of you. He left his cell number for you. Here." Sadler held out a card.

Harvey grabbed it and raced back through the press box. He found his brother standing at the buffet table.

"Harv, you got to try these burritos."

He put his hands on his brother's shoulders. "Norm, I have to go—"

"The game hasn't even started."

Harvey's pulse felt huge in his chest. "I've got to get to Providence."

"*Now*? Sometimes I wish I had your life, Harv. Anything I can do?"

"Yes. Move away from the buffet."

Harvey stepped outside the press box to call the number on the card Sadler had handed him.

"Harvey!" Coffman said breathlessly. "Where are you?"

"Comiskey Park. Where are you?"

"Listen, I couldn't find you. Where've you been?"

"I was out of town, Snoot. What's going on?"

"You've got to get back to Providence. You're not going to believe this."

"Believe what?"

"Our friend Moss hit some bimbo a couple of weeks ago. One of those escorts. He had her at his house. He had a couple of them there. Jesus, Harvey, you've got to get here and help me."

"Slow down, Snoot. How do you know this?"

"Okay, okay. Harvey, I've got a friend here, a criminal defense lawyer who's got some mob clients. He called me in New York to say some guys—connected guys—are pissed, and they want to teach him a lesson by hurting his girlfriend. Moss has this white stripper he sees regularly, and this lawyer tipped me off to get her off the street before something happens to her. Her name's Cherry Ann and I'm—I'm on my way to pick her up. I tried to get hold of you yesterday."

"Marshall's got my cell phone number."

"I didn't think of it. Listen, can you get here? You know, this is not exactly my line of work. I'd feel a lot better with you here."

"Where's Cherry Ann?"

"She's waiting for me at Teasers. That's where she works."

"Where you going to take her?"

"I don't know yet. I can't exactly take her home. Cindy won't go for it."

"Okay, take her someplace safe. When I get to Providence, I'll call your cell phone, and we'll take it from there."

He gave Coffman his own cell number. "What's this lawyer's name?"

"Bartoli. John Bartoli. I don't have the number on me. Listen, Harvey, I know this isn't my job. I was just trying to help out, calling people I know."

"It's okay, Snoot. You done good. I'll call you when I get to Providence."

As Harvey raced down the Comiskey ramps, he got hold of Detective Josh Linderman at home. "I need you," he said.

"What is it?"

"I don't have time to explain it all, I'm in Chicago right now, but Moss Cooley's got a girlfriend named Cherry Ann Smoler who strips at Teasers and apparently some wise guys have targeted her to get back at Moss for something he did to another woman. An escort. This goddamn busybody Snoot Coffman, the Jewels' broadcaster, is on his way over to pick her up at the club, but I need you to get over there and take charge of her, okay? Just protect her until I can fly in to Providence tonight. Then I'll call you. Here's Coffman's cell number, in case he beats you there."

As Harvey raced down the ramps, his body was awash in adrenaline. It was as if someone had pushed the mute button on reality. The only sounds he heard were his own breathing and, for some reason, the barking of a single concessionaire: Get your red hots, get your red hots. He saw the two managers and the four umpires conferring at home plate, then disperse. The White Sox starting team sprayed from the dugout, and everyone in the ballpark stood for the national anthem.

He stopped in the aisle of the grandstand to call Cherry Ann on her cell phone, but she didn't pick up. Instead, he left a message telling her he was on his way to Providence and to stay cool. Then he called Southwest Airlines and booked a seat on the last nonstop to Providence out of Midway Airport.

By the time Harvey got down to the wall by the dugout at field level, Art Ferreiras was at bat. Harvey got the security guard positioned at the corner of the dugout to get a message to Moss that he had to speak to him. Within seconds, Moss's face appeared around the corner.

"What's up?"

Harvey leaned over the wall to get as close as possible to Moss. "Tell me you didn't hit an escort."

"What the *fuck* are you talking about?"

"Snoot says he heard some wise guys are going after Cherry Ann for something you did to some escort from a mob-run escort service."

"That's absolute bullshit."

A fan behind Harvey called out, "Hey, Moss, nice streak!"

"Moss," Harvey said, "Snoot's in Providence, and I'm going there as soon as I get to Midway."

"Snoot? What is this bullshit? I thought you were looking for some guy in a lynching photo. Goddamn it, Bagel Boy—what's going on?"

"Tell me again you're not in some trouble you forgot to tell me about."

Moss lowered his brow and said, "Look at me, Blissberg. I'm tired of your fucking suspicions. I did not do anything to any fucking escort."

"Okay. Shit, Moss, I don't know what's going on. Call me on my cell phone in a few hours and try not to worry."

"Don't worry? What do you want me to do?"

"Pray," Harvey said and was gone, running up the aisle of the lower boxes as Art Ferreiras topped a slow roller to third and beat the throw to first by a step. Moss Cooley climbed out of the dugout and trudged to the on-deck circle.

H E got to the strip club around eight, wearing a plaid cap, tinted glasses, and the little mustache he'd bought for a Halloween costume party a few years ago. He'd phoned ahead of time, so he knew she wasn't starting until nine. Now the place had more strippers and bouncers in it than customers. What did he expect for a Monday night? Only two young guys in jeans in the seats by the runway, watching a coon girl give them the full monty. She lay on her back with her legs in a V, giving them time to inspect the unattainable merchandise, like a jeweler displaying his best diamond ring on black velvet for the impoverished groom-to-be. Three more strippers lounged on chairs in their ludicrous negligees and hot pants, smoking like their lives depended on it. One was keeping time to the horrible music by patting her thigh. He stood in the shadows against the wall.

The irony of it, finally finding out that Cooley was dating a stripper at Teasers. Where he liked to come and check out snatch once in a while himself, get a secondhand taste of what life had to offer.

All he'd wanted was to get his hands on the goddamn photo, and now he had to do a stripper.

He didn't think he'd have to do the coon, because he was confident the coon would get the message. Underneath that uniform, Cooley was just another frightened nigger.

Okay, he thought feverishly, sipping his Seagram's and Seven, I had thirty good years, thanks to Ed, a saint who kept his mouth shut, may he rest in peace. There was a stand-up guy, wouldn't sell out his buddy. But goddamn, we were stupid. Fuck Connie, though, after all he'd done. You couldn't count on women, anyway. His own daughter was dating a nigger! It was like a sick joke. You write the premise, and thirty years later God writes the punch line by having your seventeen-year-old show up with a coon whose father teaches biology at Brown! Everything was sucking him back into the past, where he didn't want to be, but where he had to go to lay it to rest. Okay, so he'd had thirty years in the clear, so what if he had to do a little wet work to nail down the next thirty?

His right hand was shaking though, his drink sloshing a bit over the rim, so he switched the glass to his left. He'd gotten out of the business a long time ago, and he didn't particularly like being in it again. He felt soft. What happened to the glib guy who'd do anything with a few drinks in him?

One of the lounging strippers got up and tried to engage him in conversation with a stupid cooing voice and a hand on his shoulder, the hand ending in purple press-on nails. The strobe was going now, making the whole scene look even less real than before. Maybe later, he mumbled, and turned from her. He walked toward the runway, then stopped, thinking these places all had to have hidden surveillance cameras, so he reversed course and left the curtained area, not looking any of the bouncers in the eye, and walked back out to case the parking lot again. He felt in his pockets for the little can of pepper spray.

He'd have to hit her with it while she was still in her car, before she got out. The parking lot was around the side of the converted brick building, away from the bouncer patrolling the entrance under the awning. He'd have to hit her and drive her out in her car.

He'd do her, but where? He had one idea that was too perfect. Once he got her in there, he'd have world and time enough to do what he wanted. The owner, as they say, was away. Of course, the owner would have an alibi. Still, who could deny that the presence of a stripper's corpse in his bedroom would implicate him? There would be suppositions and inquiries, a smokescreen of hypotheses behind which he would sit, calmly doing his job.

He leaned against a cyclone fence in deep shadow, thinking what could be sadder than a strip club parking lot in Providence, Rhode Island, early on a Monday night. How the hell could this all end in a Providence parking lot? Of all the places he'd been—Nashville, Charlotte, Spartanburg, Philly—he'd never felt safer, further from his deed, than here in this ragged little white-bread corner of the country. Another of God's jokes.

Well, he had a good one for God.

22

B Y the time Harvey had shown his investigator's license and gun permit and surrendered his pistol at airport security for safekeeping during the flight, he barely made the plane. Drenched in sweat, he buckled himself into the already taxiing jet, his second flight of the day. Ten minutes later the plane was banking eastward, following the curved foot of Lake Michigan, its waterfront dotted with quiet steel mills. He pulled the Airfone from the seat back in front of him and dialed Linderman's number.

"She never showed," the police detective said, his voice crackling. "I got here just before nine, and no one has seen her. I tried Coffman's cell, but got his voice mail. Where are you?"

"Over Gary, Indiana." Harvey looked at his watch. It was almost nine—ten on the East Coast. "Look, he's probably got her. He said he'd call me to let me know where he'd gone. I don't know whether to thank him or kill him for getting involved. Just stand by, Josh, till you hear from me."

The beverage cart docked next to his seat. Harvey drank his Scotch and pressed his forehead against the window, watching Indiana's farms darken. He tried Coffman's cell phone again and got his voice mail. He called Avis and arranged to have a rental waiting for him at the curb on his arrival. He tried to reach Mickey without success. He felt her out there somewhere below him, where one of the blazing bouquets of floodlights announced a baseball stadium.

For the next hour and a half, in the dim floating cabin, as respectful as a church, Harvey squirmed silently in his seat.

T. F. Green Airport at midnight was a harshly lit ghost town of shuttered kiosks through which a few weary travelers, drugged by distance, dragged their wheeled suitcases. Harvey clicked down the empty corridor past posters of far-flung destinations. He called Coffman again and couldn't get through. Then he called Providence directory assistance and asked for the residence number of a John Bartoli, giving two possible spellings. There was one listed in Olneyville, not where you'd expect a mob lawyer to live. Anyway, it was almost midnight and too late.

Harvey snaked up I-95 in his rental car, troubled he couldn't reach Coffman. He still had no idea where he was going. The assortment of buildings that passed for the Providence skyline slid into view ahead of him. In the distance, off to the right, the light towers of The Jewel Box stood at dark attention against some feathery moonlit clouds. On his left was the New England Pest Control building, on top of which a huge blue sheet-metal bug wearing an outsize Jewels cap crouched over the traffic like the first ominous sign of the alien invasion in a Japanese horror film.

His cell phone rang. It was Coffman finally, saying, "You land yet?"

"I'm here. Cherry Ann all right?"

"She's fine."

"No problems?"

"None, but, you know, maybe you could take over."

"Well, where the hell are you?"

"I'm over in Wayland Square. A friend's place." He gave him the address. "You know where that is?"

Harvey's heart stopped. How could he be so stupid? He was out of practice—there was no other excuse for letting himself be set up like this. Wayland Square. Jesus, how could he have missed every clue before this one?

"Harvey?" Coffman said. "I think I lost you for a minute. I asked if you know how to get here."

"Sure," he said.

"Good." Coffman repeated the address. "The front door's open."

And now he remembered why he had come to hate this work, where things always ended badly. Even success—discovering the truth—was no protection against the black hole waiting for him at the end of every case, a hole that sucked into itself all the world's alleged order and grace. And this was where he was headed now. Harvey touched the gun tucked inside his belt.

"I won't be able to get there for twenty minutes or so," Harvey said. "You okay until then, Snoot?" It would take him less than ten; he wanted to catch Coffman off guard.

"I'll be waiting for you," Coffman said and hung up.

It all made terrible sense now. Chirmside had obviously alerted Coffman that Harvey was getting warm, and Snoot was panicking. Snoot had to do away not only with Cherry Ann, but with Harvey as well. He had to get rid of the two people with a chance to match the second lyncher's face to his own. Harvey hoped to God Cherry Ann was still alive as he took the fork to I-95 East, which brought him within a few hundred yards of the hulking black freighter of a stadium where the Jewels played.

His cell phone startled him by burping out the beginning of "Take Me Out to the Ball Game."

"Yes?"

"It's me, Bagel Boy. Where do I tell this cabbie I'm going?"

"What cabbie?"

"I'm at Logan."

"You're in Boston?" An hour away by cab.

"I left after the second inning, but I couldn't get a non-stop to Providence. It took me half an inning to figure out where I belonged."

"Get your ass down here."

"Where?"

"Andy Cubberly's house. You know where that is?" He gave him the address.

"Is she okay?"

"I'm sure she's all right," Harvey told him. "She'll be fine. And, Moss?"

"Yeah?"

"I—I'm not entirely sure what's going on, so make a quiet entrance."

He exited at Gano Street and took Waterman to Wayland Square, driving the residential streets in a state of growing anxiety. He stepped on the gas, accelerating past Wayland Square's low-slung business district, turning at last onto the street of the man Harvey was now sure had gone through Cooley's locker for Snoot and found the photo. The minor-league bigot, capable only of throwing paint-filled water balloons at a parade, a child's prank, and not the real violence of which he might have dreamed. Only a few men were capable of that, and they weren't always the ones you might expect them to be.

Cubberly's bleak Tudor was dark except for the porch light and a dim glow in one of the upstairs windows. Harvey rolled past and parked a hundred yards beyond the house. The price he had to pay for not being smart enough to understand the problem until now was that he was going to have to solve it himself. He didn't know what he was going to find in Cubberly's house, but he knew he had to find it before Moss arrived.

He wondered if Coffman, knowing Cubberly's past, had recruited him all along in his campaign against Cooley, confident that Cubberly wouldn't ask questions. Or was there something more between them, a white supremacist bond, a social relationship, enlivened perhaps by some shared aspersions over dinner? Or was it something less? Was Cubberly nothing more than Coffman's unwitting cover story?

Harvey opened and closed his car door gingerly, making little sound, and walked back toward Cubberly's house, staying in the shadows. He hugged the outside of the house and made his way around to the back, listening for sounds from within, but there were only crickets, cicadas, and the sound of Jay Leno's voice and studio laughter dribbling out of a neighbor's window.

He paused at the back of the house, under the eaves, trying to settle his pulse. He dreaded what he might find inside, and what he might not find. He climbed the stoop stairs carefully. For the second time in ten days Harvey opened the back door with his lock-pick set and entered the ancient kitchen with his gun in his right hand. He left the door ajar behind him. Then he removed his shoes and padded across the worn linoleum into the empty dining room. He stopped, remembering his cell phone. He took it out of his pants pocket and shut it off. Holding his gun up near his face, he eased into the living room, searching the black forms of the furniture and the deep shadows. His eyes landed on the heavy wooden front door. It was closed tight, but the chain of the brass chain lock dangled free.

At that instant he heard a soft thump coming, he thought, from the second floor. Harvey turned and looked up the stairs at the base of the spindly floor lamp and a furry edge of carpeting that caught a hint of moonlight from the landing's casement window. As he put his stockinged foot on the first step, he felt the sudden cold pressure on his neck, just below his right ear, against his mandible.

"Please don't turn around, Harvey," Coffman said behind him

"Fine," Harvey replied.

"I'm going to take your gun now, so be still."

Harvey let him take his revolver, saying, "Would you like me to put my hands up?"

"Every little bit helps, Harvey."

"Where is she, Snoot?"

"Upstairs. Let's go. One step at a time. Remember, I now have two loaded guns."

"Okay." He started climbing, trying to swallow this humiliation.

"Straight ahead," Coffman said on the landing. "Into the bedroom. Open the door yourself."

Even before he opened the door, Harvey could hear a muffled straining inside Cubberly's room, like the distress of a small animal. The bedroom was bathed in the dull light of a gooseneck desk lamp, whose bulb Coffman had lowered to within inches of the desk. Cherry Ann Smoler was lying on Cubberly's bed, bound hand and foot with duct tape. A silver smear of tape sealed her mouth. She was wearing a black T-shirt and white jeans, knees streaked with dirt.

"Hello, Cherry Ann," Coffman said. "I believe you know each other."

Cherry Ann looked at Harvey with terror. He was no more useful than she now—an inmate of Coffman's small asylum. Harvey managed a smile and nodded at her, as if to suggest he might actually have the situation under control. But the catastrophe was now dawning on him, like a deep cut that takes a few seconds to fill with blood.

"Sit on the bed, Harvey."

Harvey sat on the king-size bed, facing Coffman for the first time. The paunchy broadcaster stood just inside the door, a gun in each hand, false mustache askew, the underarms of his short-sleeved shirt blooming with perspiration, like a cartoonist's parody of a gunslinger. He seemed to recognize the absurdity of his pose, for he quickly pocketed Harvey's gun and kept his own, an automatic with a nickel finish, pointed uncertainly at the detective.

Harvey tried to find in Snoot's fat, sweaty face the lyncher's leaner one. "Aren't you going to tape me up?"

"Tape you up? Why, I'd have to put down my gun to do that."

Just as it took more than one man to lynch a Negro. "Do you mind if I ask you a question?"

"What is it?" Coffman pulled up Cubberly's desk chair and sat on it, ten feet from the bed.

Harvey could see now in Coffman's broad movements that he'd been drinking, enough to make him dangerous, not enough to render him harmless. "My question is: What the hell are you doing?"

"Doing?" Coffman wiped his mouth with his free hand. "I'm—I'm—Cherry Ann thinks she saw me in a photograph."

Cherry Ann shook her head violently, her denial stifled by the duct tape, but Harvey knew there was no percentage in pretending.

"The lynching photo of Isaac Pettibone," he said.

Coffman's head twitched.

Then it hit Harvey. How could he have missed it? Another ball, right under his feet. "Chirmside was there, wasn't he?"

Coffman's mouth twisted. Harvey had to think hard to remember that the man before him was now a well-known radio broadcaster with a wife and two daughters.

"C'mon, Snoot. We don't have any secrets anymore. Chirmside was there too, wasn't he?"

His head wobbled for a moment on his neck before finally forming a nod.

"You can tell me."

Coffman swallowed once and said, "Clay drove."

"Clay drove, that's right. And you and old Ed Felker strung Pettibone up?"

Coffman steadied his gun hand and aimed it straight at Harvey's head.

It was Harvey's turn to swallow. He worked up some saliva

and said, "C'mon, Snoot, you don't honestly think you're going to solve anything by getting rid of the two of us."

Snoot pulled a half-full Seagram's miniature out of his
pants pocket, untwisted the cap with his teeth, and said, "It's
a damn good start."

Next to him, Cherry Ann wriggled in fear, and Harvey put
his hand on her knee to calm her. "Let me take the tape off
her mouth, Snoot. Will you let me do that if she promises not
to scream?"

"No."

"How about undoing her hands? No harm there. You've
got the guns."

Coffman shook his head.

"I don't understand you, Snoot," Harvey said ruefully. "It's
not just Cherry Ann and I who know. What about Moss? And
my friends down at GURCC. I called to let them know I'd
found their man."

"You did not."

"You're in play, Snoot. Your photo's just about to be all
over the fucking place. We're just going to have to come up
with another solution."

Coffman stared at them.

"So Clay drove," Harvey said.

He nodded.

"You and Clay have got to be the two luckiest guys in the
world. I mean, they nab your buddy, and he goes away for
thirty years while you get to go free and grow up to broadcast
Providence Jewels games. How'd you swing that?"

"Ed kept his mouth shut."

"I understand that. He did you a major solid. But what
was in it for him?" He turned to Cherry Ann. "What do you
think?" She shrugged as best she could. "What was in it for
Ed, Snoot?"

"Honor."

"Really?"

"Ed was one of the finest men I ever knew."

"Not like Clay, right? Clay sold you out for a thousand bucks ATM cash."

"Sold me out?"

"I won't say he named you," Harvey said, "but he nailed you nonetheless."

"Don't piss me off, Harvey."

"Can I have a drink? You got a drink?"

Coffman reached into his pocket, pulled out another Seagrams' miniature, and tossed it to Harvey.

"Thank you." He unscrewed the top and took a slug of it. "Here's what I think. You were sending Connie Felker dough all these years. I'm right, aren't I? She's pretty well fixed up for a retired hairdresser."

"Jesus, Harvey."

"What?"

"Where'd you get that idea?"

"I'll take that as a yes." Harvey stole a glance at his watch: a quarter to one in the morning. "You know, Snoot, you've got half the cops in Providence looking for you right now."

"No, I don't. Anyway, they'd never find me here."

"You don't think I told them where I was going?"

"No." Coffman looked startled, woozy. He pulled on the Seagram's. His eyes were glazed. He was beginning to deteriorate.

"You know, I've been in this house before. I thought Andy might be behind the lawn jockey."

"Cubberly's a dabbler."

"Not like you, huh?"

"Hate's an art, Harvey."

"Really?"

"But that was a long time ago." Coffman took a nip.

"You've got a family now. Millions of listeners."

"I made a terrible mistake."

"I think people will understand that. Take it into account."

"No, they won't."

Hate might be an art, but Coffman's real medium was words, and Harvey was beginning to think he could talk his way out of this. Unless Snoot totally freaked. But Cherry Ann didn't know this, and he could feel her growing alarm on the bed next to him.

"Do you want to know what's going to happen to you, Snoot?"

He shrugged, stealing another nip.

"There're two ways this can go. First option: you can shoot us, then spend the next day or two on the run until they catch you and convict you of three murders." Harvey ignored Cherry Ann's muted sob. "Unless of course you resist, in which case you'll die in the proverbial hail of police bullets. If you don't resist, they'll only put you away forever. You'll never be with your wife and kids again. I don't know how much dough you've put away, but your family won't have a Snoot Coffman to support them, like you supported Connie Felker. They'll know that their husband and father not only made a terrible mistake thirty years ago but is still a killer. Imagine what that would do to them. Your beautiful daughters having to spend the rest of their lives dealing with a knowledge that will color everything they feel about themselves, make them doubt everything they know, every past act of your love. Nothing sweeter than family, Snoot. That's what you're looking at there. I'm not even talking about the loved ones Cherry Ann and I will leave behind. What a fucking mess, Snoot.

"Option two," Harvey went on. "You let me take you very quietly into custody. We see if we can convince Cherry Ann here to forget that tonight ever happened. You follow me? Cherry Ann, is there a possibility that if Mr. Coffman here lets you go, you won't report his abduction, won't press charges?"

She nodded vigorously.

"Snoot, I think she's on board. That would make you completely clean in the here and now. But of course, you'd have to give me both guns. Funny thing is, Snoot, I think you'll feel a lot safer that way. It removes the temptation for you to do something stupid." He looked at his watch: one o' clock.

"Cherry Ann here, Snoot, I bet you didn't know she's going to be a chef. She's studying at Johnson and Wales. As for Teasers, well, what can I say? Nobody's perfect. You go with what you've got. I'll tell you something funny. My brother Norm, Snoot, he's the chairman of a university English department, and he once had a Ph.D. candidate who moonlighted as a dominatrix. Now she's a tenured professor in California with a closet full of dusty whips. You never know about people, right?"

And, really, Harvey thought, he wouldn't know about Snoot now if it hadn't been for a daisy chain of chance events. Chance had led Snoot to Providence and to Teasers on a night when Cherry Ann Smoler, whom chance had led to work there, was mentally recording every ringside customer with that photographic memory for men's faces refined during a childhood of chance improprieties. Then chance led Moss Cooley to Cherry Ann. Chance led Moss's friend Charlie Fathon to GURCC, where chance also led Moss and Cherry Ann to visit on one of the days Clay Chirmside was there because chance had ended the life of Ed Felker and led his wife to a box that contained photos that, by chance—who could have predicted the moment when her guilt reached critical mass?—she had donated to GURCC, where, by chance, Chirmside had observed Cherry Ann dimly recognize the face of his old partner in crime. If it were a novel, no one would believe it.

Chance was the glue without which all the infinite bits of experience would go flying off in all directions. It was the mortar with which we built the stories of our lives. Chance was like the cheap single without which a hitting streak would have ended, denying history another story.

Harvey, who was closer to the window than Coffman, heard a car approaching from down the street and coughed to cover it. "What was it like, Snoot?"

"What's that?"

"Lynching a man."

"There's a trick to everything," Coffman said, slurring his words now. He finished the miniature and threw the bottle at Harvey's head, missing him by a foot. The little bottle hit a bookshelf behind him. "I want to hurt you," Coffman said, pathetically.

"So what's the trick, Snoot?" Harvey heard the car get closer and slow.

Coffman was busy fumbling for another miniature in his pants pocket while he struggled to keep his gun on Harvey. "It's like what that guy Gordon Liddy said about putting his finger in a flame."

"What's that?" Harvey said loudly. "What did Gordon Liddy say?"

"Keep your goddamn voice down," Coffman said.

"What did Liddy say, Snoot?"

"Maybe it was *Lawrence of Arabia*. You know that movie?"

"That's a great movie," Harvey said. "I think I know what scene you're talking about."

"Do you have to talk so goddamn loud?" He swigged the Seagram's. "Keep your goddamn voice down."

"It's the scene where Lawrence is putting his finger in the fire, and the journalist—who is it? I think he's played by George Kennedy—asks him how he stands it." A car door opened on the street in front of the house.

"Unless it's Gordon Liddy," Coffman said. "I think he tells the same goddamn story."

"Right. Whoever. George Kennedy asks Lawrence how he stands it, right? How he stands keeping his finger in the flame. Isn't that right, Snoot?"

"Jesus, you talk loud."

There was a tiny sound downstairs. "Sorry," Harvey said. "Don't shoot us, okay?"

"Shut up, will you?"

"Snoot, what did Lawrence say?"

"He said, 'The trick is not to mind,' or some shit like that."

"And that was the trick for you?"

"What trick?"

"The trick to lynching a man, Snoot. What the hell do you think I'm talking about?"

"*I didn't lynch anybody.*"

"Yes, you did. You and old Ed Felker and Clay Chirmside."

"But I'm saying no one person did it."

"Of course not, Snoot. It took all three of you." Harvey thought he heard a little sound on the stairs. "What was your part, Snoot? What part did you play in the lynching of Isaac Pettibone?"

"I just put that big old noose around that nigger's neck."

"How about Ed?"

"Well, by the time I got that noose around him, he was half dead from being whacked around by Ed's putter. That's the only humane way to do 'em, you know. You've got to beat the tar out of them first. That way, they're too disoriented to fight you when you string 'em up."

Moss Cooley moved well for a big man, and it didn't surprise Harvey to see his motionless form standing now on the landing a few feet outside the bedroom, just standing there, a black mass in the dark. He seemed to be staring at the back of Coffman's head as Snoot continued to hold forth in Cubberly's chair.

"Yes, sir," Coffman said, "I'm certainly not proud of it now, but I can guaran-goddamn-tee you that we showed that nigger every possible courtesy. He was more than half out of his misery by the time we put him in the back of Clay's pickup. Ed and me, we had to stand him up on top of an old sawhorse in the back so we could get enough drop clearance to break his neck when Clay tore out of there."

Clay drove. Harvey hadn't quite understood.

"I was so full of hate back then," Coffman said, raising the miniature to his lips.

"How'd you meet Ed and Clay?" Harvey asked.

"People who hate enough have a way of getting thrown together. Actually, I met Ed at a softball tournament."

Moss came slowly out of the shadows on the landing into the faint bedroom light. Harvey thought it odd that Moss didn't look at him or Cherry Ann, but seemed completely focused on the back of Coffman's head.

"I expect people'll understand I was a figment of my habitat, a creature of my time." Coffman sucked on his miniature. He was no longer sober, no longer a middle-aged broadcaster, an upstanding citizen of Providence, Rhode Island. He was already half out of his misery. "I expect they'll cut me some slack."

Moss now stood only a few feet behind Coffman, and Harvey couldn't understand what he was trying to do until he raised his right hand.

In it was Cubberly's unsheathed Confederate officer's sword. Harvey grabbed Cherry Ann's ankle and held it tightly.

"I like the black man, Harvey. I've done a one-eighty."

Harvey wanted to speak Moss's name, tell him not to, but he knew that if he did speak his name, all bets would be off again.

Coffman wiped his mouth with the back of his free hand. "My own great-great-granddaddy was killed by cannister shot at Chancellorsville. Cut him in two. Terrible thing, to have to die just to preserve your way of life. Why the hell do you think everybody came to America in the first place, Harvey? To live the way they wanted to."

Moss, large behind the chattering Coffman, gripped the sword in two hands. Like a bat.

"The Africans didn't come here to live the way they wanted to," Harvey said.

"Don't give me that shit, Harvey. It was a better life than most of them niggers had ever known. It was better life than most of 'em ever *would* know. You don't think blacks were enslaved up North? Just because you couldn't see the shackles? Democracy was built on the goddamn back of slavery. Only reason they ever got rid of it was capitalism finally outgrew it. Morality had nuthin' to do—"

Moss swung the sword and Coffman's neck provided little resistance. His head stayed on his neck for the briefest moment before falling to the floor with a repulsive thud. It rolled over on Cubberly's carpet and looked wide-eyed at Harvey, lips poised for the next syllable he would never utter, the whole pale face trying to comprehend what had happened. The rest of him remained on the chair, his carotid and vertebral arteries pumping slurpy fountains of blood that quickly drenched his clothes and began pooling on the floor.

Violence ruptures reality. It stops the clock of being. Only later would Harvey be able to piece together a version of what he had seen, and done. He turned away with a gag, wanting to vomit. It was Cherry Ann who couldn't stop herself, and he quickly ripped the duct tape off her mouth, or else she would have choked on it. He ran into the bathroom, returned with a dampened towel, and carefully cleaned Cherry Ann's face. She had to tell him to undo her bound hands and feet.

Moss, still holding the sword, had dropped to his knees in the sticky maroon pool of Coffman's blood. His eyes were closed, and he was mumbling something to himself, perhaps a prayer.

Although he wouldn't remember doing it, Harvey took the comforter off Cubberly's bed and threw it over Coffman's body. He took Cubberly's bathrobe off the back of his closet door and covered Coffman's head on the floor. Then he turned his cell phone back on and called Linderman.

"I've got Coffman here, and he's dead," he said, and told him where. "Everyone else is alive. We need medics."

"Don't move anything."

"Come in alone, Josh. Everything's under control, but I want a moment alone with you before all hell breaks loose. We're on the second floor, and there're some elements of the situation that we need to discuss."

"Be there in five minutes."

"Thank you, Josh."

Moss was standing now, getting out of his clothes. Leaving his pants in the pool of blood. His shirt. Yanking off his shoes and socks and slipping out of his underwear. He stood naked in Coffman's blood with the sword by his bare feet.

"C'mon, baby," Cherry Ann said, standing just outside the lake of blood and extending her hand toward him. "Let's get you cleaned up."

"Let's do that," Moss mumbled mechanically. "Let's get cleaned up." He turned slowly, curiously, to Harvey. "What have I done?"

Harvey, who had been gazing into the black hole that was at the end of every case, turned to Moss. "When he turned on you with the gun, Moss, you had no choice."

"He turned on me . . . with the gun?"

"Moss, why the hell do you think you did that? It was you or him."

"Where'd I get the sword?"

"You got it on the stairs, Moss. It was Cubberly's, I think."

"And he turned on me?"

"Anybody would've done what you did."

"Really?"

"What else could you have done?" The revolving cherry of an approaching Providence squad car sprayed the bedroom with red light. "Now go get cleaned up."

23

T's said that a hitter's strength is an inch away from his weakness. That the fastball he likes to swat out of the park with some regularity will prove unhittable if you throw it an inch farther inside.

It was inconceivable that a man like Moss Cooley would actually kill Snoot Coffman, and in that way, so it helped to think that his pride and patience had been pushed an inch too far, transforming him into a different person.

And in the days following Coffman's death, Harvey kept thinking that the broadcaster's fate had been an inch away from his redemption. Had Coffman done nothing in the wake of Chirmside's report that his photo looked familiar to Moss and Cherry Ann Smoler, he might still be announcing Jewels games. But the suggestion that he had been recognized in an old photo of Isaac Pettibone's lynching had pushed him a fatal inch into panic.

Had Coffman not left Moss a headless lawn jockey, there would have been no former baseball players to ask questions and pursue the case to its bitter end. Had Coffman sat tight, which he had been doing for three decades, chances are Cherry Ann Smoler would have forgotten the old photo. Moss Cooley already had. And as long as Snoot Coffman continued to find his second-rate sexual pleasures at a place other than Teasers on a night Cherry Ann was working, the threat to his freedom would have blown over.

Information that was no longer needed trickled in, like fight fans arriving after the knockout. The computer age-imaging group that Jerry Bellaggio had recommended sent Harvey a printout of Coffman's projected appearance at fifty, based on the photo at GURCC. It was close enough. Charlie Fathon of GURCC reported that Connie Felker's car and two houses were both in her name, suggesting a standard of living well beyond the income reported on her tax returns.

More productively, GURCC investigators sifted through Chirmside's garbage, finding records of several phone calls to Coffman's office extension at Pro-Gem Palace. Armed with affidavits from Harvey, Cherry Ann, and Moss Cooley—who had heard it from Cubberly's landing—that Coffman had admitted Clay Chirmside's role in Pettibone's lynching, a contingent of investigators from GURCC, the Georgia Attorney General's Office, and the FBI showed up at Chirmside's house in early August. By the following day, he had confessed to his role in the lynching and was being held without bail pending formal charges.

After a preliminary investigation into the circumstances of Snoot Coffman's death, the Rhode Island Attorney General's Office declined to pursue any charges against Moss Cooley. It never went to a grand jury. Harvey assured the investigators that Coffman had turned around when Moss entered the bedroom, giving him ample reason to believe his life was in immediate danger. But the press coverage had already done its usual damage, and Moss went home to his mother in Alabama for a week of home cooking. He rejoined the team in Cleveland and promptly homered in his first at-bat against Rick Rusansky, the same man who had ended his hitting streak.

He and Cherry Ann Smoler continued to see each other. She took an indefinite leave of absence from Teasers, but continued her studies at Johnson and Wales. She moved into a campus dormitory, where she felt safer.

Andy Cubberly, who was cleared of any wrongdoing, nonetheless asked Felix Shalhoub to trade him. In the middle of August the team shipped him off to the Astros for another journeyman outfielder.

Harvey kept his promise, giving Bob Lassiter a long interview.

Scott Sipple, who had preceded Coffman as Jewels play-by-play man for WRIX, worked out a deal with his employer, ESPN, to come back to the broadcast booth as Jewels play-by-play man for WRIX.

In turn, ESPN asked Mickey Slavin to fill in for Scott Sipple, which necessitated her living in the Hartford area until at least the end of baseball season.

"Maybe it's for the best," she told Harvey in mid-August, walking into the living room where he was eating Doritos, guzzling Gatorade, and watching the Bears-Giants 1963 NFL Championship game on ESPN Classic Sports.

"In other words," Harvey said without looking up, "let's not think of it as a new assignment for you, but a trial separation for us."

"Something like that."

"I suppose things have gotten too lousy to last."

She waited for Harvey to look at her. "Let's just see what happens, okay?"

"You got someone else?"

"No. You?"

"Nope." He swallowed some Gatorade straight from the bottle. "Relationships wear out, don't they?" he said. "Like careers and tires."

"I don't think I've ever been so attached to a set of tires."

"I feel like giving you a hug."

"Well, get off your ass and give me one."

He rose, and they held each other for thirty seconds in the middle of the floor, swaying like two pummeled prize-fighters in a clinch, too tired to throw punches.

A week later, alone in the house, he received a phone call from Snoot Coffman's widow, Cindy. What could he say to her? Sorry your husband was decapitated? Just about everything in his life seemed better left unsaid. He waited for her to state her business.

"Sorry to bother you, but you're the only private detective I know."

"What's on your mind?"

"My daughter Tara," she began.

Harvey pictured the two teenagers in halter tops on the field in Providence, waiting for Moss Cooley to get out of the batting cage.

"The older one," Cindy Coffman said.

"Go on. I'm here."

"I think she's run off with her black boyfriend. She's been incredibly upset, as you can imagine. She's been in counseling and on sedatives. She left me a note saying, 'Don't worry, Mom, I'll call you in a few days. I need some time alone with Bryan.' That was three days ago."

The dominoes were beginning to fall. "And you've talked to Bryan's parents?"

"They haven't heard from him, either."

"Have you reported them missing to the police?"

"Not yet."

"Your other daughter?"

"Tiffany's here with me."

"Is there any reason to suppose she's in danger or has no intention of getting in touch with you?"

"I don't know. I don't think so. I'm just so worried. So are Bryan's parents. I certainly don't want to make the mistake of not acting."

"Understood."

"How would you feel about coming down to Providence

tonight and sitting down with me and Bryan's parents? Just to help us organize our thinking. You could decide then if you wanted to do more. Wanted to help us find them."

"If that would make you feel more comfortable."

"It would."

"Under the circumstances, you know, I can't take any money from you."

"Of course we'd want to pay you."

The fact was that Harvey didn't want anything at all to do with Cindy Coffman and her daughter's disappearance, yet he felt a twinge of obligation. He felt like someone at the end of an unsuccessful blind date: a good-night kiss seemed preferable, even if it falsely implied further interest, to not kissing her at all and hurting her feelings on the spot.

"All right," he said, "I'll meet with you and the boy's parents. Beyond that, I can't make any promises. Perhaps I can refer you to someone else."

Later that afternoon, Harvey was getting in his Honda in his garage when a shudder went through him. He spun, feeling that he was being watched. But it was only the lawn jockey's head, on the shelf where he had put it three weeks ago next to a bunch of paint cans. The head lay on its side, smiling insincerely at him.

He turned the head around so that it faced the wall. Then he got settled behind the wheel of his car, backed out of the garage, and started yet another journey to Providence, the city that, as if by some obscure law of the universe that applied only to him, drew Harvey back again and again.

Author's Note

Among the many works I found helpful in the writing of this novel were:

James Goodman's *Stories of Scottsboro*
Stephen J. Gould's essay "The Streak of Streaks" in
   DiMaggio: An Illustrated Life
Tony Horowitz's *Confederates in the Attic*
Joel Kovel's *White Racism: A Psychohistory*
Richard Ben Kramer's *Joe DiMaggio: A Hero's Life*
James M. McPherson's *The Battle Cry of Freedom*
Karen Simpson's independent research on the history of
   lawn jockeys
Bill Stanton's *Klanwatch: Bringing the Ku Klux Klan to
   Justice*
Diann Sutherlin Smith's *Down-Home Talk*
Joel Williamson's *The Crucible of Race*